P9-CLS-725

TRUTH

LIES

AND

MR. GREY

Also by Shelly Ellis

The Three Mrs. Greys

The Branch Avenue Boys series
In These Streets
Know Your Place
The Final Play

Chesterton Scandal series
Best Kept Secrets
Bed of Lies
Lust & Loyalty
To Love & Betray

Gibbons Gold Digger series
Can't Stand the Heat
The Player & the Game
Another Woman's Man
The Best She Ever Had

TRUTH
LIES
AND
MR. GREY

SHELLY ELLIS

www.kensingtonbooks.com

To the extent that the image or images on the cover of this book depict a person or persons, such person or persons are merely models, and are not intended to portray any character or characters featured in the book.

This book is a work of fiction. Names, characters, businesses, organizations, places, events, and incidents either are the product of the author's imagination or are used fictitiously. Any resemblance to actual persons, living or dead, events, or locales is entirely coincidental.

DAFINA BOOKS are published by

Kensington Publishing Corp.
119 West 40th Street
New York, NY 10018

Copyright © 2022 by Shelly Ellis

All rights reserved. No part of this book may be reproduced in any form or by any means without the prior written consent of the Publisher, excepting brief quotes used in reviews.

All Kensington titles, imprints, and distributed lines are available at special quantity discounts for bulk purchases for sales promotion, premiums, fund-raising, and educational or institutional use.

Special book excerpts or customized printings can also be created to fit specific needs. For details, write or phone the office of the Kensington Sales Manager: Kensington Publishing Corp., 119 West 40th Street, New York, NY 10018. Attn. Sales Department. Phone: 1-800-221-2647.

The Dafina logo is a trademark of Kensington Publishing Corp.

ISBN: 978-1-4967- 3133-3
First Trade Paperback Printing: April 2022

ISBN: 978-1-4967-3134-0 (e-book)
First Electronic Edition: April 2022

10 9 8 7 6 5 4 3 2 1

Printed in the United States of America

Thanks to Andrew for always having my back and always encouraging me to bet on me.

TRUTH

LIES

AND

MR. GREY

Prologue

June 2008
Washington, DC

"Have a seat! Can I get you anything? Whiskey? Tequila? Or are you a bourbon kinda guy?" Maxwell asked with a grin before gesturing to the bar cart laden with bottles, decanters, and glasses.

Cyrus Grey slowly lowered himself into the leather armchair facing Maxwell's desk and unbuttoned his suit jacket. "Sure, I'll take a whiskey on the rocks."

As Maxwell poured his drink, Cyrus could hear the thumping beat of R&B music filtering through the office's walls and door. It was from the dance floor two stories below, where more than five hundred people were currently partying the night away. Being a numbers guy, Cyrus did a quick calculation in his head of how much money Maxwell likely pulled in per night between the cover charge and bar. Inwardly, he smiled, because he knew a portion of that money would soon be his; he was to join Maxwell as co-owner of The Spot, DC's premiere nightclub. In fact, Cyrus was here tonight to finally sign the paperwork.

Maxwell handed him his glass, then took the leather chair behind his desk. "Thanks for comin' down here so late, Cy. I know not everybody's a night owl like me, bruh."

"No problem! I would've come here at four o'clock in the morning if you asked me to. You know I'm ready to get this done." He leaned forward eagerly in his chair and glanced at a stack of binder-clipped papers on the desk. "Is that the contract?"

Maxwell followed Cyrus's gaze. "Uh, no. No, it isn't." He shifted in his chair. Maxwell's grin was now replaced with a grimace. "Actually, Cy, that's why I asked you to come down here tonight. We've known each other for a while now, and it didn't feel right sayin' something like this over the phone."

Cyrus's stomach dropped. That didn't sound good. He leaned back, bracing himself for what he was about to hear next.

"Look, I thought about it," Maxwell began, "and I don't know if it's such a good idea for us to become . . . you know . . . business partners."

Cyrus's jaw tightened. Fury bubbled inside him, but he forced himself to keep the volcano from erupting. It wasn't always good to show your emotions. It was like showing your hand in a game of poker.

"But that's what we agreed to," Cyrus began in an even voice. "I loaned you the money to invest in your club, and you said you would grant me a portion of the ownership. You'd make me co-owner."

He'd given Maxwell more than a quarter of a million dollars. Cyrus hadn't made him sign a contract outright because Maxwell had given him some song and dance about how it all had to be done under the table for tax reasons. Rightly or wrongly, Cyrus hadn't given Maxwell's request a second thought. He'd gotten used to working with clients who didn't believe in contracts—just a dap and your word.

Sure, Cyrus had told his fair share of lies. He claimed he had a master's degree from Stanford when he didn't. He didn't have a master's degree at all. He claimed, as a financial consultant, that he had clients like the DC mayor and Redskins coach Jim Zorn, and even Hollywood celeb clients like Denzel Washington, John Legend, and Jamie Foxx. None of that was true either. Cyrus was a self-made man—creating himself from scratch. But he considered those little white lies compared to this, compared to reneging on a deal.

Maxwell nodded and waved his dark hand. "Yeah. Yeah, I know! But like I said, I had a chance to think about it, and I'm just not good with working with other people, Cy. I'm pigheaded. I like to go my own way. Trust me, bruh. I'm doing you a favor!" He chuckled.

"We . . . agreed," Cyrus said through clenched teeth.

Maxwell nodded again. "I know. But it ain't like we signed anything! It was just a . . . a gentleman's agreement."

"And part of being a gentleman is keeping your goddamn word!"

"Hey!" Maxwell said, narrowing his eyes and pointing at him. "Watch your tone!"

"Or what? What the hell are you gonna do?" Cyrus challenged.

The office fell silent. The DJ switched to another song on the dance floor below as the two men glared at each other across the office desk. Suddenly, Maxwell broke into another grin. He tossed back his head and laughed again, hearty and loud, showing almost all his teeth, infuriating Cyrus even more.

"Cy, get the hell outta here, bruh! We can duke it out if you want to, but the only thing that will happen is you getting thrown outta this club and banned from ever coming back." He tilted his head. "Now, I know you run with a rough crowd. Sometimes, a black man has to in order to get where he needs to go. Shit, I've done it myself. But they're the gangbangers, Cy. Not us. We're businessmen. We understand business. We also understand what constitutes binding agreements. We didn't sign a contract. It's your word against mine. You can come after me in court if you want," Maxwell shrugged, "but you know damn well you'd lose. I'll pay you back the money with interest if it'll make you feel any better. But I am not giving you half of my club. That's it. Sorry, bruh."

Cyrus slowly rose from his chair, swallowing his pride like he was swallowing down a boulder. It took all his willpower not to leap across the desk and start pummeling Maxwell in the face, but he knew the other man was right. It would only end up with him evicted from the club and probably in jail. And he likely had no legal recourse for Maxwell's disregard of their verbal agreement either. They'd had no witnesses present when they made the deal. The litigation would just be long and expensive—one man's word against another's. And frankly, at this point, he wasn't convinced that Maxwell would even pay him the money he was owed. Maxwell's word meant nothing.

Cyrus wouldn't take the loss and just ignore this disrespect, though; he would have to take care of it another way.

"I do want my money back with interest," he said, buttoning his suit jacket again, "and don't ever ask me to borrow another dime in your whole goddamn life. You hear me?"

"Understood," Maxwell said, nodding and already looking disinterested.

Cyrus turned and walked toward the office door.

"Enjoy the rest of your night!" Maxwell called to him,

almost mockingly. "Tell the bartender I said all your drinks are on the house!"

Cyrus didn't respond. Instead, he walked into the hall, slamming the door behind him.

Five minutes later, Cyrus found Tariq standing at the bar, chatting up a young lady in a short black skirt and a bedazzled, sequined top.

"Tariq! Tariq!" Cyrus shouted, cupping his hands around his mouth so he could be heard over the cacophony of voices and blaring music.

Tariq whispered something to the young woman before strolling to Cyrus's side. "What's up?" he asked. "You finish your business? You sign the papers?"

Cyrus had taken Tariq under his wing a couple of years ago, showing him the ropes of financial consultancy. He was more than a decade younger than Cyrus, but when they'd met, Tariq had seemed confident, capable, and wiser than his years. Considering that he didn't even have a high school diploma, Tariq was a surprisingly quick study. He was good with numbers, too. But he was also good at a few other things you couldn't learn in school. He had a skillset that Cyrus hadn't employed so far, but he would tonight.

"No, we didn't sign the damn papers," Cyrus replied tersely. "Maxwell said he isn't gonna make me co-owner."

Tariq rolled his eyes. "Man, didn't I tell you he was full of shit? Didn't I tell you? He didn't even sound like—"

"I don't need any 'I told you sos,' Tariq." Cyrus reached into one of his suit jacket pockets. "I need a solution. I need you to take care of it."

Tariq frowned. "What am I supposed to do?"

Cyrus hesitated for only a second or two before pulling out one of his business cards and a gilded pen—the very pen he'd brought tonight to sign the contract. But he'd still put the pen to good use. If he couldn't sign an agreement to make him and Maxwell business partners, he'd use the pen to sign Maxwell's death sentence.

Cyrus wasn't a gangbanger like Maxwell said, but that didn't mean he would let a slight like this go unpunished. If Cyrus had learned anything from dealing with clients in the underworld, it was that you had to maintain your rep. You couldn't let people think that you were a pushover. A punk. A sucker. Or they would always take advantage of you, and Cyrus Grey would not be taken advantage of.

"Here's his address," Cyrus said, lowering his voice and scribbling on the back of the card. "He doesn't get home until five A.M. most of the time, and he lives alone."

"Okay . . . and?" Tariq stared down at the card. "What are you telling me that for? Why are you giving this to me?"

"Why do you think I'm giving it to you?"

"What? You want me to beat his ass?"

Cyrus slowly shook his head. "It's past that point."

Tariq squinted. "Wait. You want me to R-I-P this nigga?"

Cyrus nodded, making Tariq suck his teeth.

"Cy, come on! I know you pissed, man, but no. No! I don't do that shit anymore! I could've just stayed with my crew if that was the case. I came to you for something different. You told me that you could hook me up. Put me on some new shit. Not the same ol', same ol'."

Cyrus took a step closer to him. "You like that expensive motorcycle jacket you're wearing? You like your ride?"

Tariq bit down on his bottom lip. He was annoyed, but he had no right to be, in Cyrus's opinion. Cyrus was simply asking Tariq to do what he was hired to do.

"Well, you have those things because of me, Tariq," he continued, pointing at his chest. "One hand washes the

other. That's what we agreed to in the beginning. Remember? Maxwell may not understand a gentleman's
agreement, but we do. And both of us have to live up to it.
Maxwell wouldn't be the first dude you've handled. Don't
act brand-new on me. Just do it. You do this . . . you stick
with me, and we'll go places. We'll go farther than you
ever imagined. I can promise you that. Sky's the limit,
Tariq."

Tariq glowered at him a beat longer before snatching
the card out of his hand. "Fine," he mumbled before
loudly exhaling and walking away.

"Tariq!" Cyrus called out, making the younger man
pause and turn back around to face him. "And don't make
it quick. I want him to feel it."

Tariq nodded, then continued across the club. Cyrus
watched until he reached the exit. Then he turned back
around and glanced at the bar.

Might as well have a drink, he thought.

After all, Maxwell had said it was all on the house.
Hopefully, he'd at least keep that promise. It was the bare
minimum of what the club owner could do after aggravat-
ing Cyrus and wasting his damn time.

Cyrus saw an open spot at the marble counter. He saddled up to the bar, raising his hand to get the bartender's
attention, but he stopped short when he saw a woman
standing on the other side of the bar, about twelve feet
away, who made him do a double take.

Damn, she's beautiful, he thought.

She was petite, tan, with a cute button nose and long
hair that she was now tossing over her shoulder. She wore
a skin-tight, low-cut wrap dress that showed all her lus-
cious curves. This was a woman who attracted attention
like a spotlight was following her around the room. She
currently seemed to be getting unwanted attention from a
dark-skinned brother who was trying his damnedest to

chat her up, but she didn't look remotely interested in him. The mystery woman raised her glass to her ruby-red lips and locked eyes with Cyrus across the bar. He winked at her. She lowered her glass and smiled before giving him a saucy wink back. In less than a minute, Cyrus made his way to her side of the bar.

"Hey, baby," he said, making her and the man she was standing with whip around to face him, "sorry that call took longer than I thought it would. I'm back now."

"Oh, that's okay," she replied, quickly catching onto Cyrus's farce. "I had Tony, here, to keep me company and buy me a drink, but I told him I came here with my man and he'd be back soon."

"Thanks for getting her a drink, brotha," Cyrus said, thumping a now-disgruntled Tony on the shoulder. "I got it handled from here, though."

Tony nodded awkwardly and walked off. Cyrus leaned his elbow on the counter as he towered over her. She was such an itty-bitty thing. "I'd buy you a drink, but it sounds like he already took care of that."

"He did." She let her eyes slowly travel over Cyrus. He noticed that her gaze lingered on his Rolex and his Gucci tie clip before resting on his face. "But maybe you'll make better company."

"I can certainly try." He extended his hand. "I'm Cyrus, by the way."

"Vanessa," she said before shaking it and licking her lips.

Cyrus smiled.

So he wouldn't get half of the club like he'd wanted, but based on the way this beautiful creature was looking at him like he was a prime rib with a side of mashed potatoes, he suspected he might get something else good tonight. And he was right. Two hours later, he and Vanessa left the club together. He took Vanessa home to his skyrise condo on Massachusetts Avenue, and she did her very damnedest to take care of him in his bedroom, giving Cyrus a night he would never forget. On the other side of town, Tariq simultaneously took care of Maxwell, making sure the club owner wouldn't live to see another dawn.

All in all, it was a good night. One that Cyrus would remember for a long time, because it showed how he never let things get him down. Because no matter what, he knew he could not . . . would not lose. No matter what it took, he'd always find a way to come out on top.

Chapter 1

Vanessa

"Nessa! *Nessaaaaa!*" Cyrus yelled from upstairs.

His voice ricocheted like a sonic boom from their bedroom door, down the hall, and then down the stairs to Vanessa Grey as she stood at the kitchen counter, assembling his lunch—a club sandwich with tomato bisque and chips—on a serving tray.

Her husband of twelve years may still be mostly bedridden from the gunshot wounds he'd suffered almost two months before, but nothing seemed to be hampering his mouth. He was as loud and demanding as ever.

"What?" she shouted back irritably over her shoulder as she poured pomegranate juice into a glass.

"What the hell is taking you so long, woman? I'm starvin'!"

She sucked her teeth. "Well, you can starve to death for all I care, you son of bitch," she muttered before slamming the glass onto the wooden tray, making juice slosh over the side.

Vanessa had been catering to Cyrus since he'd arrived home from the hospital—feeding him, washing him, clothing him, disinfecting his wounds, and changing the bandages. And she'd hated every minute of it. It was bad enough that he had cheated on her for years, even marrying two other women behind her back while he was still married to her. It was bad enough that he was now blackmailing her to stay in their joke of a marriage by holding evidence of her affair with her eldest son's soccer coach over her head. (He'd threatened to email that photographic evidence to everyone from the other soccer moms to their children's stuffy school principal.) But now Cyrus was making Vanessa cater to him like some handmaiden and nurse all rolled into one. It was a slow torture she endured daily.

She still couldn't believe how her life had gotten to this point. She'd gone from worry that her affair would end her marriage to fury at hearing about her husband's other wives and now, wanting nothing more than to be rid of Cyrus—all in a matter of months. Vanessa was willing to do just about anything to end this living nightmare, including killing her husband, something she'd never thought would have entered her mind a year ago, let alone a decade before that, when she'd made it her mission to seduce and ensnare the handsome, wealthy Cyrus Grey.

Vanessa now opened one of the kitchen drawers to retrieve a spoon. As she did, her eyes landed on a bottle of Clorox spray she'd left sitting on the counter yesterday after she'd scrubbed down the kitchen. Her eyes then shifted back to Cyrus's glass of pomegranate juice. Maybe she could pour a little into his drink. Not too much so he would taste it, but just enough to kill him. If he died, this whole ordeal would be over. No more Nurse Vanessa. No more Pain-in-the-ass Cyrus. She reached for the bottle.

"Nessa! Did you hear me?" Cyrus shouted again, making her jump in alarm and snatch back her hand. "Where the hell is my food?"

Vanessa grumbled. Instead of grabbing the bottle of cleaning fluid, she grabbed a spoon and slammed the kitchen drawer shut.

She wouldn't poison her husband—not today anyway. It was too risky; a coroner might find traces of the bleach in his system.

She'd have to stick to the plan and let her lover, Bilal, kill him for her. She just hoped Bilal did it soon. Though she had to admit Cyrus being laid up in his bed at home most of the time didn't make carrying out their murder plot any easier.

"I'm coming, damn it! Stop yelling!" she shouted back before grabbing the tray and trudging out of the kitchen and later up the stairs to their bedroom.

Vanessa eased the bedroom door open with her shoulder and found Cyrus sitting up in the center of their California king in maroon silk pajamas.

Though the bed was easily big enough for two, Vanessa hadn't slept in here with her husband since he'd arrived home. Instead, she slept in one of the guest rooms two doors down the hall. She'd told their three children she'd made the move to the other room because she wanted to give their father space to spread out and get comfortable, anything to expedite his full, healthy recovery from the shooting. But the truth was, the less time she had to stay in the same room with Cyrus, the better. And she suspected Cy knew the truth and hadn't asked her to stay in here with him for that reason.

Besides, if they slept in the same bedroom, she couldn't

vouch that she wouldn't try to strangle or smother the bastard in his sleep.

"Lunch is served," she now announced dryly as she carried the tray to his bed.

"Took you long enough," he muttered.

She set the tray on his lap. "Even if I didn't come up at all, you would've been fine. You could skip a meal or two, honey." She poked his growing paunch through his shirt, making him swat her hand away.

Cyrus had never been a man with sculpted muscles, but he'd always been solidly built—her own John Henry, with a bald head, big arms, and tree-trunk thighs, like the folk hero. That is, until recently. Cy had gone from frail, when he first returned from the hospital, to now almost doughy after being in bed and stuffing his face for so long. He even worked from his bed now, grazing on snacks as he typed emails and made business calls.

Vanessa glanced at the opened bags of nacho chips, chocolate chip cookies, and trail mix that sat on his night table. If she didn't kill him, all the food he was eating certainly would.

"Don't worry about me. I'll be up and around sooner or later and get back to my old fighting weight," he assured her before taking a bite from his sandwich.

She turned away. "Let's hope it's sooner rather than later," she tossed over her shoulder with a withering glance as she strolled out the bedroom.

A half hour later, Vanessa was finishing up her own lunch when her doorbell rang. She rose to her feet and walked out of the kitchen through the living room and into her foyer. When she swung the front door open, she saw her mother, Carol, standing on the welcome mat in a tank top, capris, and kitten-heeled sandals.

"Hey, Mama," she said tiredly.

"Hey! How's the patient?" her mother asked as she cocked a finely arched eyebrow over her sunglasses. "Still alive, I assume?"

"Unfortunately," Vanessa whispered before cutting her eyes at the stairs. "Let's go outside to the deck and talk."

Her mother nodded as she stepped inside and shut the front door behind her.

"You don't look too good, sweetheart," her mother said as she trailed behind her across the house. They winded their way through the spacious living room and sunroom.

"Oh, thanks," Vanessa replied sarcastically.

"I mean it, baby! Are you getting a good night's rest? When's the last time you got a facial, or at least an exfoliation treatment? You can't neglect yourself, Nessa. You're a woman of thirty-seven. You have to maintain what you have, my dear!"

As Vanessa neared the French doors leading to the rear of her home, she caught her reflection in the windowpanes. Her mother was right. She didn't look like herself. She was wearing a wrinkled, nondescript sheath dress rather than the clingy, designer dresses and outfits she usually wore that showed off her petite, curvy figure. Her glossy, dark curls were haphazardly pulled into a bun at her nape because she hadn't been in the mood to style her hair in days. There were bags bigger than Birkins under her eyes. And worst of all, she was starting to look pale, especially next to her mother, whose soft, brown skin had taken on the warm radiance it always did at this time of year. Vanessa hated it when her own skin lost its healthy, golden glow. She had Cyrus to blame for all of this.

"I've just been down lately," she mumbled to her mother. She swung open one of the doors and stepped onto the two-story deck.

Her mother closed the French doors behind them. Both

women headed to one of the patio tables, squinting at the blinding afternoon sun that now hovered in a cloudless sky.

"I haven't had much energy for self-care thanks to Cyrus," Vanessa continued. "Taking care of his big, lazy ass is a twenty-four-hour job."

Carol pulled out one of the table chairs and looked over her shoulder at the overhead windows, searching for the man himself. When she didn't see Cyrus and was reasonably sure he wasn't eavesdropping, she sat down. "Well, hopefully you won't be taking care of him too much longer, honey," her mother whispered. "Any progress on that little project of yours?"

Vanessa shook her head as she sat in one of the chairs on the opposite side of the table. "Nope. Bilal can't really do anything while Cyrus is staying home all day." She inclined her head. "I guess we could try to do it while I'm out on errands and the kids are away at day camp. Maybe he could break-in, do a fake robbery, and . . . you know . . . get the job done, but I really don't want him to do it here at the house." She winced. "It could get messy, and it might creep out the kids."

"Hmm, I see your point," her mother said, pursing her lips. "Now, explain to me why you two decided not to do it as he was leaving the hospital."

Vanessa groaned. It was still a touchy subject for her. She and Bilal had discussed the plan about a dozen times, then had to abruptly abort the mission only hours before it was supposed to take place.

"He was supposed to walk up and shoot Cy as he was being wheeled out to our car," she said, dropping her voice to a whisper again. "He was supposed to wear a ski mask . . . you know . . . so his face would be covered and everyone would think it was the same guy who tried to kill Cy the first time. But the night before I found out that Diamond and her pimp boyfriend were charged with Cy's attempted murder. If the cops already have the guy who says he did it, Bilal couldn't very well pretend to be him, could he?"

"I guess not." Her mother slumped back in her chair, removed her sunglasses, and tossed them onto the patio table. "Too bad that other wife of his didn't succeed the first time! All your problems would be taken care of."

"Maybe," Vanessa said, though she still wasn't convinced the cops had arrested the right person.

She wasn't fond of Diamond, Cyrus's third wife, by any estimation, but she found it hard to believe the young woman would try to have Cyrus killed. Diamond had defended him fiercely to both Vanessa and Noelle, Cyrus's second wife, the last time they were all together—the *only* time all three women had agreed to meet once they learned of one another's existence. Vanessa grudgingly had to admit that Diamond seemed firmly smitten with Cyrus. And Cyrus was equally convinced of her innocence, insisting to Vanessa that Diamond wasn't the culprit and he knew who really was behind his attempted murder— though he refused to name names. But still, the cops said Diamond's boyfriend had confessed to the shooting, claiming he'd received a gold chain as payment. And the cops wouldn't charge her with the crime unless they had credible evidence against her, would they?

"So what are you gonna do?" Carol now asked. "Just hope your husband heals faster and finally gets off his ass and out the house? I thought you had a deadline with this. Didn't you tell that boy toy of yours that you were pregnant months ago? Won't he start wondering why you aren't showing?"

"I gave him a copy of one of my old printouts of Zoe's ultrasounds to buy some time. I altered the dates on my computer so it looks like I took it a couple of weeks ago."

"How inventive! I guess he believed it, then?"

Vanessa nodded. "He started crying. He keeps the printout on his refrigerator."

"Oh my goodness!" Her mother threw back her head and cackled. "The dumb pretty ones never cease to amaze me!"

Vanessa didn't join Carol in her laughter. The truth was, she was starting to feel a bit guilty for lying to Bilal about being pregnant. He was so excited at the prospect of becoming a father, musing about what the baby would look like and how he hoped they were having a boy.

"But I'd be okay with a girl too, bae," he had assured her just yesterday over the phone. "I'll be happy either way!"

She didn't enjoy lying to him about something like this, but she didn't know what alternative she had. He wouldn't have agreed to murder Cyrus if she hadn't told him about having a baby on the way.

"Well, hopefully," her mother said as her laughter tapered off, "he's finally able to take care of your husband for you in the next month or so. Or you'll have to dig up another ultrasound photo, I suppose, or maybe start wearing a damn pillow underneath your clothes when you see him."

"Let's hope it doesn't get that ridiculous," Vanessa muttered.

Though she had another printout saved on her computer, just in case, *and* a pillow on standby.

Chapter 2

Cyrus

Cyrus listened to the front door slam shut, then to his wife's and mother-in-law's voices until they receded and disappeared. They must have gone to another part of the house. He waited one minute ... two minutes ... three minutes before shifting aside his tray on his lap and setting it on the bed beside him. He then tossed aside his bedsheets, threw his legs over the side of the mattress, and rose to his feet.

Cyrus winced a little as he stood, but the pain was fleeting. It wasn't sharp either. It was more like a lingering soreness from stiff muscles after working out too hard, nowhere near as bad as it had been a month ago, or when he first arrived home from the hospital—though he would never tell his wife Vanessa that.

Whenever he stood up from the bed when she was around, he made a big production of groaning and moaning, of leaning most of his weight on her shoulder as she guided him to the bathroom. She thought he couldn't make it to his bedroom door without her help. But the truth was, when she and the children weren't home, he freely walked around the house, even up and down the stairs by himself. He'd ventured outside a few times to sit in the patio chairs and smoke a cigar on the deck. He was building up his endurance. Cyrus figured in a week or two, he should be ready to venture from home on his own, though he had to do it carefully so hardly anyone knew what he was doing, including Vanessa.

Part of the reason he was pretending to still be an invalid was because the longer he stayed "sick," the longer his lawyers could put off his bigamy trial. The other reason was because there were advantages to seeming weak; it was an easy way to catch your enemies off guard, and Cyrus Grey had many enemies.

He walked across his bedroom and peeked into the hall, finding it empty and quiet. Usually, the house would be filled with little, energetic bodies and a wall of sound— television soundtracks, video game explosions, and the shouts and laughter of his children as they ran from room to room—but Cy Jr., Bryson, and Zoe were away at day camp right now, doing craft projects and sailing in paddle boats. They wouldn't return until later that afternoon.

Cyrus walked down the silent hallway and caught a glimpse through Cy Jr.'s bedroom window of Vanessa and Carol sitting on one of the outside decks. The two women were reclining in the patio chairs under the shadow of an umbrella. He could see they were talking. Cyrus strolled into his son's room, stepping over discarded clothes, game cartridges, and books. He watched as his wife and mother-in-law talked, as they leaned their heads together and whispered to each other. He frowned.

What were they talking about?

Nothin' good, he surmised.

He didn't trust Vanessa. He hadn't trusted her since he'd found out she was cheating on him.

He'd been confronted with the truth about his wife's infidelity when he saw the photographs the investigator had taken of her with her weak-ass side nigga. But Cyrus had secretly suspected something was off with her before he got evidence. For weeks Vanessa had seemed less than excited when he returned home after being "away on business." At least, that's what he always told her, but more than likely he was with one of his other wives—Noelle or Diamond.

Vanessa had stopped fawning over him like she used to in the old days; she no longer cooked him big, elaborate meals anymore or met him at the bedroom door in a negligee. Instead, she'd reheat leftovers from the night before, or loudly be snoring before he even climbed into their bed. And he'd noticed when he was home that she would disappear for hours at a time, claiming to be running errands, but she didn't come back with anything.

He'd told Tariq, his business partner and confidante, about his observations and growing unease.

"She's cheatin' on you," Tariq had said casually in his usual blunt manner.

"No, she's not! Not Nessa. Somethin' else has to be goin' on. She would never cheat on me."

"Why not? You cheat on her!"

Cyrus had contemplated Tariq's words. "Shit. You really think she's cheatin'?"

Tariq had only laughed in reply and walked out of his office, like it was the stupidest question he'd ever heard.

Tariq was right in both regards, of course. Vanessa was, indeed, cheating, and Cy had been having affairs of his own for years, and had even married other women while he was still married to Vanessa. But he'd never done anything as tawdry as fucking one of his women in the back seat of a car in a public park, like Vanessa had done with her lover. He'd never been that reckless. Anyone could have seen Vanessa and her lover together—a jogger or a gaggle of moms on a playdate pushing strollers. How could she have been so stupid? So tacky? He'd given her more credit than that. And to add insult to injury, Vanessa had cheated with a man with no money or status: a twenty-something soccer coach who worked part-time at a gym, a guy who wasn't worth the dirt on his shoes. After all Cyrus had done for her, after how well he had taken care of her unemployed, spendthrift ass for all these years, *this* was how Vanessa repaid him?

He now stared at his wife and his mother-in-law through the window, squinting until his eyes were narrowed into slits, trying his best to read their lips from this distance. Did he see Vanessa say the words "kill him"? Did her mother say something about money? Maybe they were talking about killing him to get his money.

"Jokes on y'all. I don't have any more," he muttered.

And he wasn't that easy to kill, either. He'd already had one brush with death thanks to Tariq. That backstabbing bastard had set up the shooting, but Cy had survived.

"Jokes on that motherfucka, too," he now whispered.

But it still angered him that he hadn't seen it coming. Neither had he anticipated that Tariq would steal his wife, Noelle.

Tariq and Noelle had seemed friendly for years. Cyrus had never picked up anything more than that when they were together, but maybe he had been ignorant to the obvious signs. Maybe it had been Tariq's mission to seduce and steal her from Cyrus all along. That could be why he had plotted his murder.

Noelle now thought she had herself a winner with Tariq. She believed Tariq was a good guy she could trust, but little did she know she now had an even bigger liar and con artist than Cyrus—and a deadlier one at that.

Tariq had been a shooter for many years for the Nine

Crew in DC during his younger days, and what he'd done weren't your average, low-level drive-bys. No, Tariq was more skilled than that. He handled the higher profile hits, the ones that required the shooter to get in and get out quickly and unseen. Tariq had even used his skills to execute the occasional "favor" for Cyrus to protect their business interests. Cyrus had lulled himself into thinking that after years of friendship and being in business together, after so many shared secrets and crimes, Tariq would never turn on him, but his old friend had proved him wrong.

They still ran Greydon Consultants together because—despite everything that had happened—business was still business, and Cyrus wouldn't let anything get between him and his paper. But he kept a close eye on Tariq and had marked him for payback. He was just biding his time until he could execute it.

With Vanessa, Tariq, and Noelle no longer in his corner, Cyrus had no one he could turn to except Diamond, who was out of prison for the time being. He had put up the money for her bail, dipping into his already tenuous savings, but she was barred from contacting him per the conditions of her release. They managed to sneak the occasional phone conversation every now and then, but that was it.

It wasn't much of a sacrifice for him, though, because sometimes he wasn't eager to talk to Diamond. She had caught him off guard when he started to hear stories about her past: the prostitution, the pimp boyfriend, and the other murder trial in which she'd testified. He'd thought she was just a wide-eyed hostess at a classy restaurant in Baltimore, a college dropout with a good heart but lack of direction. He hadn't known she'd been turning tricks and masturbating on the web as horny strangers paid to watch. Why hadn't he researched her better? It was yet another example of him letting down his guard and being made a fool of.

Well, not anymore, he thought.

Cyrus Grey wasn't a fool. Cyrus Grey didn't cower. He would regain control of the situation, including the women in his life.

He turned away from his son's bedroom window and walked out of the room and down the hall to one of the guest rooms. He glanced over his shoulder, listening for the sound of footsteps or voices. He heard neither. He eased open the door and stepped inside.

The scent of Vanessa's signature perfume hit him as soon as he entered. She'd been staying here for less than two months, but she had already added her own little touches, switching out the blinds for satin curtains, adding her mahogany makeup table and a plush fur ottoman. He strolled across her bedroom to her makeup table. Again, he glanced at the guest room doorway to make sure no one was there and reached into the pocket of his silk pajama shirt.

Cyrus had worried that when she'd jabbed his stomach earlier she may have felt it, but she obviously hadn't or she would have said something. He now removed it from his pocket: a remote, voice-activated recording device the size of a USB. He'd gotten it from the private detective he'd hired. Turns out there was some legal loophole that allowed you to put recording devices in your own home, so Cyrus had done it to aid in the investigation of his wife's affair—and he'd kept the device when the investigation was done. Now, he was using it again. He didn't know what Vanessa was plotting against him, if anything, but Cyrus wouldn't be caught by surprise this time around. He was done with that shit.

He peeled off the adhesive tape on the backside of the device, bent down, and attached it to the underside of her makeup table, far enough in the shadows so she couldn't see it. He then flicked a switch, stood upright, and smiled.

"I gotcha now, bitch," he whispered before walking out of the guest room.

By the time he heard his mother-in-law say her good-byes a half hour later and Vanessa closed the door behind her, Cyrus was already back in his bed, finishing his lunch.

"Nessa! Nessaaaaaaaaaaaaaaaaaaa!" he boomed. "Come and get this tray! I'm done!"

Chapter 3

Noelle

Noelle Grey's eyes fluttered open when she heard the gentle pulse of her alarm clock. Her bedroom was still shrouded in darkness, thanks to the drawn window blinds, but she could see the sun trying to peek its way through. She shifted to stretch but couldn't because Tariq's arm was linked around her waist as he dozed. He was still spooning her from behind, staying in the same position he'd been in for most of the night. She laughed silently to herself.

To be honest, she didn't want to get up yet, either, or to move. She was perfectly content to stay wrapped in his embrace with him snuggled behind her. Noelle liked the comfort of Tariq's presence and the reassurance that came with it. Tariq was a good man who had protected and nurtured her from the beginning. All those years she'd thought he'd been kind to her as a favor to Cyrus. But the truth was, he'd really done it because he was secretly in love with her, but had held back out of respect for his friendship with Cy, and for their marriage. But now that everyone knew her marriage to Cyrus was a sham and she knew her husband was a liar and a crook, there was no point in either of them holding back anymore. And it was the best decision Noelle had ever made.

Tariq finally began to stir behind her. When his hold around her loosened, she eased forward and started to throw her legs over the edge of the bed, but stopped short when she felt his arm clamp around her waist again.

"Uh-uh, where do you think you're goin'?" he whispered huskily into her ear, drawing her back to him. At his question, the hairs on her neck stood up. The skin on her arms lit with goose bumps of anticipation.

"I was getting up," she said, smiling at him over her shoulder. "I thought you were, too."

"Nah, not yet." He then brushed his lips along the nape of her neck, leaving a series of butterfly kisses along her spine.

She felt him ease up the hem of her silk nightie, lifting it up her hips and torso, kissing her back and shoulders the entire time. Following his silent command, she raised her arms so that he could tug it off, then she bit down on her bottom lip to stifle a moan as he dipped a hand between her legs.

The love Tariq showed her daily with sweet gestures and kind words was only a close second to the love he showed her in the bedroom. Noelle had never put a huge emphasis on sex, seeing it as something pleasurable and even exciting with the right partner, but definitely not anything worth risking it all for. But Tariq made her rethink that idea. She couldn't say exactly what he did or how he did it, but sex with Tariq was something she didn't know if she could go without for very long.

Noelle spread her legs to give him more access, feeling herself grow wetter against his fingertips, twisting, turning, and whimpering all the while. He nibbled her earlobe and nipped and licked the skin along her shoulder blades as he did it, and she felt his erection nudging at her bottom, begging to be let in.

Tariq could bring her to orgasm just like this in a matter of minutes. He'd done it enough times that she knew he could. She could certainly feel herself getting close right now. He was pushing her to the brink, to the point she was panting and moaning. Then, suddenly, he pulled his hand away. He went for her throat, catching her by surprise. She tensed. He was usually so tender; he'd never been aggressive with her before.

"Tariq," she whispered with a nervous laugh, "what . . . what are you doing, baby?"

But he didn't answer her, perhaps lost in the passion of the moment. He continued to kiss her shoulder and nibble at the skin.

She began to panic when the same fingers that were bringing her pleasure less than a minute ago now clamped around her windpipe. His grip tightened. She couldn't speak anymore. She could barely breathe. Was he trying to kill her?

Noelle reached up to tug Tariq's hand away.

"Stop," she squeaked. "Stop! Let go! You're choking me!"

"Trust me," he finally whispered against her ear. "Trust me, baby."

She hesitated.

Trust him? He was damn near strangling her and he expected her to not fight back, to not shove him off and run away screaming bloody murder? But Tariq had never hurt her before, and he'd promised that he never would.

She stopped tensing. She pulled her hand away from his wrist and closed her eyes, even though every fiber in her at that moment told her to do the opposite. She wanted to breathe.

Tariq slid inside her with one swift thrust that made her

cry out. He then pounded into her over and over again, increasing the tempo. He loosened his hold around her neck, but only a little, and the throbbing between her legs increased by tenfold. Her body was dancing on edge of something she hadn't experienced before. It frightened and exhilarated her.

Noelle grabbed the mattress. She had a death grip on his arm. When the orgasm hit her, he released his hand from her throat. She gasped for air, and not just because she could finally breathe unhindered. She shouted out. She screamed for God. Noelle had never felt something so intense, so exquisite. When it ended, it left her shuddering all over. Tariq came soon after, holding on to her for dear life, jerking with each wave and spasm that crested over his body until they both lay still and sweaty on the wrinkled bedsheets.

"Are you ever gonna wake up, sleepyhead?" Tariq chided playfully.

Noelle opened her eyes, pushed herself up to her elbows, and yawned. "I *did* wake up—and then some rude person made me exhausted all over again," she grumbled, though she still shivered with delight at the memory of their early morning tryst. She glanced at her alarm clock on her night table and smacked her lips. "Damn! It's seven thirty already?" she groaned.

"Yep," he said as he slid into his suit jacket.

Tariq was wearing a custom-tailored, navy-blue, pin-striped suit today, with a crisp white shirt that stood out against his caramel-hued skin. A gold clip was on his tie. Gold cuff links adorned his sleeves. He always looked so put together, damn near Godlike in suits, which was a good thing, considering he seemed to wear them almost exclusively. In fact, Noelle had only seen him two ways: in a suit or naked.

"I've got to head out now if I have any chance of making it to work by eight fifteen," he said, pausing mid-motion. "*What?* What's with the face?" Tariq adjusted his tie. "I don't have a lot on my plate today. I'll be out of the office by five. We're gonna meet up later. Trust."

"It's not that." She adjusted the stack of pillows behind her, propping them up against the headboard so that she could sit up and face him. "I just don't understand how you can keep going into work every day knowing who Cyrus is . . . what he's done. Your business is tainted, Tariq. It could have gotten him killed. Doesn't that bother you?"

Tariq had revealed to her months ago that one of the reasons Cyrus may have been shot was because he'd stolen money from one of the clients of their financial consultancy firm. She'd been shocked to find out her husband's business was connected to the criminal underworld, but considering how many other secrets Cyrus had hidden from her, it wasn't completely surprising.

She watched now as Tariq let out a long sigh. It sounded more like a grumble. He then sat down on the edge of the bed beside her.

"Noelle," he began in a measured voice, "we already talked about this, baby. I told you that I'm dissolving my partnership with Cy, but I can't do it overnight. We still have clients we have to answer to. I still have a business to run."

"A business with criminals," she corrected, making him narrow his dark eyes at her.

"Not all our clients are criminals. Some are regular people who paid us a fee to invest their money. I'm still responsible to them." He braced his hands on both sides of her legs. "It's gonna take a few months to start my own operation and move over my clients. Until then, I'm still a partner in Greydon Consultants. It is what is, baby."

"Look, I understand how businesses work. I have one of my own! Remember? But I know what funded that business and I can't . . . I *cannot* walk through the door every day knowing what I know. It just feels wrong!"

"So, what are you saying? You're just gonna give up on your shop? You're shutting down Azure?" he asked, referring to her women's boutique in Ballston, Virginia, that she'd opened a few years ago with her husband Cyrus's help and funding.

"I don't see how I have any choice but to shut it down! We've been in the red for years. Cy's money is what kept the doors open. And now that I'm no longer talking to Cy and I've filed for an annulment, he isn't paying my bills anymore. Not at the shop—not here. He's what was keeping everything afloat, but I'm done with him. It's over! He can keep his dirty money and his lies as far as I'm concerned."

"Wait. He cut you off? Why the hell didn't you tell me? So how are you even paying your mortgage? Who's paying the utilities?"

"I have a little money saved up. It should hold me over for a few more months, but after that . . . after that, who knows? The house can go into foreclosure, or he can have it outright. I'll move on. I'll survive. I was fine before him. I'll be fine without him!"

"But you don't have to let it go into foreclosure. You're right. You don't need that nigga! Not with me around. How much do you need for everything? How much are your monthly expenses? I mean . . . what are we talkin' here? Ten thousand? *Fifteen*?"

She moaned impatiently. "I didn't tell you this because I wanted you to loan me money, Tariq. I'm just explaining that I know what it means to—"

"It's not a loan. I'm *giving* it to you. You can have the

money outright." His eyes scanned over her face. "I'd be happy to help you."

Of course he would. Tariq had been nothing but kind, supportive, and honest with her through all the trials and tribulations her husband had put her through, from finding out that Cy was secretly married to two other women, to him lying about his ability to father children and give her the baby she'd badly wanted. With every heartache, Tariq had offered her a pep talk and a shoulder to cry on and she loved him for it. But kindness and affection was one thing—she would take all that he was willing to offer in that regard. Money was a different matter.

She raised her hand to cup his cheek, stroking his goatee with her thumb. "Thanks, love. That's a sweet offer, but . . . no. No, I couldn't accept it."

"Why not?" he cried. "If you don't have to lose your home . . . if it allows you to keep your shop . . . if it keeps you from having to fire those women who work for you, which I know you don't wanna do, why not just take the money? When your shop makes a profit, you could handle your expenses yourself. Until then, just think of it as a monthly gift. No strings attached."

She lowered her hand from his face and began to squirm uncomfortably. It was like Tariq was wrapping his hand around her throat again and slowly squeezing, applying pressure.

She trusted him, but Noelle knew the truth: There were *always* strings attached when it came to money. She realized that now. Even when they weren't stated explicitly, you knew what the conditions were. Because Cyrus had paid most of their bills, bought the house and cars, and was co-owner of Azure, she hadn't wanted to rock the boat too often in their marriage, outside of pestering him to have a baby. He'd supported and taken care of her so she'd felt it was her duty to do the same—even when he'd raised her suspicions and made her doubt his fidelity and honesty.

Noelle realized now that one of the reasons she'd ignored so many alarm bells with Cy was because he pretended to be such a good husband, including a good provider. But she didn't want another relationship tainted with money and those types of power dynamics. She wanted her relationship with Tariq to be different, to be better. It couldn't be if he started financing her life.

"Look, you're a woman with integrity. I get it. That's one of the things I love about you, baby. But sometimes you gotta do stuff that doesn't look good on paper if it's for the greater good," Tariq urged, as if reading her thoughts. "You need a place to live. Your employees need a place to work. Just think about it, okay?" Tariq gave her a quick peck. "You don't have to decide right away. Think about it for a little bit and get back to me." He shifted, pushed up the sleeve of his suit jacket, and checked his watch. "We're gonna have to save this for later, though. I better get going or I'm gonna be late."

Noelle tossed aside her bedsheets and rose to her feet. She spread her arms and stretched. "I guess I should finally get up, too. I should probably make an effort to run my business while I still have one," she muttered.

Tariq let his eyes slowly rake over her naked body, at the glistening dark skin, long legs, round behind, and pert breasts. He licked his lips. "On second thought," he said before reaching up, grabbing her hand, and yanking her so that she shouted out in surprise and landed sprawled on top of him. He kissed her neck and shoulder. "I don't have any phone calls or meetings scheduled this morning. I can get in a little late today. Get that fine ass over here, girl."

Tariq began to nibble her earlobe and neck again, making her squeal. "Stop! Stop!" she yelled between giggles. "At least let me brush my teeth first! You know damn well I've got morning breath. I can taste it."

"I don't mind a little morning breath. I love you anyway." He gazed down at her. His eyes went soft again. "You know I love you, right?"

She nodded, trailing a finger along his cheek. "Yeah, I know. And I love you, too."

"Good. And don't forget it." He kissed her bare shoulder one more time and rose from the bed, adjusting his suit as he did it. "I should finally head out now. I'll see you this evenin'. Okay?"

"Okay," she said, and blew a kiss to him.

But as she watched him walk out her bedroom door, her winsome smile faded. Her thoughts were plagued with the problems she now faced and Tariq's offer to fix them for her. Whatever decision she made, she knew it wouldn't be an easy one.

Chapter 4

Diamond

"Two Bud Lights and a whiskey on the rocks, Jake," Diamond said as she ambled up to the bar with her serving tray. The bartender nodded before grabbing a stein and turning to the beer taps. While he poured, Diamond glanced over her shoulder at the half-empty barroom.

It was illegal to smoke in bars and restaurants in Maryland, but the owner of Finley's Tavern in Baltimore didn't seem to care. Several of the patrons were lighting up in the booths, drinking, talking, and cussing up a storm as they smoked. She'd heard a patron had once complained that smoking in the Tavern violated the health code—and *he* was the one who got kicked out. The first week she'd worked there, her eyes had watered from the haze. She'd looked like she was crying. She'd coughed and hacked like she had tuberculosis. Even her hair and clothes smelled like smoke at the end of each night. But now she was used to it.

Waitressing at Finley's Tavern was light-years away from the hostess gig she'd had for two years at The Seneca restaurant. The patrons there had ordered seared scallops and pureed potatoes with glasses of merlot. Here, they were happy with beer, burned onion rings, and nachos coated in neon-orange cheddar cheese. She'd had to wear silk blouses and high heels at The Seneca, but she could show up at the Tavern in a pair of ripped jeans and a tank top and no one would bat an eye. The Tavern didn't pay as much, but with tips, it still paid her enough to cover her expenses, and she'd been grateful to get it. Since her criminal case had drawn national attention, jobs were hard to come by. But like smoking inside the bar, the manager didn't care that she was facing an attempted murder charge. As long as she showed up on time, could carry a tray without spilling drinks, and didn't steal from the till, she was fine with him.

Diamond watched as the bartender set the steins and glass on her tray. She turned away from the counter with the drinks in tow, prepared to head back to the table of grizzled truckers who were talking about last night's Orioles game. But when she spotted someone familiar step through the Tavern's swinging glass door, she came to a halt.

It was Darius Mercer—her defense attorney.

He had just shown up one day while she was in jail, claiming he represented her. She'd thought he was with the public defender's office, or that maybe Cy had hired him, but she found out neither was true.

"So who hired you?" she'd asked him. "Who is paying for all this? Lawyers aren't cheap."

"No one. I'm working pro bono," he'd told her while flipping through his files.

"But why?"

Why would he take her case for free? What could he possibly get out of this?

He'd shrugged. "You're a high-profile client. This case has gotten national attention. If I could get you off this charge—"

"Then you raise your profile?" she'd asked suspiciously.

"Something like that. But as long as I keep you from serving twenty years to life in prison, does it really matter?"

He'd had a point.

Now she watched as Darius took a few steps into the Tavern and looked around him, probably in search of her, but he didn't notice her watching him. He coughed into his fist and waved at the haze around him. With his horn-rimmed glasses, drab gray suit, and his leather satchel thrown over his shoulder, he had to be the nerdiest-looking Black man she'd ever seen in her life. Well, that wasn't true. He was maybe a distant second to Steve Urkel. He had absolutely no swag and stood out like a sore thumb among all the other men in the room, making her laugh to herself. But he was a nice enough guy, and he was helping her for free, so she tolerated him—barely.

Diamond walked toward the table of customers, smiling as she did it. "Here you go," she said as she set their drinks in front of them.

Darius finally spotted her and walked toward her. "I waited at your condo for over an hour," he said. "I don't like having to chase you down. Did you forget that we were meeting there at five?"

She glanced over her shoulder at him as she tucked dollar bills into her apron pocket. "Hello to you, too," she muttered.

"This is not funny." He pushed his glasses up the bridge of his nose and glared down at her. "We were supposed to meet today. We were supposed to go over the crime scene and you were supposed to show me what happened—and you didn't show up!"

"Yeah, sorry about that. You got my message, though, right?" she asked as she walked to another table to take their order.

"No, I didn't get your message or I wouldn't have been there waiting," he argued while trailing behind her. "And you canceled our last meeting before this one. You can't keep doing this, Diamond."

"Hey," she said as she approached the other table with her order pad in hand, "what can I get you fellas?"

"Don't ignore me," Darius said tightly behind her. "Look, you aren't my only client, and I don't have to chase the others down because they value my work and my time. I can't do my job if you don't let me help you. We have a hearing next week. Your trial comes up in a few months and I'm trying my very damnedest to keep you from rotting in prison for the rest of your life, and you don't seem to give a shit!"

The two men sitting at the table did a double take and Diamond's polite smile withered.

"I'm sorry, gentlemen. Can you give me a sec?" she asked them. Diamond then whipped around and faced Darius, giving him the once-over. But he didn't flinch under her withering gaze; he stood his ground. She decided to give him a piece of her mind anyway.

"First of all, don't you ever talk to me like that."

He opened his mouth to respond, but she held up her hand to cut him off before he could.

"Second of all, don't tell me what I give a shit about. You don't know me and you don't know my life. I'd rather die than go back to that damn place," she muttered under her breath.

Her stay in prison before a judge finally granted her

bond had been the worst month of her life. They'd taken everything from her—from her braids to her dignity. And it didn't help that one of the girls she used to turn tricks with in the old days had told everyone on the cellblock that she was a snitch, that the only reason why they were arrested in the first place was because Diamond had called the cops and tried to turn in Julian, but managed to get herself arrested in the process. That didn't exactly make her the most popular girl in jail.

The whole experience had changed Diamond. She wasn't as kind or as trusting. In fact, the *only* person she still trusted was Cy.

"Thirdly, I have to keep a roof over my head," she continued. "I have bills to pay. Yes, I was supposed to meet you this afternoon, but the other waitress called out sick and the manager called me in to work her shift. He didn't give me a choice, Darius. I have to keep this job!"

For the first time, her lawyer's hard façade softened. He looked a little less annoyed.

"And speaking of jobs, I have to do mine. So if you aren't gonna sit down at one of the tables and order somethin', we're gonna have to save this for another day."

She watched as he gritted his teeth, as his nutmeg-hued face flushed a shade of pink and his nostrils flared. He looked like he wanted to continue arguing, but instead he muttered, "Fine," before walking to one of the empty booths and sitting down.

She then returned her attention to the table of men who had been waiting patiently.

A few minutes later she walked to Darius's booth and found him drumming his fingers on the sticky tabletop, staring blankly at the wall paneling.

"Sorry for the wait," she said.

He turned away from the wall and slumped back

against the cracked pleather seats that were probably just as sticky as the tabletop. "What's another five minutes compared to the *hour* I've already waited?"

She set a beer in front of him, deciding to ignore his sarcasm and offer an olive branch.

"Uh, thanks," he said before shoving the bottle aside, "but I don't drink."

Of course you don't, she thought. He was so straitlaced and uptight, she doubted he would ever let alcohol pass his lips. Or do anything else the average person would consider fun—like the very idea was a moral failing.

She once had a trick like that. He was one of her regulars—a Mennonite from Western Maryland who came to DC just to see her. He'd pay her three hundred dollars to stand naked in front of him in his hotel room. He didn't touch her and wouldn't let her touch him. He wouldn't even touch himself. He'd just stare at her for an hour or so, smile, nod politely, thank her for her time, and be on his way, only to do the same thing a few months later.

She now wondered what would have happened if she'd caressed the Mennonite's face or sat on his lap. He probably would have died of a heart attack right there in the hotel room. She bet if she did it to Darius right now, he'd react the same way.

"Do you have anything else?" Darius asked hopefully. "A glass of ice water with lemon, maybe?"

She gave a saccharine smile. "Sure! Would you like sparkling water or tap?" she asked sarcastically. "Would a Perrier suffice, sir?"

"A simple no would have sufficed," he muttered before leaning his elbows on the tabletop. "Anyway . . . back to the reason why I'm here. So while I was at your old building, wasting time, waiting on *you*, I got a chance to talk to Richard, the security guard."

"Oh yeah? And what did he say?" she asked eagerly.

She hadn't spoken to Richard since the day of her arrest. He had been a sweet guy. Always helpful. He was also one of the few people besides herself who may have actually laid eyes on the man who had really shot Cyrus. He had confirmed that he'd seen the guy at her condominium the day before the shooting, and she'd told the police as much, but they never followed up.

"His description definitely matched yours. He said he remembers seeing the guy, and he could probably point him out in a lineup if he had to."

"That's good! No, that's . . . that's great! Damn, that is such a relief. So we can—"

"No, it's not great." Darius licked his lips. He hesitated. "He doesn't want to testify. He said he won't take the stand. He definitely doesn't want to be cross-examined."

"*What?*" She sat down on the other side of the booth, forgetting that she was supposed to be waitressing. This wasn't the news she'd hoped for. "Why won't he testify?"

"Something about being nervous speaking in front of people."

"You mean like stage fright?"

"Maybe. He seemed like an anxious guy. Or maybe it's more than that. Maybe he's just not sharing the real reason. I could subpoena Richard and force him to testify, but I'd really prefer not to do that. Hostile witnesses aren't fun and far from reliable. He could hurt your case more than help it."

"Should I talk to him myself? Maybe he'd do it if I asked him . . . if I *begged* him to do it."

"No, don't do that. It's not a good idea. Even if he agreed to testify, we don't want to make it seem like we pressured him to do it. He said he wished you the best, but he doesn't want to get involved. He said he's moving out of the city, too." Darius paused again. "Something about him not being able to take life in Baltimore anymore, especially after what happened to you and your husband. Frankly, I think the guy is scared, Diamond."

She leaned her elbows on the table and dropped her head into her hands. She closed her eyes, praying this was all a bad dream. She was counting on Richard to help her case. If she didn't have him to back up her testimony, she didn't have any other witnesses. Cy said he had already told the cops it wasn't her who was behind the shooting, but they believed he was just a man in denial, refusing to think the worst of his wife.

"Hey," Darius said, placing a hand on her forearm, "look, I'll try talking to him again. Maybe in a week or two. Let's give him a little time to think about it, though. Don't lose hope. Okay?"

His hand was warm and slightly callused.

Maybe it was because she hadn't been touched by any man in months except maybe the brush of customers' fingers when she handed them change or a receipt that her arm started to tingle a little at Darius's touch. The sensation was surprising and unnerving—yet so familiar. She looked up, expecting to see Cyrus's smiling face. Instead, she saw Darius gazing at her earnestly. He wasn't her man and her man should be here with her, holding and reassuring her. Not Darius.

She snatched her arm away and sat upright. "How can I not lose hope? He was the only witness we had. He was the only person who could speak for me. You won't let me testify in my own defense!" she shouted, making some of the patrons turn from their drinks and onion rings to glance at her.

"I just . . . I just don't think you'd be a very sympathetic witness on the stand," he whispered.

"*Why not?*" she pointed at her chest. "What is so damn intimidating about me?"

He pursed his full lips and seemed to hesitate before he

spoke again. "You're not intimidating. That isn't the right word for it. It's just that jurors . . . jurors aren't always open-minded. When it comes to female witnesses, a certain type is what they consider more trustworthy . . . more believable. Because of your past . . . the things you've done, it could be a challenge for us to—"

"You mean no one is going to believe an ex-hooker whose pimp is accused of shooting her husband."

Darius went silent. He didn't respond.

"So because I used to turn tricks that means I also must be capable of planning a murder?" she pressed on. "Is that what you're saying?"

"No, I don't think that, but . . ."

"But?"

"But . . . the jurors might."

Of course they would, she thought sullenly.

The jurors wouldn't believe her like the detectives didn't believe her when she'd told them what had really happened that day when Cyrus was shot, when she'd told them what she saw. She'd said the same story about a dozen times and it always fell on deaf ears. No one would believe her because it was much easier for them to believe the lie than the truth, because the lie fit the narrative they'd already created about her in their heads. They all believed she was a lying vengeful whore who just wanted to steal Cy's money and leave him for dead. And here Darius was, insisting he could perform a small miracle by making a jury conclude the complete opposite about her and believe she was innocent.

This is such a joke, she thought.

She shouldn't have depended on him. She couldn't depend on anyone but herself and Cy, her one true protector. She had to finally take control of this situation, or it was only a matter of time before she would end up in jail again, and she couldn't go back. She refused.

"I have to go," she said, sliding out of the booth, rising to her feet. "I can't keep sitting here with you. I've got to get back to work."

"Wait! We still have to talk about the crime scene," he called to her as she walked back across the barroom. "Diamond! Diamond, come on! So one setback and you're just gonna throw in the towel?" he shouted after her, but she ignored him and walked to the bartender to give him her orders.

When she turned back around, Darius was gone.

Chapter 5

Vanessa

"Mommy, can I have more money for my card?" Bryson yelled, shoving his game card into his mother's face, yanking her attention.

Vanessa turned from searching around the arcade to look down at her son. "Uh, yeah, sure, honey." She reached into her purse to pull out her wallet.

"Can I have some money, too, Mommy? Puhleaaaaase!" her daughter, Zoe, cried over the arcade cacophony, bouncing on the balls of her feet, making her pigtails flap around her ears.

"Yes, baby," Vanessa said after absently pulling out two twenty-dollar bills. She handed them both to Bryson. "Split the money between you and your sister and put some on her card, too."

Bryson nodded before snatching the bills out of her hand. He then ran off.

"Wait for your sister! Don't separate, you two! You hear me?" she yelled after them as she watched her younger children scamper across the arcade.

Usually her eldest, Cy Jr., would be around to watch his

little brother and sister for her, but he was off with his friends yet again. Cy Jr. didn't seem to want to be around the house or his family so much anymore. Vanessa suspected his absence had less to do with preteen independence than him coming to terms with his father's secrets, lies, and the embarrassing revelations that followed.

Zoe and Bryson only vaguely understood that their father was accused of marrying two other women while he was still married to their mother. They'd accepted Cyrus's half-assed explanation that the allegations were "all just a big misunderstanding." But Cy Jr., now eleven, was a lot wiser and less gullible than his siblings. He was also more sensitive to the news coverage and neighborhood gossip about his father and family.

Vanessa knew Cyrus's lies hurt Cy Jr. just as much as they had hurt her—if not more.

But Mama will make it right, Vanessa thought as she glanced around the arcade, on the lookout for her lover, Bilal. *I'll make sure that son of a bitch never hurts us again.*

She was meeting Bilal here today to regroup and come up with another plan to murder her husband. They had been in a holding pattern for months and were finally ready to discuss their next move. But she and her lover had to be more careful now how and where they met. Ever since Vanessa had found out that Cyrus had a private investigator following her and Bilal in the early months of their affair, she'd been paranoid. She was always wondering if her phone calls and texts were being monitored or that maybe someone was trailing them. So no more clandestine meetings in the park that would end in passionate lovemaking in the back of Bilal's car, hookups at his apartment while Cyrus was away on business, or quickies at her house while Cyrus was in the hospital. Now she and Bilal only met in busy places where they could barely hear each other, let alone worry about anyone listening to their conversations.

She'd told Bilal she'd meet him here today at Play Palace—a giant, noisy arcade where she sometimes took the kids. It had seemed like the perfect cover, but she hadn't considered how hard it would be to find him in here.

After a few more minutes of searching, she finally spotted him standing by one of the glowing, blue hockey tables about twenty feet away. All the tables were taken by teenaged patrons who were screaming, leaping, and making the black disks zip back and forth across the tables' surfaces at lightning speed. Bilal was the only one over there not focused on any of the games. Instead, he was gazing around him, probably in search of her, like she was in search of him.

Vanessa walked straight toward him, drawing close before he finally noticed her.

"Oh, uh . . . h-hey, Mrs. Grey! F-f-funny running into you here," he stuttered awkwardly, making her loudly sigh.

Could he be any more obvious?

"We don't have long. The kids will start looking for me soon," she whispered to him, then walked around him. She took a few more steps and inclined her head, motioning for Bilal to follow her. She kept walking to a series of video games in one of the arcade corners after noticing that only a few patrons were back there. She climbed into one of the glass gaming booths where a bloodthirsty zombie with arms outstretched was on screen. Bilal climbed into the leather gaming chair beside her.

"How you doin', bae?" His eyes raked over her, but instead of seeing lust bloom in those dark irises like she usually did, she watched as Bilal frowned. "You don't look too good."

Well, damn, she thought.

First her mother, now him? Vanessa knew she was a little off her game lately, but she didn't know she looked *that* bad.

"You haven't seen me in a whole three weeks and those are the first words outta your mouth? 'You don't look too good'?"

"I didn't mean anything by it! I mean you just look tired. That's all. But it makes sense considering . . . well, everything."

"Yeah, this stuff with Cyrus is starting to wear me out," she conceded.

"No, I meant the baby. But waiting hand and foot on that nigga in your condition is bound to make it worse. I bet you're tired."

Oh, yeah. The baby.

She was supposed to be pregnant. She forgot about that occasionally, especially because the only person whom she had lied and told she was pregnant was Bilal.

Vanessa nodded. "It is and . . . and *I am!* I am so tired, honey. So very, very tired," she moaned softly, playing it up over the sound of bombs and lasers from one of the video games nearby.

"I'm sorry, bae. I want to get you out of there and away from him. That son of a bitch is no good for you! He's not good for the baby, either!"

"I know. And we—me and the baby—will be able to get out eventually. We'll finally be one big family like we hoped. We just have to come up with a new plan."

"But what new plan? What the hell do we do?" Bilal whispered. "You said we can't take him out at your house. You said to wait until he leaves and—"

"But he never leaves except for doctors' appointments. He can barely walk."

"So maybe we can do it when you take him to the doctor. I can wear the ski mask and—"

"No, you can't! The cops already caught the guy who wore a ski mask at the last shooting. He confessed. Remember? You'll just look like a copycat. It's too obvious."

"So then I have to sneak in and do it at your place. We've got no choice, bae!"

She thumped her head back against the leather headrest in frustration and closed her eyes.

Bilal was right. Their options were becoming increasingly limited. But it still felt too risky to do it at the house. The children weren't there during the day thanks to summer camp. With Cyrus still so ill, she could disappear from the house without raising anyone's suspicions, but only briefly. That left about an hour or so for Bilal to get the job done and get in and get out, unseen. What if something went wrong? What if he got caught? What if *they* got caught? She hated Cyrus and wanted him gone, but she didn't want to go to jail for the rest of her life. She didn't want to lose her children. There was so much at stake.

"Fine, then. We'll set a deadline," she resolved. "If he doesn't get better in a month, then . . . then we'll do it at the house. I don't like it, but I don't see what other choice we have. We can't wait around forever."

"Yeah, you're gonna start showing soon." He glanced at her stomach. "We gotta do it before that happens. You know my mama said she started showing with me as early as the third month," he rambled. "She said it was probably because she didn't do more sit-ups before she—"

"Bilal," Vanessa snapped, cutting him off, "I don't really want to hear about your mother's stomach muscles right now. Okay?"

"Aww, bae, this is really stressing you out, ain't it?" he asked as she started to rub her temples in a feeble effort to soothe her budding headache.

"Stressing her out" was putting it lightly. She felt like she was stuck in a prison cell with no visible bars or cinder-block walls, but whatever she did, she couldn't get out of it.

"I wish I could make you feel better. Give you some peace." Bilal raised his hand to caress her cheek, making her eyes flutter open.

Vanessa wished he could give her some peace, too. It would be the perfect answer to her headache. In fact, she wished she could give *him* a piece—a piece of ass, that was. But they hadn't made love in more than two months, not having the time and opportunity to do so. She longed for it, though, to have his arms around her and him thrusting between her legs. She licked her lips hungrily. Vanessa wanted her sexual fix so bad she swore she could taste it. This man had led her to form quite a habit.

Vanessa turned to face Bilal, gazing at his handsome face, zeroing in on his kissable lips. She could almost feel his lips against hers and his tongue inside her mouth. She tingled at the memory of the ghostly trail of his facial hair along her inner thighs.

He must have been reading her mind because he leaned forward and kissed her and, God help her, she kissed him back like a starving woman who had been tossed a few succulent scraps of meat. She fisted the collar of his shirt in her hands, dragging him closer so the kiss could deepen. The kiss became almost ravenous. Vanessa shoved aside one of the plastic machine guns between them and was almost straddling him in the gaming chair. Their heated moment probably would have gone further than that if it wasn't for a little girl, screaming, "Mommy!" nearby, breaking the spell. The girl sounded a lot like her daughter, Zoe.

Vanessa pulled her mouth away and shifted back, looking around her frantically. She didn't see her daughter or her son—to her relief.

"What? What's wrong?" Bilal asked.

"We can't do this here," she whispered, easing back into her chair. "Not with all these kids around. Anyone could see us!"

Her children included.

"But I want you, bae," he said, reaching for her again, biting his lower lip. "I want you so damn bad, girl."

But she grabbed his hand and held it tight, tugging it away from her face. "And you *will* have me as much as you want—when all of this is over."

He slowly shook his head. "I don't think I can wait that long!"

She glanced down at his crotch, at the bulge in his jeans, and took a deep, shuddering breath. She didn't think she could wait that long, either.

"Text me in a few days," she said. "We'll meet. I'll find a way."

"But I thought you were worried about being followed. I thought that's why we—"

She raised a finger to his lips. "Don't worry about that."

Vanessa was certainly starting to worry less and less if Cyrus found out she was still seeing Bilal, especially the more he pissed her off.

Bilal gritted his teeth, not looking convinced until she took his thumb into her mouth and began to suck it almost as a demonstration of what was to come. He grinned.

"I promise, baby," she whispered.

They shared one last, quick kiss—far too quick for her liking, but it would have to do—before she tore her mouth away from his, and rose from her chair. She walked back across the arcade, feeling Bilal's eyes on her all the while. As she crossed the crowded space, she spotted her children.

"Mommy! Mommy!" Bryson yelled. "I got four hundred points!"

"Did you, now?" she asked as he and his sister crashed into her. "Well, I guess we better get your prize, then."

"No, I want to play a few more games! Can you give me some more money?"

Her children then grabbed her hands and led her away, but her thoughts remained with Bilal. Vanessa was already eagerly looking forward to when she would see her lover again.

Chapter 6

Cyrus

Cyrus opened the door to his garage and walked down the wooden stairs to his BMW. Before he unlocked the car door, watched the headlights flash, and climbed inside, he made a quick check of everything, patting the pockets of his shirt and linen pants.

Wallet. *Check*.

House keys. *Check*.

He reached around and felt the metal grip of the handgun tucked into the waistband of his pants.

Gun. *Check*.

It was a tight fit. Vanessa was right about one thing: he had put on some weight. Maybe it was time to go up a few inches in the waist if he was gonna start carrying around this thing all the time. Ever since he'd been caught off guard with the shooting at his Baltimore condo in May, he didn't want to leave the house without a weapon. He even kept a loaded Magnum in his night-table drawer. He'd resolved that this time, if someone shot at him, he was shooting that motherfucka right back.

Cyrus opened the car door and climbed inside. He pressed the button overhead on the garage door opener and listened to the metallic cranking sounds, to the whine of the cables as the door slowly opened, revealing his driveway. He backed out and paused to take another quick glance around him, hoping that none of his neighbors were home and, more importantly, they weren't watching his departure.

He hadn't wanted to go out today. He hadn't wanted to ruin his act as a bedridden invalid this soon after he'd arrived back from the hospital, but the email he'd received yesterday hadn't left him much of a choice. Today was as good a day as any to do this excursion, though his time window was slim.

Cy Jr. was at a skate party with his friends and Vanessa had taken Zoe and Bryson to that headache-inducing, hell-on-earth known as Play Palace. She would finish up their afternoon with a pizza lunch and then drive back home. That gave Cyrus about two hours to do this— maybe less.

He backed all the way onto the street, turned left, and followed the road leading out of his neighborhood. He was headed to DC. It was a necessary journey, the first step to right a wrong that had been committed against him. He was going to meet the person who had sent him the email yesterday, someone claiming to know who'd really shot him. He knew who was behind the shooting, the grand mastermind: It was Tariq, of course. But he still didn't know who had pulled the trigger. The person said they could give Cyrus the info he needed—for a price. They'd refused to speak by phone and only agreed to meet in person.

Cyrus had been incredulous at first, and paranoid. He wasn't stupid; he didn't want to walk straight into yet another trap. He'd initially refused the meeting, but the person gave him details about the shooting in a follow-up email, details that only someone who had been there on that day or had been given firsthand knowledge could have known. He was intrigued enough to take the risk, but again, he wasn't stupid. He had agreed to meet the person, but would only do it armed.

His BMW gradually made its way through the suburbs and streets lined with single-family homes to the fast-moving lanes of the beltway and, finally, to the city. The scenery was a lot less serene here. Brick homes gave way to steel and concrete. Manicured lawns were replaced with chain-linked fences. Cyrus slowly gazed around him. He knew these tarnished streets well. It was places like this where he had started his business. This was where he'd found his first "investors." He'd hustled hard to make it out of the concrete jungle, but he should have known that he would be drawn back one day, like some human boomerang. It was inevitable when you ran high-stakes cons like his.

The meeting spot, he discovered, was near the end of a dead-end street. Cyrus stopped the car and sat idle in front of the storefront, gazing up at the exterior.

"The fuck is this?" he murmured in bewilderment.

Ray's Bar & Lounge, the place where they were supposed to meet, wasn't a glamorous spot by any means. There were grates over the windows. Old, ripped flyers covered the bullet-proof glass. Steel bars were on the doors. The "Y" in Ray's was busted in the storefront sign.

This was a place you went to get drunk during the day because you had nowhere else to be. This was a place where you disappeared to because no one would ever be crazy enough to come looking for you here. This was the end of the road, literally and metaphorically, and this "meeting" was definitely starting to feel more and more like a setup.

Cyrus pulled into a small lot next door, beside a gas station that had seen better days. A minute later, he pushed open the door to the bar and lounge.

It was dark inside even though it was midday, and the sun was achingly bright outdoors. The only visible video camera in the bar seemed to have its lens pointed up, permanently focused on the water-stained ceiling for some reason. Cyrus squinted as his eyes adjusted to the darkness. His gaze landed on the bar first, where a wrinkled, dark-skinned bartender stood smoking a cigarette and wiping down the counter. When he saw Cyrus he paused and tugged the cigarette from his mouth.

"Can I help ya?" the bartender rasped.

"I'm lookin' for somebody," Cyrus replied. "He told me to meet him here. Has anyone else come in here?"

Instead of answering him, the bartender's gaze drifted away and landed on one of the booths in a shadowy corner. Cyrus turned to look in the same direction and found a man who was sitting alone holding up his hand, beckoning Cyrus toward him. Cyrus strolled across the lounge.

The man was nursing a drink even though it was only eleven o'clock in the morning. As Cyrus drew near him, he could see he wore cornrows and had a series of tattoos all over his face and neck.

The mystery man lowered his glass and leaned back. "What's up, man? Have a seat, bruh!"

As Cyrus sat down on the other side of the booth, he assessed him. There was something familiar about him, but Cyrus couldn't put his finger on what—or why.

"I ain't know if you was gonna show up," the man said, eying him right back.

"I said I would, didn't I?"

"Yeah, that you did." The man nodded before taking another sip. "But I'mma be honest, I don't know if I would've if I was you."

"Why?" Cyrus raised his brows. "Should I be worried? You planning on killin' me?"

"Nah, nothin' like that!" The man chuckled. "But you never know with these kinda things. Anything could happen."

"Yeah, well, I'm a guy who likes to take chances," Cyrus said dryly. "I wouldn't have gotten where I am today if I didn't. So what do I call you? What's your name?"

"You don't need my name. You just need my info."

Cyrus nodded. "Okay, then. So what did you have to tell me?"

The man set down his drink and leaned forward again. "I can give you the name of the dude who set you up. Give me twenty grand and I'll tell you."

Cyrus chuckled. "I ain't giving you twenty grand for that. I'm not giving you one red cent. I already know who set me up. I wanna know who fired the bullet."

"Why you wanna know that?" he asked, sounding anxious for the first time. He began to rub his legs underneath the table, lingering on his knees. It was a nervous habit. A tell. If the man was playing a game of poker and holding a hand of cards, he'd be well on his way to losing right now based on all the fidgeting he was doing, Cyrus noted.

"Because I'm curious and I don't like puzzles with missing pieces. Never have."

The man sitting across from him didn't respond. His hesitancy and the fidgeting was starting to make Cyrus suspicious.

"Do you know who shot me?" He tilted his head. "It wasn't you, was it?"

"Nah, bruh!" He laughed, rubbing his knees again. "But I could find out for you."

He was lying, but Cy wasn't sure what he was lying about—shooting him or that he was capable of finding out who did it.

"And how would you go about doin' that?"

"I don't know," he said with a shrug. "I know people. They tell me things. I can get info. Wouldn't be no problem."

"And how do I know you're not bullshittin' me just to get some money? I need something to let me know you're not full of shit . . . that you're legit. Giving me your word doesn't cut it."

He'd had men in the past give him their word and only been made a fool of for believing them.

"All right. I got you." The man nodded, looking almost smug. "You said you already know who arranged the hit. So I guess you already know it was that nigga Tariq Donohue. You work at his company, right? Y'all know each other?"

"I work at *his* company? *His* company?" Cyrus's jaw tightened. "It's *our* goddamn company! My name is on that damn plaque on the front door *above* his! I started it. I funded it from the beginning. I brought him in. Is that what Tariq told you . . . that it was his company?"

"Nah, he ain't tell me. I just thought that—"

"What else did he say to you?" Cyrus could feel his heartbeat accelerate. A vein was starting to bulge along his temple. "What other lies did that motherfucka tell?"

"Nothin'! He ain't say nothin', I swear!" He held up his hands. "Shit, I've never even spoken to the dude. I don't even know him. The streets be talkin', that's all," the man explained. "I heard about him. People tell me things! I can find out what you need. I can find out who shot you."

Cyrus took a deep breath, getting his anger back under control. He couldn't afford to lose focus and get side-tracked by his hatred towards Tariq. "And how . . . how much would you charge for it?" he asked calmly.

"Only half the price I told you since you already know part of it. Leave it to me to find out the rest."

Cyrus considered the man's offer until he noticed his

arms as he lowered them back to the tabletop. It wasn't the web of veins or the purple bruises that showed the remnants of a nasty drug habit that drew Cy's attention, but the tattoos. One tattoo, in particular. He spotted a gothic nine on the inside of the man's forearm. Cyrus had seen that tattoo before. Tariq had one. It was the mark of the DC gang to which Tariq was once affiliated. It was where Tariq got his big start and Cy had gotten money to fund and start his financial consultancy firm. Two of the lieutenants in the gang had even been among Cy's first clients. His job had been to take their drug money and make it look legit.

"You were part of the Nine Crew?" Cy asked, gesturing to the man's tattoo.

The man glanced down at it and nodded. "Yeah, back in the day."

"I remember y'all. You used to run this city," Cyrus continued.

The man grinned, lowering his hands. "Sure did! I tell the young ones comin' up that y'all shoulda' been here twenty years ago. We commanded respect back then. You ain't have to worry about folks actin' up. We handled shit. Didn't need no police. *We* were the police!" he said, pointing at his chest proudly.

"You used to be a tight network of dudes, too. I remember y'all had each other's backs."

"Shit," the man uttered slowly as he slumped back in the booth, then sucked his teeth. "Not no more! Most of them niggas either in jail or dead now. The ones that's left act like they forgot the code. I wouldn't have to hustle like I do if my crew still had my back. Them niggas know I'm strugglin'! But a lot of them wanna act like we ain't tight no more. Like this don't mean anything," he said, gesturing to his tattoo. "They too good for a gutter nigga like me! So I watch my own back. Fuck them!"

"Did you know Tariq used to be a Nine, too?"

"Nah, I ain't know that," the man said, rubbing his knees again.

You lyin' son of a bitch, Cyrus thought.

Based on that tattoo alone, Cyrus suspected this man knew Tariq. Now he was convinced he did as he watched the man do yet another tell, showing that he was lying. He was hiding too many secrets, telling too many half-truths or outright lies. Cyrus didn't trust him one bit. Sitting here in the bar, he felt his rage flare up again at the idea that the bastard now trying to shake him down for cash could very well be the same one who had shot him months ago and left him for dead.

I should kill him, he thought. He should reach across the table and strangle him right here in the barroom. Usually, he would give a job like that to Tariq. In the early days, when someone crossed Cyrus and did him sideways, Tariq was there as the enforcer to make sure that offender didn't dare do it again. But Tariq was no longer at his side. He was no longer in his corner. Cyrus would have to handle this on his own.

"So when can you get me the info I need?" Cyrus asked, not letting on what he now knew.

"I say give me a week." The man finished the rest of his drink. "I should be able to get the info by then. I'll hit you up when I'm ready and we can meet here again. Then you can pay me the five stacks."

Cyrus nodded. "Sounds like a deal."

He reached across the table and held out his hand for a shake. The man reached out, too, and shook it, unaware that he only had a minute or so left to live. "Talk to you in a week, bruh."

Cyrus grinned. "I'm counting on it." He then slowly slid across the booth and rose to his feet, pretending to grunt as he did it.

"Eh, you all right there, bruh?" the man asked, wrinkling his nose at him.

"I am now," Cyrus said as he reached behind him and tugged out his Magnum.

The moment he saw the weapon, his eyes went wide.

"Don't do it," Cyrus warned as he watched the man reach for one of his pockets. "Or I'll shoot until I run out of bullets, and I got a lot of them."

In response, the man eased his hand away and instead held up both at his sides in a sign of surrender. "You got it, bruh," he said shakily. "You . . . you got it."

"Just answer one question. Answer it honestly and I'll let you go. I won't shoot. Understood?"

The man loudly swallowed and gradually nodded.

"No more bullshit, because I'll know if you're lying. Did Tariq pay you to try to kill me? Was it you that day who shot me at my place in Baltimore?"

The man hesitated before nodding again. "But it ain't like I wanted to do it," he rushed in explanation. "I didn't even know you! He just told me that I had to—"

He didn't get the chance to finish. Cyrus unloaded two bullets—one in his head, the other in the center of his chest.

"Oh, shit! Oh, goddamn!" the bartender yelled, dropping the glass in his hand, making it shatter on the floor. He turned to run for cover, perhaps to the back of the lounge or beyond the swinging doors of the barroom. But he only made it two steps before Cyrus raised his arm again and fired, shooting him three times between the shoulder blades and making him fall face-first onto the wall display of dust-covered liquor bottles. The bartender then crumpled to the floor, taking several bottles with him, landing in a pool of blood and spirits.

Cyrus strolled across the lounge and ambled up to the bar. He leaned over the counter and peered down at the bartender, watching as he took his last breaths. The old man gave one final gasp. His terrified eyes went vacant.

"Sorry," Cyrus mumbled to the dead man. "Nothin' personal."

Unfortunately for the bartender, he just happened to be at the wrong place at the wrong time.

Cyrus leaned back and looked around him, surveying the mess. He glanced again at the camera still pointed up at the ceiling, now grateful that it hadn't been pointed at the bar or lounge. He hated dirty work like this, but it had to be done. Cy tucked the gun back into the waistband of his pants before walking out of the barroom and back into the sun. He tugged a pair of dark shades from his shirt pocket, taking a few seconds to let his eyes adjust again before he walked back to his car and headed home.

Chapter 7

Noelle

"Noelle, can I speak with you for a sec?" Miranda, Noelle's assistant manager, called out after softly knocking on her office door.

"Uh, yeah. Sure! Just . . . uh . . . just give me a minute, please!" Noelle shouted as she scrambled to gather the stack of envelopes and papers strewn across her desk.

They were all overdue bills for her boutique, Azure— the electric bill, the water bill, and bills from clothing vendors. Some were first notices but others were second notices in bright red ink and all caps. The letters threatened to cut off service or to contact lawyers if payments weren't remitted immediately. Just looking at them made Noelle's chest flush with heat under her silk blouse. It made her sick to her stomach. She wanted to gobble down another Zoloft just to calm her overwrought nerves, but she resisted the urge.

She had no idea how to make the bills go away, to pay all the money she owed. No, that wasn't true. She *did* have a means to pay it; Tariq had offered to handle her debts and all her monthly bills from now on. But she wasn't willing to go down that road. At least, not yet. And she'd be damned if she'd go back to Cyrus. She wouldn't go groveling to him for more money even if her life depended on it.

But you can't let this drag on forever, a voice in her head cautioned.

Of course she couldn't. But she'd do it for a bit longer until another solution presented itself, or she had no options left—whichever came first.

Noelle shoved the envelopes into a desk drawer and closed it. "You can come in now," she called out. When Miranda opened the door, Noelle pasted on a congenial smile. "Hey! What's up?"

Always the saleswoman and brand promoter, Miranda was wearing a pale-blue, sleeveless cotton dress today from their own collection. She had accessorized it with a pearl necklace and earrings set they also sold at the boutique. Miranda now tucked a lock of dark hair behind her ear, unwittingly showing off one of the earrings. She seemed to hesitate. She didn't return Noelle's smile, either. Instead, she quietly shut the door behind her and stepped farther into the small office.

Noelle's brows crinkled together as she gazed at her friend and employee with concern. "What? What's wrong?"

"Umm, I . . . I checked my bank account today," Miranda began.

"Okay?" Noelle said, shifting uneasily in her chair.

"I know I'm one of those crazy people who still prefers paper checks. It's my weird quirk. I get it," she said, throwing up her hands as her cheeks flushed pink. "Well, anyway, I deposited my paycheck last week and was surprised to see the money still wasn't there today. I mean . . .

usually, it doesn't take this long to deposit," she said while wringing her hands anxiously. "So I called the bank. I thought maybe it was a mistake on their end, or that the check had deposited and I just couldn't see it online yet for some reason. Well, long story short . . ."

Too late, Noelle thought tiredly.

"The bank said it wasn't a mistake." Miranda stopped wringing her hands and took a deep breath, making her freckled shoulders rise, then fall. "The check bounced, Noelle. I guess for insufficient funds."

Noelle's stomach plummeted. There had been money in that account last week. She had checked it personally because it was the one she used to pay Miranda's and the salesclerks' wages. Unlike the other bills, she would never put off paying her staff. She knew it could mean a late rent or student loan payment for them, or no food on the table. And besides, they worked hard. They deserved to be paid on time. But obviously, Cyrus hadn't considered that, or cared when he took money from the account. It was the only way the money could have disappeared. He was the only other person who had access to it.

You bastard, she thought. After all Cy had done to her, after all he had put her through, he was punishing her all over again.

"I'm so . . . *so* sorry!" Noelle reached for one of her cabinet drawers and removed her purse. She opened it and pulled out her checkbook. Her hands were trembling a little as she did it. "How much do I owe you? Seventeen hundred, right?" She flipped open the checkbook, grabbed a pen from her desk, and began to write Miranda's name on one of the checks. "Again, I'm so sorry this happened. I guess I better check in with Janise and Tasha to see if—"

"Noelle," Miranda said, holding up her hand, taking a step toward her desk, "look, you don't have to apologize. Mistakes happen. But is . . . is everything okay? I mean . . . is there something I need to know?"

Noelle stilled mid pen stroke. She slowly looked up at her. "What do you mean?"

"I mean, is there something you need to tell me? You can, you know! I realize a lot has been going on these past couple of months. You've had a lot of stuff happen to you. Your husband getting shot, then that whole . . . well . . . bigamy thing. . . ."

Noelle didn't know if she would describe what Cyrus had done under such simple terms as the "bigamy thing," but she understood where Miranda was coming from. It was still something even Noelle struggled to wrap her head around and clearly articulate in words.

"I'm leaving Cyrus," she began. "He and I are done. But needless to say, it hasn't been a clean break. He's making it very . . . very difficult."

"Difficult how? If you don't mind me asking."

Noelle was starting to feel light-headed again under Miranda's intense gaze. She didn't want to get into this, but she felt like she owed Miranda an explanation. She couldn't continue to keep her in the dark about this stuff.

"Cy . . . Cy controlled lots of things in our marriage— the purse strings, in particular. He's co-owner of Azure, too. He handled a lot of expenses and—"

"And now he doesn't anymore," Miranda said, going from intense to resigned. "So that's why my paycheck didn't go through?"

Noelle nodded. "He's likely the reason. Yes."

"So he's pulled all his money. What does that mean for Azure?" Miranda took a few steps to her desk. "What does that mean for *us*, Noelle? Are you saying you can't pay us anymore? Are you going to have to let all of us go? Close down the shop?"

"No! No! I mean . . ."

Noelle cringed. Why was it so damn hot in here all of a sudden? She felt like she was about to break into a sweat. Her stomach flipped. Then flopped. She was getting queasy.

"I mean I don't think so," she whispered.

"You don't think so? So you don't know for sure if you'll have to close down Azure?"

Noelle felt cornered, like whatever answer she gave wouldn't be the right one. She felt like her husband had pressed her up against a wall and she couldn't get away, even if she tried. Cyrus had forced her into this situation, and now she had the stark choice between her pride and ideals versus closing down the shop she loved and firing women she cared about.

"Look, I don't want to let you guys down." She lowered her eyes, no longer able to hold Miranda's gaze. "And this shop has been my dream for . . . forever, but I . . . I . . ."

Words disappeared. She could no longer think of any. That's when she lost the battle to her light-headedness and her stomach. When she opened her mouth again, it wasn't to speak. Noelle just barely managed to grab the trash can beside her desk before she leaned forward and threw up.

Noelle arrived home several hours later. She stepped through the front door and kicked off her high heels, leaving them on the hardwood where they had fallen, too tired to bend down and retrieve them. The house was dark and achingly silent. She flipped a switch, making her living room and kitchen blaze with light. She then headed to the stairs to climb to the second floor.

It was one of the few nights in the past few weeks when she would be home alone. She would usually be at Tariq's place in DC, or he'd spend the night here, but he had texted her earlier that he would have to cancel dinner plans—he was working late. Under normal circumstances she would be disappointed by the news, but an evening home alone gave her the chance to do what she had been putting off doing.

Noelle walked down the hall to her bedroom. She'd re-decorated in here since leaving Cyrus, removing all his old things, including his armoire and his clothes, giving them all to Goodwill. She had been so relieved when she'd done it. After the guys who loaded the furniture and garbage bags full of stuff on the truck had left, she'd twirled in a circle, fallen back on her bed, and laughed. She'd felt freer . . . lighter, knowing that Cyrus was out of her life. She'd told herself that all her problems were now behind her. She didn't realize how wrong she was.

Noelle now removed her leather belt before tossing it along with her purse onto her bed and heading straight to her bathroom.

Vomiting in front of Miranda had given her a reprieve. The other woman had been too concerned with making sure Noelle wasn't dying to bother continuing their con-versation about the future of Azure. She'd gotten her something to drink and hovered over her for most of the afternoon to make sure she was okay and didn't need to go to a doctor. Noelle guessed she should've been relieved that the vomiting had been a distraction, but she wasn't. This was the third time she had thrown up this week. The first time she had excused it as food poisoning—bad shrimp or undercooked chicken she must have eaten. The second time she'd convinced herself that maybe it was a lingering stomach virus, even though she hadn't developed any other symptoms. But like her dire finances, Noelle couldn't continue to deny the reality of the situation, especially now that her period was late.

She hadn't breathed a word of this to Tariq, of course. Yet another secret worry she was keeping from him. No, they hadn't used condoms as consistently as they should have. And she should have gone back on birth control weeks ago, like she'd planned, but had only scheduled the appointment with her doctor instead, taking whatever time slot the receptionist had available. Noelle hadn't thought it necessary to tell Tariq what was happening, assuming, perhaps naively, that her period would come eventually, like it always did, or the vomiting would just stop. But now she might have to tell him if her suspicions were correct.

Noelle took a deep breath, bent down, and opened one of the cabinets beneath the double sinks. She quickly found the box of pregnancy tests in the wicker basket with her ovulation tests and thermometers, remnants of a time when she had been obsessed with getting pregnant, when she had prayed to have a baby with Cy. She'd intended to throw the basket away, assuming after ending it with Cyrus that she wouldn't need it anymore.

"Jokes on me," she muttered.

Noelle quickly removed the test kit from the box and plastic packaging and did the same process she had done dozens of times before. She flushed the toilet, washed her hands, and waited for about a minute, hoping against hope that the test was negative.

It seemed ironic that now she was praying for the opposite of something she had prayed so avidly for only months ago.

She looked at the indicator and instantly felt her knees buckle, making her grab the counter to steady herself.

Oh, shit, she thought as she stared down at it, reading the word, "Pregnant" in bright blue ink. So it was true. And now she was left with another conundrum and even more overwhelming choice than the last one.

Chapter 8

Diamond

Diamond halted in front of the glass doors of the twenty-five-story condominium, hesitating before she reached for the handle. It had been two months since she'd been back here. In fact, she could remember the last day she had walked on this stretch of sidewalk. It had been while she was in handcuffs, being led away by the Baltimore PD to a waiting police car.

She couldn't tell her lawyer, Darius, that she kept skipping showing him the crime scene because she had been avoiding coming back here. She hadn't set a foot in the building, even when the moving guys came to pack up the place. Any other woman would have wanted to supervise the crew handling her clothes, jewelry, and furniture, but she hadn't. Diamond had even left the task of cleaning out her fridge for the maintenance staff.

Every time she tried to make her way back here, to the home she'd shared with Cyrus, she'd feel sick to her stomach—which was what she was feeling right now. Each time she was gripped by fear at the prospect of showing her face to all her old neighbors. She could just imagine the derision in their eyes or outright disgust on their faces. They probably heard all the stories about her—the truth and the lies. How could they have not heard them? It had been all over the evening news and in newspaper articles for weeks.

But I've gotta go in there, she told herself, despite the embarrassment and shame. She had to do it if she stood any chance of saving her own hide.

Diamond took a deep breath and tugged the glass door open. She stepped inside the building, walking past a line of gold mailboxes and under the two-story, white-coffered ceiling and chandeliers that looked like glowing dandelions. As she neared the reception desk, her espadrilles sank into the plush floor rugs. She ignored the people who strolled by her and kept her eyes focused on the redhead sitting at the desk.

Richard was diligently watching the video monitors that showed the building's four elevator compartments and basement. He was probably on the lookout for any unfamiliar faces or shady characters roaming the building. He'd apologized to Diamond for letting the shooter get in that day back in May, for not stopping him when he had the chance. But now he had a chance to finally help her, and for some reason, he wasn't.

Frankly, I think the guy is scared, Diamond, Darius had told her back at the Tavern.

But she was scared, too—downright terrified of spending the rest of her life in prison. And she knew that was a strong possibility if Richard didn't testify on her behalf.

The young security guard didn't notice her walking toward him. He was too engrossed by the monitors. But when she drew near the desk and leaned against the black-lacquer counter, he looked up and did a double take.

"*Mrs. Grey?*" he whispered, almost in awe.

"Hey, Richard."

"I didn't expect to see you here." He rose to his feet and then sat back down, as if he wasn't sure whether to sit or stand. "No one told me."

"No one knew. I wouldn't know who to tell anyway. I don't live here anymore. Remember? I just decided to . . . you know . . . stop by. I haven't been here in weeks. I thought . . ."

Her voice trailed off when she noticed him looking over her shoulder. She turned to follow his gaze, but found no one there. She turned back around to face him again.

"Is everything all right, Richard?"

"Oh, everything's fine! I was just seeing if anyone was coming up from the downstairs office. Because you're here, I mean."

She frowned. "Why would anyone come up from the office for me?"

Richard took a hesitant glance around him. He eased forward in his chair and dropped his voice to a whisper. "I really wish you would've told us you were coming, Mrs. Grey. The manager told me to alert him if I saw you in the building." He shook his head. "I can't let you up-stairs without his permission. I'm sorry."

"I wasn't trying to go upstairs. I didn't come to get any-thing. I came here to talk to you."

"Oh!" He sat back and pursed his lips. "Is this about what your lawyer asked me about last week? About testi-fying?"

She nodded. "He said you don't want to do it."

"It's not that I don't want to do it, Mrs. Grey. It's just . . . it's just that I can't."

"Look, I know you might be scared or intimidated to speak on the stand. To be honest, I would be, too, but right now you're the only person I've got on my side. You're the only one who could back up my story."

"I know and I'm sorry, but—"

"If you don't testify, it's my word against the cops, and we all know who everyone is gonna believe," she rushed out. "They're already painting me as some murderous mastermind when I had nothing to do with it. Even my husband knows I would never do anything like that!" She paused, watching as Richard's face fell, as his eyes lowered to his desk. "You believe I did what they said I did, don't you? Is that the real reason why you won't testify?"

"No! No, it's not that." He took a quick look around him. "I'm sorry, but I can't talk about this here."

He was blowing her off. She should have expected as much, but she was still disappointed.

"I have to take my lunch break in about an hour," he continued, surprising her. "The other guard, Blake, takes over while I'm out. I usually grab a sandwich and a soda at the deli down the street. I could meet you there."

She had to be at the Tavern in about an hour and her manager wouldn't be happy if she showed up late, but Diamond was willing to risk his anger to keep talking to Richard and convince him to help her.

She gradually nodded. "Sure, I'll . . . I'll meet you there."

Exactly an hour later, like clockwork, Richard walked through the door of Angelo's Deli. She was already sitting at the counter waiting for him, sipping absently from a glass of lemonade and picking at a bag of plain potato chips. Richard saddled up to the padded stool beside her and sat down.

"A Reuben and a pickle with a Coke. Thanks," he said to the man behind the counter, perhaps Angelo himself. Richard then removed his black baseball cap with his security firm's logo and set it at his elbow. He turned to Diamond. "Thanks for waiting for me, Mrs. Grey."

She raised her glass. "It's not like I had much of a choice." She took a sip.

"Look, I know you're in a tight spot."

"That's putting it lightly."

"But I can't testify," he continued. "My job would be at stake. The company I work for . . . they don't want me to get involved. They don't want to bring bad publicity to them. I could get fired."

"Trust me, I'm not trying to get you fired." She closed her eyes, struggling to find a possible solution. "Maybe if I talked to your boss. Maybe if I explained the situation and—"

"It's not just that." He sighed. "My fiancée . . . she's scared. We just got engaged three months ago, and when she heard about what happened to Mr. Grey, and then what happened to you . . . well, she told me that I should stay as far out of it as possible. I mean, what if that guy who shot Mr. Grey comes after me if I testify and say that I saw him come to the building? What if he comes after my fiancée or . . . or my family?"

"He won't come after you. He won't! He—"

"How could you know that, though? How could you be sure?"

The truth was that she couldn't be sure. The tattooed assailant still hadn't been arrested, thanks to the police being obsessed with their theory that she and Julian had committed the crime.

Diamond sometimes wondered what had happened to the mysterious gunman. Why hadn't he come back to make a second attempt on Cyrus's life, especially when he realized Cy wasn't dead? Cyrus's other wife, Noelle, had insisted that Cyrus had crossed the wrong people, and they were hell-bent on punishing him. Why hadn't they done anything since? It made her wonder if maybe there was a piece of this puzzle she still didn't know about. Perhaps there were some questions about what happened on that day in May that were left unanswered. Either way, the gunman was still out there, so Richard's and his fiancée's worries probably weren't unfounded.

"I can't put her at risk," Richard continued. "I can't put my family at risk. I'm . . . I'm so sorry, Mrs. Grey, but I can't."

Just then the guy behind the counter sat a plate with a wax-paper-wrapped Reuben sandwich with a pickle skewered on top in front of Richard. He set a bottled Coke beside it. Diamond watched as Richard unwrapped his sandwich and took a bite.

"I'm gonna end up going to jail, Richard, and it'll be for a long time," she said, now resigned to the truth. He stopped mid chew. "I'm gonna go to jail for something I didn't do."

He slowly set down his sandwich and turned to face her. "I'm a big believer that things always work out in the end. I bet they will for you, too, Mrs. Grey."

She let out a sad laugh. If only she had the luxury of believing in fairy tales like he did. She hopped off her stool and grabbed her purse.

"I wish you the best! I really do," he called to her as she began to walk off.

"Yeah, thanks," she muttered before turning back around, swallowing her disappointment and bitterness. She then pushed open the deli's glass door and stepped onto the sidewalk. As she did, she felt the weight of the moment fall upon her. That was it. That was her last chance at freedom.

As Diamond began to walk back to her car, she felt as if the world was crumbling around her. Even when Julian had been arrested the first time and the police raided their apartment, even when she'd had to flee and leave all the other girls behind—the only real family she'd ever known, no matter how messed up their "bond" might have been— Diamond had never felt alone like she felt right now. She'd never felt so abandoned. She needed something . . . *someone* to soothe her because she was utterly lost. She needed her husband. She had to be with Cyrus.

Chapter 9

Vanessa

"Let's spread out here, Mama," Vanessa said, spotting a group of empty lounge chairs near the Olympic-sized swimming pool where a couple of dozen people were already taking laps and splashing around in the blue water. Out of the corner of her eye, Vanessa saw a boy cannonball off the diving board, sending up a big splash and making the nearby lifeguard blow his whistle.

"Fine." Her mother huffed under the sweltering sun before tossing her rattan beach bag onto one of the chairs. "Though I still don't know why we're here anyway. You've got a perfectly good swimming pool at your house!" The older woman then fanned herself, wrinkling her nose at a squealing gaggle of children who ran by them.

"I just thought it would be good to get out for once. Give the kids a chance to play with some of their friends," Vanessa lied as she sat down and began to rub sunscreen on her son Bryson's shoulders. She motioned for Zoe to turn around so she could do the same. Meanwhile, she took a furtive glance around in search of Bilal.

For once, planning a murder wasn't on the agenda. They were meeting here today for the long-overdue secret rendezvous she had promised. At first she had balked at the idea of hooking up at a public pool.

"What the hell do you take me for? One of your tacky little gym hos?" she'd exclaimed over the phone.

"Nah, bae, I know the guy who has the keys to the pool house. They usually rent it out for parties and stuff. But one of their rentals backed out at the last minute. He said we could have it all to ourselves this Saturday between the hours of eleven o'clock and two."

"*To ourselves?*" she'd repeated, more than just a little incredulous.

"Yep," he'd whispered, "all to ourselves."

The promise in his voice had been too tantalizing to resist, even though she knew the risk that came with such a meeting. What if someone caught them? What if it got back to Cyrus? But she was under so much stress, and with Cy still alive, there seemed to be no apparent end in sight to the private hell she was enduring. A few hours with Bilal could be just what the doctor ordered. They just had to be careful.

Vanessa now did another quick glance around the pool as her mother got comfortable, reclining back on the chair beside her.

So where the hell was Bilal? He should be here by now.

"Can we go in the pool, Mommy?" Bryson asked.

"Yes, honey. Go swim," she said to him and Zoe, shooing them away. She watched as her children scampered off. "And don't run!"

"Honestly, Nessa," her mother said, lowering her Chanel sunglasses and gazing over the top of them at her daughter, "why are we here? I thought the point of having your own pool built was so you could use it anytime you wanted. It's certainly a lot more private." She grimaced. "If we were there, we wouldn't have all these loud, sweaty people around. That's for sure!"

"Mama, why do you insist on talking about regular people like they're peasants?"

"Because they are, as far as I'm concerned." The older woman shoved her sunglasses back up the bridge of her button nose. "I didn't marry three wealthy husbands because I was enamored with being 'regular,' sweetheart. I put up with a lot of bullshit so I wouldn't have to be that anymore."

Her mother then reached for a women's magazine in her beach bag, flipped it open, and began to read an article about finding peace, humility, and your inner Zen. The irony wasn't lost on Vanessa.

Just then, she glanced over her shoulder and caught a pair of washboard abs in her periphery. She looked up and saw they belonged to Bilal.

He was standing near the diving board, next to a young woman in a tiny yellow bikini. The young woman laughed and playfully slapped Bilal's shoulder. Bilal leaned toward her ear and said something that Vanessa couldn't hear, making the woman laugh even harder.

You gotta be kidding me, she thought with annoyance, watching as Bilal's companion twirled her braids around her finger. He was supposed to be meeting Vanessa today and here he was, flirting with some hussy by the pool. She should've known he couldn't focus on one piece of ass at a time.

He must have sensed her watching him because he stole a glance in her direction and gave her a knowing smile. He then said something and kissed the young woman's cheek before walking off.

Vanessa loudly sucked her teeth.

"What?" her mother asked, lowering her magazine. "What's wrong?"

"Nothin'," Vanessa said, rising to her feet and adjusting her sarong around her waist as she did it. "I'll be right back."

"What do you mean, you'll be right back? Where are you going?"

"I-I have to go to the . . . the ladies' room," she said, sounding as flustered as she felt. "Just watch the kids, will ya, Mama?"

She then walked in the same direction Bilal had gone, following him to the pool house, ready to give him a piece of her mind.

She found him less than a minute later. The pool house looked less like the trendy, decked-out cabana she'd hoped for and more like a community center rec room with a few fold-up tables and metal chairs, a couple of pleather couches, and a flat-screen TV. When she walked into the room she saw that Bilal was leaning against one of the tables.

"So you made it?" he asked with a grin.

She closed the door behind her and stalked toward him. "Yeah, I made it! Though I don't know why the hell you asked me to come here when you already had pussy lined up elsewhere!"

He cocked an eyebrow. "What?"

"I had to drag my mother and my damn kids here to see you, and I find you kissing up on some bitch in a tacky yellow bikini!"

"Girl, what are you talkin' about? *You're* wearing a bikini!" he said with a chuckle, pushing himself away from the table. "And I wasn't kissin' up on nobody. I was just sayin' high to a friend."

"*A friend?* Yeah, right! And I may be wearing a bikini, but I went classy old Hollywood." Vanessa gestured to her one-shouldered, Badgley Mischka two-piece. She then haughtily raised her chin into the air. "There's a difference. Your little friend went classic *hoochie!*" She stomped her leopard-print kitten heel. "I should've known you'd pull this shit! I must be out of my damn mind to—"

She didn't get to finish. His mouth was firmly against hers, smothering any more arguments she could make. His tongue slid inside her mouth as his hands cupped her ass and he roughly tugged her against him, kissing her senseless, grinding his pelvis against hers. Bilal then pulled his mouth away, making her stare up at him dazedly. He was beaming.

"I love it when you talk your shit, bae," he growled in a husky whisper. "It turns me on. But you know damn well I ain't focused on any other woman but your crazy ass."

He then kissed her again and eased her back so that she was pressed flat against the pool-room wall. He yanked down her bikini bottom, shoving it down her hips and knees until it pooled at her ankles. She was damn near panting by the time his hand was between her legs, rubbing her there, making her wetter than the pool deck outside.

"You like that, bae?"

"You know I do," she moaned, squirming her hips, unable to resist.

"Well, you'll like this even better."

He then dropped to his knees on the rug, raised one of her legs, and rested her thigh on his shoulder. She was already quivering when she felt his beard brush the inside her thigh. Her legs almost caved when Bilal began his handiwork. His mouth and tongue flicked, dove, and sucked, and her moans became even louder. Vanessa had to bite down on her wrist to keep the swimmers and sunbathers outside the pool house from hearing her.

"You know what, bae," he said after abruptly pulling his mouth away. He gazed up at her from between her legs. "I still can't get over how flat your stomach is. I mean, when are you—"

"Please shut up," she whimpered, pressing his head back between her thighs.

Thankfully, he stopped talking like she'd ordered and got back down to business. It didn't take her long to reach orgasm right against the pool-room wall. She almost suffocated Bilal in the process as her thighs squeezed his head, and she groaned.

"Damn, warn a brotha first!" he said, rising to his feet a few minutes later. He glared down at her. "You tryin' to kill me?"

"Don't worry." She yanked down his swim trunks. She licked her lips and wrapped her hand around his already erect manhood. She began to stroke him. "I'll make it up to you."

She shoved him back onto the sofa and straddled him. She lowered herself and he slid inside so smoothly that she shuddered with delight all over again. This was what she wanted. This was what she had longed for for weeks and weeks and had been denied thanks to her husband.

Bilal lifted her and flipped her onto her back on the couch cushions, catching her by surprise.

"You like that? You like that, bae?" he asked as he pumped his hips.

"Oh, yes," she groaned, dragging her nails down his back, then reaching down to grab his ass and hold him in place. She'd keep him here forever if she could.

"When that husband of yours is dead and gone," he whispered, "I'm gonna fuck you like this, every day and every night," he promised while gazing down at her. He then raised one of her legs, plunging even deeper. "You hear me, girl?"

She nodded frantically. "I hear you! I hear you, baby!"

"And when I'm done with you, it won't be no more shit talkin'. When I'm done with you you ain't gonna be able to walk straight."

"Yes! Yes! Oh, God, yes!" she moaned, closing her eyes and bucking beneath him. "Give it to me!"

By the time Vanessa left the pool house forty minutes later, she and Bilal had made love on the sofa, against the wall, and on top of a minifridge. She strolled along the pool's edge, feeling invigorated. She'd been right; meeting up with him was just what the doctor ordered. Her head was clear. Her spirits were high. She was once again ready to conquer the world and murder her husband so she could get the same treatment from Bilal every day and every night, like he'd promised.

"Well, there you are!" her mother exclaimed, lowering her magazine. "I thought you got lost."

Vanessa adjusted the towel on her chair. "No, just ran into an old friend on the way back from the bathroom. Haven't seen her in years! Guess time got away from me."

"Mm-hmm, I bet," her mother murmured before flipping another page in her magazine. "Hope you had enough time to clean up afterward."

Vanessa had been about to lower herself onto her chair but stopped and wobbled on her heels at her mother's words. "W-what?"

"I said, 'I hope they clean those bathrooms, dear!' You never can be sure with these public pools. They're always so dirty."

"Oh . . . oh, yes, it was . . . i-i-it was . . . fine," Vanessa stuttered.

She could have sworn her mother had said something else. But she didn't get the chance to linger on it because her son and daughter soon came running toward her, soaking wet and wanting her attention.

Chapter 10

Cyrus

Cyrus groused as he strolled past the monkey bars for the third time, where several children squealed, laughed, and played. He glanced down at his wristwatch. His third wife, Diamond, was late, and he hoped she would get here soon. The group of mothers sitting on a bench near the seesaws were starting to look at him strangely, perhaps wondering why a grown man with no child kept circling the playground like a hawk.

They probably think I'm some pedophile and wanna call the cops on my ass, he thought in exasperation. *Where the hell is she? Never should've agreed to meet her here.*

He probably shouldn't have agreed to meet her at all, considering that he was still pretending to be incapacitated. And after killing the two men at Ray's Bar & Lounge about a week ago, he'd decided it was a good idea to lie low as well. So far, no cops had come knocking at Cyrus's door, asking where he had been the day of the murders, but he didn't want to tempt his luck. He still had a lot more to accomplish, so he'd stuck to the house and stayed in his bed, making plans and biding his time.

But Diamond had sounded so desperate over the phone yesterday, when she'd called him on his cell. She'd begged him to see her in person, even though she knew she could get thrown in jail if the cops found out she'd been anywhere near him. She claimed it was worth it. She said that she was at the end of her rope and unsure of where or to whom to turn.

"I need you, baby!" she'd cried, making him roll his eyes as he listened. "I'll come to you. I'll come to your house. I *have* to see you, Cyrus! I mean it."

"You know you can't do that. Nessa and the kids are here. They—"

"Don't talk to me about Vanessa and your damn kids! I'm your wife, too, aren't I? Either meet me somewhere or I will drive right up to that house you live in with that high yella, stuck-up bitch and bang on the front door until you come out! I don't care who sees me! Those are your choices."

He'd grumbled, knowing it was futile to keep arguing, that she wouldn't take no for an answer.

Diamond had always been so sensitive, so unsure of herself. When he'd met her, she'd been like a frightened, stray kitten. All you had to do was offer her a bowl of milk and a pat on the head and she'd purr contentedly and be yours forever. That's what he had loved about her. She wasn't like his other wives—aloof like Vanessa or argumentative and demanding like Noelle. Diamond had asked little of him and been content with what he'd had to offer. But now everything had been thrown out of whack thanks to that son of a bitch Tariq. Now everything and everyone was in disarray and misbehaving, including his precious Diamond.

Today had seemed like the perfect day to meet up with her, because Vanessa would be gone for hours. She claimed she had a long list of errands to do.

"I can't stay stuck in the house serving you, Cy, or ferrying your kids everywhere. I actually have things to do," she'd said over her shoulder before sashaying out their front door.

But he wasn't so sure if that's where she'd gone. Listening to audio recordings from the device under her makeup table, he'd noticed his first wife had been taking a lot of late-night phone calls lately. He hadn't heard who she was speaking to last night, but she'd ended one call with "See you soon, love."

He suspected she was hooking up with Bilal again, which infuriated him. But he'd deal with that mess with Vanessa later. He had enough on his plate today.

"Cy! Baby!" he heard a high-pitched voice scream from behind him.

Cy whipped around and found Diamond running across the park's rolling lawn to the playground at full speed, drawing amazed stares as she did it, including from the moms perched by the seesaws. Diamond leaped into his arms, crashing into him and making him wince as their bodies collided.

They hadn't seen each other in a while, but it certainly wasn't worth all these theatrics.

"Oh, baby! Cy, I missed you," she gushed as she linked her arms around his neck and kissed his forehead and cheeks. She was crying as she did it. She gazed up at him lovingly. "I've missed you *so* much! You look so good!"

He wished he could return the compliment, but he couldn't because she didn't look quite like the girl he remembered. She'd lost so much weight that he could feel bones where before there had been soft, supple skin. Diamond had always been curvy, but that didn't seem to be the case anymore. Her body showed the trials she had been through, that she was *still* going through.

"Come on," he said, lowering her back to the ground. He then unwound her arms from around his neck. "Let's go for a walk. It'll give us some privacy."

He noticed they now had an audience. Even a few kids on the playground were staring at them curiously. The whole point in meeting in a park far away from home was to be inconspicuous, for no one to know he was here.

Diamond linked her arm through his as they walked along the sidewalk leading them to a short, wooden bridge over a sleepy creek. She was giddy, almost bouncing on the balls of her feet as they strolled along the path.

"Baby, I'm so happy to finally see you in person. You don't know how hard it's been without you."

"Happy to see you, too."

"I was so scared that day you were shot, Cy." She reached up and rubbed his chest, trailing her hand over where the bullets had hit him. "I didn't know if you were gonna make it."

"I was worried I wouldn't make it, either," he confided. "My doctor said it was pretty touch and go that first couple of days. I guess I had somebody lookin' out for me."

"Thank God! You know I wanted to see you at the hospital after you woke up. I was on my way there that day when I got arrested. But I never got to go. They took me to jail, Cy. Paraded me in handcuffs in our own damn building. I was so embarrassed and scared! I'd never been so terrified in my life. I didn't understand what the hell was happening. The cops wouldn't explain anything to me."

"I'm sorry you had to go through that." He wrapped an arm around her.

"I don't know who was worse—the inmates or the guards back in jail. They both made my life a living hell in there. I always had to watch my back. I couldn't sleep. I could barely eat." She glanced down at herself. "That's why I look this way. Prison was the best diet plan I've ever had."

"You'll put the weight back on. You'll get better."

"It doesn't matter if I put the weight back on. Not if I have to go back. I don't wanna go back there, Cy. I can't!"

"And you won't."

"But they think I did it. Julian, my ex, told them I did, but he's lying. You know that, right?"

"Absolutely, baby! I wouldn't be here if I didn't believe you." He tightened his hold around her shoulders as they began to walk across the bridge.

"You still trust me, don't you? You know I would never try to hurt you."

"Of course. I already told you that."

"And you still love me?"

She was giving him those sad kitten eyes again. *Reassure me, Cy*, they said. *Give me my head pat and my belly rub. Make it all better.*

"Of course, baby. What a silly question to ask. I never stopped lovin' you." He raised her hand to his lips and tenderly kissed her knuckles.

"And you still love them, too?"

"Still love who?"

"Vanessa and Noelle."

He lowered her hand and slowed to a stop beside her, caught off guard by her question.

Cyrus should have anticipated it, though. Both Noelle and Vanessa had already confronted him about the others, about the lies he'd told them—and had decided to punish him for it. Diamond's confrontation was long overdue, he supposed. But did his little kitten have claws like the rest of his wives? Was she about to bare them at him?

"Why are you asking me that?"

"Because I just want to know. I-I mean, it's okay if you do," she stuttered, shrinking underneath his stern gaze. "I understand that men sometimes . . . well, have more than one woman in their life. To fulfill their . . . their needs. I would have understood if you told me about them, Cy." She lowered her gaze. "I wish you would have told me the truth. It hurt that you didn't trust me enough to tell me."

"It hurt that I didn't tell *you* the truth?" His face hardened as he removed his arm from around her and turned around to face her. "Well, is there a reason why you didn't tell *me* the truth? Is there a reason why you kept secrets from me?"

She blinked in surprise. "Wha-what do you mean?"

"I mean I know that Julian dude wasn't just your ex. He was your pimp, too, wasn't he?"

Diamond opened her mouth, then closed it. She loudly swallowed.

"Was he your pimp like those stories said?" Cy persisted.

He hadn't forgotten all the stuff he'd heard about Julian, or the many other things he'd learned about Diamond since the news came out after her arrest, though Cy had tried his damnedest to forget. He tried not to imagine the other dozens, maybe hundreds of men she'd slept with besides him. He tried not to imagine the seedy motel rooms Diamond had probably "worked" in, and the sweaty wads of bills left on night tables and bathroom counters when her work was done.

Instead, Cy tried to recall Diamond exactly as he'd met her two years ago—as the bright-eyed, charming hostess standing behind the counter, who'd welcomed him to her restaurant and asked his name. But what he remembered and what he imagined kept blurring together. He'd remember her back at The Seneca, but instead of her wearing her usual classic black dress or silk blouse and skirt, she was wearing a bustier and thong. Instead of escorting a guest to their table, she'd lick her lips, grab their hand, and lead them across the restaurant to one of the bathrooms.

Those visions tortured him. It made him feel powerless and filled him with rage.

"I'm sorry I brought up Noelle and Vanessa, baby," she finally whispered, sheepishly looking up at him again. "I shouldn't have. We don't have to talk about any of that stuff. That's your other life. That has nothing to do with us. And what's past is in the past, right? None of that matters anymore. I just want to be with you. I just want to have my man back." She went for his lips, but he pulled away.

"No, the past isn't in the past. Thanks to you and your dishonesty, it's in the here and now because this is the first time I'm learning about all that shit you did before we met." He glared down at her. "Now I want you to answer my question. How long did you prostitute yourself out for that nigga? Did you do it by choice—or did he make you do it?"

Diamond didn't respond at first. Instead, she looked away, focusing on the other side of the creek and a family of ducks that were waddling their way along the embankment. She was being stubborn, just like Vanessa and Noelle. It annoyed the hell out of him. He wouldn't stand for it, especially not from her.

No more misbehavin', he thought. *I'm not putting up with that shit anymore.*

Cyrus gripped her chin and roughly turned her face toward his.

She stared up at him in shock. He had never manhandled her before.

It usually wasn't his style, but she was pushing him. Diamond was pressing all the wrong buttons, and she would see what happened when those buttons were pressed.

"Answer me."

"I did it for . . . for two years," she whispered as the tears flooded her eyes again.

"And did you do it because you wanted to, or because he made you do it?"

"Cy, stop! That hurts!" She reached up to tug his hand away, but he didn't budge.

"It's *supposed* to hurt. Now answer me."

He roughly shoved her back against the bridge's wooden railing, making her take a panicked glance over her shoulder even as he loomed over her.

"What are . . . what are you doing? Stop! I'm gonna fall!"

She might, he mused while his grip on her chin tightened. The railing may not be able to bear her weight. *Not this cheap ass plywood,* he thought.

It could snap, and she'd go tumbling onto the creek bed, onto the jagged rocks and sticks below. Diamond wouldn't die from a fall at this height, but she might bleed badly—just as bad as that lying piece of shit he'd shot in Ray's Bar & Lounge back in DC.

And just like him, she'd deserve what was coming to her.

"Cy," she whimpered. Her back arched even farther. Her ponytail dangled in the air. She started to quake and tremble more than the rippling waves in the creek below. "Cy, please!"

"Answer me and I'll let you go."

"At . . . at first it was because I wanted to do it. I-I needed the money for school," she said, as big, fat tears ran down the sides of her face and a snot bubble formed in her nose. "And then I did it because Julian made me do it. I-I-I couldn't quit even if I wanted to!"

He finally released her. Cyrus took a step back and she stood upright, pushing herself away from the railing.

Diamond took a wary glance at the creek again and then stared up at him. "Are you crazy?" she cried, raising her hand to cup her chin. "I could've fallen! You could've pushed me over that thing!"

"I could have." He inclined his head. "But I didn't. Just remember that."

She lowered her hand from her face. Her reddened eyes went wide.

"Don't ever keep secrets from me like that again. Do you understand me?"

She slowly nodded. "Y-y-yes."

She looked terrified, which was just how Cyrus liked it. Terror begot reverence. Respect.

"Good," he said, now feeling much better. "We should head back. I should get back home before Nessa does."

He reached for her again, and she flinched and stepped away, like he was about to hit her. Cyrus slowly smiled. His little kitten was scared of him now. That was to be understood. That was part of the process when a master brought his pet to heel, but he could be soft-handed, too. He'd reassure her, if that's what she needed right now.

"I'm not gonna hurt you, baby. I would never hurt you," he assured her, ignoring the fact that he had hurt her only a minute ago.

He took one of her hands within his own. He could feel her tense a little, but she didn't pull away. He wrapped an arm around her and steered her back the way they came, believing that now he had at least one wife back under control.

One down, he thought as he and Diamond walked side by side. *Two more to go.*

Chapter 11

Noelle

Noelle cursed under her breath as her doorbell rang.

"Coming! Coming! Just a sec!" she yelled over her shoulder. She opened the oven door and waved frantically at the smoke billowing out of it. Noelle coughed and raced to press the button next to the stove's hood to turn on the ventilation fan before her little cloud set off her kitchen smoke alarm.

The doorbell rang again. She then heard a knock. Noelle didn't have to look at the video monitor perched on her console to see who it was. It was Tariq and, of course, he was right on time—per usual.

He thought they were meeting up for a regular night in: a takeout dinner, a movie, and then raucous sex before they both fell asleep in each other's arms. But she had planned something more elaborate and much more sedate tonight. She'd even set the table and lit taper candles. She was hoping to butter him up with good food and wine before she finally broke the news that she was pregnant. Noelle had never been much of a cook, but she figured she could handle premade, stuffed Cornish hens, dinner rolls, and a salad.

"All you have to do is set the oven to three-seventy-five," the smiling older woman behind the sales counter at Whole Foods had assured her. "Pop the hens in the oven. Let them cook for twenty minutes or so and you're good. It's pretty simple!"

But obviously she and Noelle had underestimated just how culinary-challenged Noelle was. Turned out something that was "pretty simple" for most was still a task she could manage to screw up.

She used her oven mitts to remove the tray of burnt Cornish hens before tossing them onto the stove top in defeat. She then stalked to her front door.

When Noelle opened it she found Tariq smiling. Seeing her expression, though, his smile quickly faded. He raised his nose and sniffed the air. "What's burnin'?" he asked.

"Our dinner," she muttered, before motioning him inside and heading back to her kitchen.

Tariq shut the front door behind him and strolled across her foyer. He cocked an eyebrow and removed his suit jacket before tossing it onto one of the armchairs he passed. "Wait. Don't tell me you actually tried to cook, sweetheart."

"It wasn't cooking! Not from scratch anyway. I just had to heat it up," she said, motioning to the hens, whose skin were now cracked and blackened, like they were suffering from a bout of the bubonic plague. The dinner rolls hadn't fared any better. They were now sitting in her microwave, as hard as rocks.

"If you only had to heat it up, what happened?"

She flapped her arms helplessly. "I'd turned on the broiler instead of the oven. I realized my mistake when it was taking so long to cook. So I turned on the oven and raised the temperature so it would cook faster, but then it . . ."

She stopped when she realized Tariq was pursing his lips, trying to hold in a laugh. She dropped her hands to her hips. "It's not funny."

Saying that made him laugh even harder. He nodded as he strolled into the kitchen, holding his stomach. "Oh, yeah, it is! We both know your ass can't cook! Why did you even bother?"

"Because I wanted to do something nice. I wanted to make tonight special. And now I've fucked it up! It's like nothing . . . *nothing* will go right anymore!" she lamented. "Everything is messed up."

"Hold up. Hold up! Calm down. It's not worth all this. We can still make tonight special, baby." He wrapped his arms around her and drew her close. "We don't need food for that." He then lowered his mouth to hers for a kiss, but she shifted away and pressed her hands against his chest, holding him off.

"Stop, Tariq."

"Why?"

"It's just . . . nothing," she huffed, wrenching his arms from around her waist, stepping out of his embrace. She walked around her kitchen island and headed to the adjacent dining room. "Let's just eat. The salad is still okay."

He trailed behind her again, following her through the dining room entryway. "Lucky for us, you don't have to cook lettuce, tomato, and vinaigrette, huh?" he asked with a smirk as he pulled out a chair.

"Are you done with the jokes?"

Tariq held up his hands in mock surrender as he sat down. "Hey, I'm just trying to lighten the mood. You seem kind of uptight right now and—"

"Well, you're not lightening the mood," she snapped as

she grabbed two wooden serving forks and began to angrily toss the salad inside the bowl sitting at the center of the dining room table. "You're just . . . you're just pissing me off!"

"Sorry. Shit! Didn't mean to." He watched her with widened eyes. "Uh, are you done with that salad?" he asked uneasily, pouring himself a glass of wine.

"No! Why?"

"Because you look like you're trying to murder that thing. Keep going and we'll have nothing left to eat tonight."

She slammed down the serving forks on the table and fell back into her chair. Noelle shook out a dinner napkin and tossed it onto her lap. She grabbed her fork and knife, as if preparing to eat, but looked down and realized she had nothing on her plate. She tossed the utensils back to the table and raised a hand to her forehead, trying to steady her breathing. Maybe it was the pregnancy hormones. Maybe it was time to up her Zoloft dosage. Either way, she had to get herself back under control.

"You all right, baby?" he asked.

"Yes, I'm fine!" She paused, deciding it was pointless to lie. "No . . . no, I'm not. Not really. I'm just a . . . a little anxious. I'm sorry if I took it out on you."

Tariq squinted at her as he took a sip of wine. "Anxious about what?"

"Everything!" she cried, dropping her hand. "You know how things are right now with Cy . . . with the boutique. And now I've fucked up dinner."

"It's just food, Noelle. I keep telling you that."

"No, it's not." She tossed her dinner napkin to the tabletop. "Everything is spiraling out of control, and no matter what do, I can't—"

"If I recall, I offered to help you with that. Well, not dinner," he said, glancing over his shoulder at her smoke-filled kitchen, "but all the other stuff. Just tell me how much money you need for the house . . . for the shop, and I'll take care of it."

"But I don't want you to take care of it," she said tightly, now annoyed all over again that their conversation was drifting off topic.

She'd wanted to tell Tariq that she was pregnant, had even planned out the dinner sequence and rehearsed her whole speech, and now it was all falling apart because of burnt Cornish hens. How was she going to find the courage to tell him she was pregnant and that she wanted to keep the baby?

Who the hell would believe I can keep my shit together long enough to raise a child?

"But if I helped you take care of it, maybe you'd be less anxious," he argued.

"That's not it. It won't solve anything. It'll just be something else for me to agonize over and worry about."

"Look," he began. He reached out, placed a hand over hers, and squeezed. "I know none of this shit is easy. I can only imagine what you're going through. I'm not trying to make things harder for you. I'm trying to make it *better*. I just wanna help."

She exhaled. "I know you do, honey."

"But we don't have to talk about any of that tonight. We'll just chill and enjoy each other's company like we always do." He released her hand and grabbed the bottle of wine sitting at the center of the table. He poured more into his glass, then extended the bottle to do the same for her. "Let's eat some salad. Drink some wine—"

"No wine for me. Thanks," she murmured tiredly, placing her hand across the top of her glass.

"Since when?" Now he was squinting again. "You *always* drink a glass of Moscato with dinner. Sometimes two."

"Well, not tonight. I probably shouldn't anyway."

"*Ooookay*," he said slowly, then let out an uneasy laugh. He set down the bottle. "I'm still waiting for the reason why, though."

She didn't respond.

Tariq shifted in his chair and loudly grumbled, "Come on, baby. What's up? There's something else goin' on besides a burned dinner. Something you're not telling me. It's written all over your face. What is it? Did Cy do something else? Because if you need me to handle his ass . . . if you need me to say something to him, I can—"

"No! No, it's not Cy—for once." She took another deep breath and closed her eyes. "I'm . . . I'm pregnant," she whispered, finally saying the words. "I took a pregnancy test about a week ago. I took another one today, just to make sure it wasn't a fluke, and . . . and I got the same result. I'm pregnant. I wanted to . . . to tell you as soon as I found out, but I was just so . . . so scared because I don't want you to think I did this on purpose or—"

"Why would I think you did it on purpose?"

Noelle opened her eyes to look at him. To her surprise, Tariq didn't look shocked, angry, or happy; he didn't look like anything. Instead, he was taking another sip of wine and gazing at her expectantly. Based on his facial expression, she could have just told him the time and he would have responded with equal nonchalance.

"Well, because . . . because I wasn't on birth control."

He nodded. "Yeah, you mentioned that once or twice."

"And we didn't always use condoms."

He chuckled. "Be honest, baby . . . *most of the time* we don't use any."

"My point is," she said, now feeling more than a little exasperated, "I wasn't actively trying not to get pregnant, and I wanted to have a baby for a long time. I told you how long Cy and I were trying. We were at it for over a year. I was consulting a fertility doctor. And then you and I are together for a couple of months and suddenly," she snapped her fingers, "I pop up pregnant. Some men would think—"

"That you tried to set them up," he finished for her, taking another sip of wine. "That you tried to trap me into giving you the baby you always wanted."

She gradually nodded, making him loudly exhale and lower his glass back to the table.

"Noelle, I know how this shit works. You know how many women I've been with? A lot! I don't get trapped, and plenty have tried. I know how to watch my back and cover my ass. You weren't actively trying not to get pregnant, but I wasn't actively trying *not to get you pregnant* either. I bear just as much responsibility for this as you do. I knew the risks we were takin'."

She wanted to be relieved by his response. He didn't blame her. He wasn't angry. But that didn't mean he wasn't expecting her to get an abortion. He said he loved her, and she knew she loved him, too, but that didn't mean he felt they were ready to be a family. Noelle wasn't convinced they were ready, either, but she was at least willing to try. If he said no, she'd just go it alone.

Being a single mom isn't what I envisioned, but it wouldn't be the end of the world, she tried to convince herself.

"It was a risk," Noelle began hesitantly. "And I feel stupid that I let . . . that *we* let it happen. I'm too old to be this careless. And frankly, I couldn't think of a worst time to get pregnant. I'm trying to get an annulment from my husband who I found out is married to two other women. I'm running out of money. At the rate I'm going, I'll probably be broke by the end of the year. I'll lose the shop. I might even lose the house. How can I take care of a baby right now?" She paused again. "But as crazy as it sounds, I wanna keep it. I wanna have this baby, Tariq."

He didn't answer right away. He took a gulp of wine and set the empty glass back on the table. Noelle braced herself for him to stand up, say, "Well, on that note," grab his suit jacket, and walk out of her home, never to be seen again.

Instead, he gradually nodded. "Good. Because I think you should," he said.

"I should . . . what?"

"I think you should have the baby. It's not crazy! You'll get your annulment. Cy can't hold out forever. And you won't go broke as long as I'm around. I would never let you or our baby not have a place to live. I swear it on my life."

"Tariq, you don't have to—"

"No, I *do* have to," he said firmly. "I do, Noelle. I get that you want to take care of yourself. I get that you don't wanna owe me anything, but if you're really serious about having this baby, it ain't just about what you want anymore. You need help. Let me help you. We can do this."

Noelle winced like she had just taken a bite of one of her blackened Cornish hens. She had prepared herself for rejection, for having to go this alone. But she hadn't expected him to embrace this so enthusiastically.

"Oh, come on, girl!" he lamented. "Stop being so damn proud."

But it wasn't just pride. How could she explain that she trusted Tariq enough to let her choke her in bed, but not enough for him to take care of her? How could she tell him that even though she loved him with all her heart, a part of her still feared he would pull the rug from under her like Cy had when she'd needed him the most? She didn't want to feel that vulnerable again. The prospect was terrifying, but she might have to be if she was going to have this baby with him.

"I love you," he assured. "You believe that, don't you?"

"Yes," she answered softly, "but I also believed the last man who told me that."

His face changed at her words. His eyes went hard. "I'm not Cy."

"I know that, but you can understand why I'm gun-shy, right? We were married for four years . . . *four years*, and that whole time Cy pulled the wool over my eyes! He lied to me. *You* lied to me to protect him, and—"

"You're never gonna forgive me for that, are you? You're gonna hold that shit over my head forever, aren't you?"

"I'm not 'holding it over your head.' "

"Yes, you are!" He leaned forward and gazed into her eyes. "Look, if I could change the past, I would—but I can't. Cy and I were partners. I watched his back and he watched mine. And I followed him into the fire . . . I was his soldier because I thought that's what I was supposed to do. I thought I owed him for showing me the ropes, for bringing me into the business. The only thing . . . the *only* thing that made me turn on him was you, baby. I saw how he treated you, what he did to you. I knew you deserved better."

But you didn't warn me, she wanted to correct him, but didn't.

Tariq had only told her the truth about Cyrus when his hand was forced, when the shooting and its aftermath made her husband's elaborate house of lies crumble brick by brick. It was only then that Tariq told her about Cyrus's other wives and dirty business deals. If the shooting hadn't happened, would Tariq have allowed her to stay lost in the dark? She wondered about that more than she cared to admit.

"I want to show you better," he continued. "I want to

show you what it's like to be with someone who really loves you and is willing to put you first." He grabbed her hands, clutching them within his own. "Let me show you."

She hated when he did this, when he offered her his heart in his hand. It always came off so tender and vulnerable. And Tariq was not a man who easily bored himself. Yet he'd done it for her, again and again. How could she reject him? How could she possibly turn away someone who loved her this much, especially when she wanted to embrace that love and give as much in return?

She slowly nodded. "Okay," she whispered.

"Okay?"

"Okay! I just hope you don't regret this later."

I hope I don't regret this later, either, she thought.

"Like that's even a possibility." He leaned across the table and kissed her.

Chapter 12

Diamond

"Damn it!" Diamond said as she dropped and spilled one of the plastic steins of beer on her tray, making one of her customers leap back from the table, barely missing the beer spilling all over him, too. "I am so sorry! Let me clean that up, sir."

She set the stein upright and reached for the napkins stuffed in her apron pocket. She began to wipe frantically at the mess she'd made.

It was the third drink Diamond had spilled today. She'd also brought the wrong drinks and meals to tables, screwed up her orders, and had to comp customers because of her mistakes. Diamond's mind was just too distracted to concentrate on her work. Her nerves were too shaky. She'd been that way since meeting up with Cyrus yesterday.

She'd hoped seeing her husband would be the calming balm to make all her worries go away. Instead, seeing him had done the opposite. Cy hadn't acted at all like himself. The man she knew, who would run her bubble baths and massage her feet at night, would never grab her face and dangle her over the edge of a bridge, no matter how angry he was after finding out she had hidden her past from him. The man who made love to her and held her in his arms until she fell asleep would never threaten her. Diamond didn't know who that man was that she'd met in the park yesterday. He certainly wasn't her beloved husband. He reminded her more of her ex, Julian, who had abused her verbally and then physically when words alone didn't work anymore.

Why had Cyrus changed so much? Was it stress from the shooting, or the fallout of the discovery of his secrets that was making him unstable?

Or was he really like this all along? a bleak part of her wondered.

"I need a refill, Jake, and please make it quick," she said a couple minutes later as she set the empty stein on the bar counter. "I knocked this one over."

"*Again?*" the bartender asked, cocking his gray eyebrow as he placed the stein under the tap. "Rough night, huh?"

"You could say that," she mumbled while leaning back against the counter and looking around the room.

Just then, the Tavern's glass door swung open. When she saw who had stepped inside she let out a groan. It was Darius, her lawyer, though she didn't know why he was here today.

He had forgone the suit and was just wearing slacks and a dress shirt with the sleeves rolled up, like he was preparing for a fight. She didn't have a meeting scheduled with him, and he sure as hell didn't drink alcohol. Why was he here? Why did he keep ambushing her like this?

"Doesn't he have other stuff to do?" she murmured under her breath.

She grabbed the stein that the bartender handed to her and walked back across the room, but Darius was close at her heels. He marched straight toward her. His expression was severe. His brow was lowered.

"You went to see him anyway?" Darius asked her as she handed the customer his drink, painting on a smile as she did it.

"Let me know if you need anything else, sir," she said to the patron before she turned to face Darius. "You're gonna stop just showing up at my job like this," she whispered through clenched teeth. "Or you're gonna get my ass fired."

"Even when I asked you not to, you went to see him anyway. Why would you do that?" Darius challenged as he followed her across the barroom.

She looked at him in surprise. How had he found out that she went to see Cyrus? How had it gotten back to him already?

"I had to see him," she said over her shoulder.

"No, you didn't. You could've backed off and let me handle—"

"Look, he's my husband, Darius! I don't care what the law says. I didn't try to kill him. It's not right that they banned me from seeing him. You know that!"

This time Darius was the one who looked surprised. "Wait. Wait! You went to see *your husband* too? You went to see Cyrus?"

"Yeah. Isn't . . . isn't that what you were asking me about?"

"No!" he yelled back. "I went to do a follow-up with Richard McKenzie to see if he changed his mind about testifying on your behalf, and he said he'd already talked to you last week, even though I told you to give him a break. When the hell did you go see your husband? Why the hell would you do that? Don't you realize they could throw you back in jail?"

Diamond glanced at Jake, who was staring at them openly, listening to their conversation. She noticed several of the Tavern's patrons were now doing the same.

"That *is* her," one patron said as he chewed his nachos and pointed with cheese-covered fingers at Diamond. The rest of the diners at his table followed his gaze. "The one who tried to kill her husband. I thought she looked familiar."

Shit, Diamond thought. They probably weren't going to tip her now that they'd recognized her.

Thanks a lot, Darius.

"I'm taking a five-minute break, Jake," she said as she untied her apron from around her waist and slapped it onto the counter. "I'll be back. Come on," she called to Darius as she began to walk to the Tavern's door.

"Hey! Where you goin'?" Jake yelled after her. "Who's gonna cover your tables?"

She didn't answer him. Instead, she shoved open the swinging door to the Tavern and stepped onto the cracked sidewalk, into the balmy air of evening.

The Tavern was located in Little Italy, not far from the high-rises and swanky restaurants along the Baltimore Harbor where she used to work, but the scenery was a lot less glitzy down here. The Tavern was sandwiched between three-story brick buildings: Isabella's Ristorante and a no-name plumbing store. Diamond walked to the end of the block, near a narrow alleyway behind a parking garage, and motioned for Darius to follow her. When they reached a secluded spot away from the foot traffic, she turned to Darius with her arms crossed over her chest.

"What was that about? Why would you put me on blast at *my job*, Darius? I told you that I have to keep it. I have to pay my goddamn bills!"

"You're worried about paying your bills when you could be in handcuffs right now!" he shouted back at her.

"Why would you go to see him? Are you out of your damn mind?"

"Because I missed my husband! I'm sorry if you don't understand that. I'm sorry if you think it's stupid or crazy. But I had to see him."

"No, you didn't. Just like you didn't have to go behind my back and track down Richard. I asked you to let it settle . . . to let him think about it for a bit . . . and you did the opposite! I told you in the beginning you were barred per the terms of your release from seeing or even calling your husband."

She rolled her eyes and mumbled angrily as she listened.

"And you did that, too! You seem hell-bent on ignoring my advice and going back to prison for a long damn time! You're making my job ten times harder than it should be!"

"So why don't you just quit, huh? It's not like you're getting paid to stay here anyway. If I'm such a pain in the ass as a client, why don't you just move on?"

Darius fell silent. His face went slack and ashen. He took a step back from her.

She regretted the words as soon as they'd come out of her mouth. She didn't want Darius to quit. She couldn't do this without his help, without his know-how. There was no way she could walk into that courtroom without Darius at her side, defending her before the judge and jury. But what had happened yesterday with Cy and the stress she'd been under for months had finally broken her. She was lashing out, but she'd done it to the wrong person.

"I wish I could quit," he said bitterly. "I wish I could walk away and leave your ass high and dry. You're the worst client! You don't listen. You couldn't make it to an appointment on time to save your life," he argued, counting off the laments on his fingers. "Building a defense that the state isn't gonna poke more holes through than Swiss cheese will be hard enough without you fighting me at every goddamn turn. I am fighting an uphill battle here, Diamond, and you don't seem to care! A lot of lawyers would have given up by now, and honestly, maybe I should. Maybe I should take your advice and drop you. That seems like the best choice."

She closed her eyes.

So that was it. He was quitting. She'd lost her very last chance at freedom. But Diamond's eyes fluttered open again when she felt his cool hands on her bare skin. He'd placed his hands on her shoulders. She looked up to find him gazing intently at her with his dark, soulful eyes.

"But I know in my gut . . . in my heart . . . that you didn't do this. I know you didn't try to kill your husband. And that's why I'm still here."

Feeling his hands on her, hearing his comforting words, Diamond broke a little more. Her seams ripped open by another few inches. She blinked as tears flooded her eyes. This was exactly what she'd wanted Cy to do. This was all she'd needed from him, but he hadn't done it. Instead, he'd bullied and frightened her.

And now Darius was doing the opposite—giving her what she needed and craved, making her skin tingle where he touched her and making her chest flush hot underneath her T-shirt. Responding this way to him felt like a betrayal to her husband, but she didn't want to fight it. Not after feeling abandoned for so long.

"But I'll step down if you want me to," Darius continued, dropping his hands from her shoulders, "if you think you can get better representation somewhere else, I'll—"

"No! No! I don't want another lawyer. I didn't mean what I said. I just . . . I just . . ."

The tears spilled over then, and she didn't know why she did it, but she crashed into his chest, wrapped her arms around him, and started to sob.

He didn't react at first. He just let her sob into the cotton of his shirt. After a few seconds he tentatively wrapped his arms around her, too, and held her close. He didn't say anything. He didn't try to shush her or reassure her. He just let her cry—and it felt amazing. The sludge of so many emotions began to seep out of her—anger, pain, and mistrust. She finally felt a little relief.

Her cries tapered off. She stepped back and he released her. Diamond wiped her eyes with the backs of her hands.

"Thank you for . . . for letting me do that," she whispered between sniffs. She gazed at his shirt. It was soaked now and smeared with her makeup.

He shrugged. "It's okay. You were probably overdue for a good cry."

"You're right." She slowly nodded. "I was."

"Well, if you risked your freedom to do it, I hope seeing your husband at least helped a little."

"It . . . it did," she lied, forcing a smile. "It helped a . . . a lot."

"But you know you can't do that again, Diamond. You realize that, don't you? I mean it! No more secret meetings. Not until all this is over and—"

"I-I know. Trust me. I won't."

This time she was telling the truth. She wouldn't see Cyrus again, unless it was in a courtroom. If she saw him in person, she didn't know which version of her husband she would get—Dr. Jekyll or Mr. Hyde. She didn't want to run into his darker alter ego again. It frightened her too much.

"And I've been thinking about your trial," Darius continued. "Now that we know for sure that Richard is out, maybe we should let you take the stand in your defense after all."

She gazed up at him in shock. "But . . . b-b-but I thought you thought it was too risky. That I wouldn't make a good witness."

"Yeah, but now I'm second-guessing that decision. Everyone, including me, has been speaking for you. Maybe we should give you a chance to speak for yourself . . . tell your own story." He smirked, and for the first time she could see the handsome man lurking behind his awkward exterior. "If you could piss me off and still win me over, maybe you can do it with a jury, too."

Diamond wanted to hug Darius all over again because she was so grateful. But she didn't. She figured she'd been emotional enough for one night.

"Thank you. Thank you so much, Darius."

"So we need to start prepping you to testify. I want you to take me to the crime scene. I want to get our stories straight. And I need you to be diligent about this. Don't fight me anymore. Be on time. Be ready."

She nodded. "Yes! Yes, I will be. I promise! I won't let you down."

He glanced over his shoulder at the parking garage. "I should get going. I'm behind on work for some of my other clients. It's gonna be a late night."

"Thank you, Darius. Thank you for not quitting on me."

He shoved his hands into the pockets of his slacks. "Let's make a pact not to quit on each other, okay?"

She nodded again.

"See you soon, Diamond."

"See ya."

She watched as he walked off and disappeared around the corner leading to the garage's stairwell. She surprised herself because for once she wasn't loathing seeing him again. She was actually looking forward to it.

Chapter 13

Vanessa

"Come on, Mommy!" Zoe cried as she ran down the sidewalk in her pink leotard, white tights, and ballet slippers, dragging her sequined dance bag behind her. "We're gonna be late!"

Vanessa puffed air through her inflated cheeks and wanted to stomp her feet like she was a disgruntled child, not a mother. She grumbled as she climbed out of her Mercedes SUV and slapped on her dark-tinted sunglasses, armoring herself. She slammed the car door shut and trudged behind her daughter to the glass doors of Miss Sabrina's Dance Academy.

The truth was Vanessa didn't want to be here today.

Her mother had been taking Zoe to her dance classes for weeks, but the older woman said she was getting tired of it taking up her coveted time during the weekend.

"I have other things to do than ferrying your children. Besides, you're gonna have to show your face around there at some point anyway, my dear," her mother had said over the phone only yesterday. "You can't avoid those bitches forever!"

By "those bitches," her mother was referring to the dozen or so dance moms, aka frenemies, that Vanessa socialized with at the Academy. Most of them were moms of students in Zoe's Kinderdance class. Vanessa had lunch with a few of them. They'd even planned fundraisers together. Vanessa had been one of the queen bees of their group, lording her fit body, sexy looks, happy marriage, and expensive car and clothes over them. And she'd loved every minute of it, accepting the other moms' adoration and envy with glee. But now that Cyrus's bigamy story and shooting was making headlines, they all knew Vanessa's perfect image and life was just a mirage. And she bet they were all laughing at her behind her back.

Laughing their big, fat asses off, she thought as Zoe went running through the Dance Academy's door. Vanessa trailed in after her.

She wasn't fooled by their concerned phone calls and texts.

"Call me back, girl," Nicky, one of the dance moms who also happened to be her neighbor, had said in one of the voice mails she'd left on Vanessa's cell. "I know what you're going through can't be easy. I mean, if *my* husband had done anything like what Cyrus did to you, let's just say they wouldn't have to track down the person who tried to murder him, because I would've done it myself."

Vanessa now saw Nicky standing against the wall, along with a few of the other dance moms who were waiting with all the little girls now huddled in the hallway, preparing to get into one of the dance studios where practice would begin.

Vanessa's stomach clenched.

She would have to be around these women at least an hour and a half, until class was over. She would have to use memories of the time she and Bilal spent together at the pool house a week ago to fortify her. Even now, she got flashes of it at odd moments, of their bodies intertwined, of the feel of him between her thighs. It made her tingle all over. She craved another sexual interlude with her lover, but she knew she couldn't this soon.

Not too long, though, she promised herself, like a kid who gave up chocolate for Lent and knew a whole smorgasbord of candy bars awaited her at the end. *Not too long from now*, she thought as she approached the other mothers.

When Cyrus was finally gone she could be with Bilal whenever she wanted. Until then, she would continue to keep their affair on the low.

Vanessa beamed as she strolled toward the mothers. Zoe ran instantly to her gaggle of friends.

"Nessa!" one of the mothers cried. "Where have you been, girl? We haven't seen you in months!"

"I've just been busy at home with the kids," she said, removing her sunglasses. "You know how it is."

"And nursing your husband, I bet," another one volunteered, placing a hand over her bosom, feigning concern. "We all heard what happened to Cy, honey. So devastating! How is he now? Is he doing better?"

"Yes, much . . . much better," Vanessa said, her smile tightening. "His recovery is going well! He should be up and about any day now."

"He isn't doing that *already*?" Nicky asked.

Vanessa paused at her question. Confused and somewhat irritated that she was even asking it. "Of course not. He was shot in the chest three times, Nicky."

"I know! I just thought . . . well, because—"

"Advanced Kinderdance!" the dance instructor called out as she opened the studio door, cutting off Nicky midsentence. "Ladies, we're ready for you."

Vanessa watched as the giggling little girls all fell into a single-file line and made their way through the open doorway. As the door closed behind them, the mothers took their seats in the nearby waiting area.

Vanessa sat down at the end, setting her handbag on her lap. To her great annoyance, Nicky took the padded chair beside her.

"Hey!" Nicky said.

"Hey," Vanessa answered in a monotone, staring at the wall in front of her.

"Look," Nicky continued, leaning toward Vanessa's ear, "I'm sorry about that question I asked about Cy. You know . . . about him being up and moving around already."

"It's fine," Vanessa mumbled.

You can't help it if you're stupid, she thought before shifting a few inches to her left to put some distance between her and Nicky, but Nicky just scooted closer to her.

"I only asked because I thought I saw Cy driving past the house a couple of times."

"What?" Vanessa did a double take, suddenly whipping around to face her. She couldn't have heard what she'd thought she heard. "That's not possible. Cy's still on bed rest, like I said. He can barely walk into the hallway without holding on to my arm."

Nicky squinted. "*Really?* Because I could have sworn I saw him driving around a couple of weeks ago. And I saw him again last weekend. Saturday, I think." Nicky seemed to consider it for a moment. "At least, I thought it was him. It definitely looked like his silver BMW. I was walking to the curb to get the mail and I waved at him when he was driving by, but I don't think he saw me."

Vanessa blinked rapidly. If Nicky was to be believed, Cyrus would have been out of the house likely the same afternoon that Vanessa was with Bilal at the pool. No wonder he hadn't complained when they'd come home later than expected. Maybe he was away on a little errand of his own.

Had he been pretending to be bedridden all this time? Was he even home right now?

"That son of a bitch!" Vanessa shouted as she shot up from her chair, making Nicky lurch back and the other mothers turn to stare up at her.

"What?" Nicky asked, looking alarmed. "Did I say something wrong?"

"I'll . . . uh . . . I'll be right back. I-I left something in . . . in my car."

Vanessa tossed her purse strap over her shoulder. She then fled to the Dance Academy's doors.

She raced across the parking lot to her Mercedes and drove off with tires squealing.

Twenty minutes later, in record time, Vanessa made it back to her neighborhood. She drove so fast onto her block that she almost passed her own house. She slammed on the brakes just in time, making her lurch forward in her seat and wince as her seat belt tightened across her chest. She gazed up at her house.

Nothing looked amiss. She saw the same brick exterior and black shutters, same ionic columns and emerald-green front door. The red flag on their mailbox stood up, showing that the mailman had already arrived. Maybe Cyrus was still inside, lying in bed, waiting for Vanessa to return and wait on him hand and foot.

Maybe Nicky is full of shit, she thought.

She pulled onto her driveway and pressed the garage door button, watching as it slowly opened. She drove forward, prepared to pull in the garage in her spot between her husband's BMW sedan and his Aston Martin convertible, but stopped short when she noticed his BMW was gone.

She threw on the emergency brake, opened her car door, and hopped out. She then strode to the front door, leaving her car door gaping wide.

"Cy! Cyrus!" she shouted as she stepped inside her home seconds later.

Silence greeted her. Her boys were at their friends' houses, her daughter was still at dance class, and her son-of-a-bitch husband obviously wasn't home.

"Cy! You lyin' piece of shit!" she yelled as she stormed up their staircase to the floor above. She walked straight down the hall to their bedroom, threw open the door, and found their California king empty, along with the rest of their bedroom.

She stood in the center of the room with her hands balled into fists at her sides, seething with rage.

So Cyrus wasn't still bedridden after all. All those weeks he'd had her feeding and clothing him.

"Damn near wipin' his ass," she hissed.

He could have done it all himself. Instead, he'd let her continue to be his maid and his nurse. She'd bitten her tongue and held back her fury all while doing it. And for what? Only for him to take glee in manipulating her, in making a fool of her all over again.

"That son of a bitch. That son of a bitch!" she screeched.

She then stalked toward their bed and ripped off the comforter and sheets, throwing them to the floor. She picked up their alarm clock and hurled it at the wall, screaming like a banshee as she did it. It shattered into more than a dozen pieces. She picked up one of the plastic shards and began to stab one of their decorative pillows with it, pretending the pillow was Cy, pretending she was killing him like she wanted. As she vented her rage, the cotton flew in all directions. The mattress became as white as a fluffy cloud.

When Vanessa fell to the floor with exhaustion, she saw her hands were covered in blood. She'd cut herself in her frenzy. She let her head plop back against the bed and closed her eyes as she gulped for air. Slowly, her breathing returned to normal. Gradually, her heartbeat slowed.

"Pull yourself together. Pull yourself together. Pull it together," she whispered to herself.

Eventually, she did. And that's when she realized all was not lost. Cy had lied about being bedridden like he'd lied about everything else, but that meant that she no longer had to wait around for him to be up and moving for her and Bilal to finally take their chance. She no longer had to worry about her children stumbling onto a macabre scene in their own home. Now they wouldn't have to do it in her house. They could come after Cy anywhere.

No more waiting, Vanessa resolved. It was finally time to kill her husband. She rose to her feet. First, she needed a stiff drink, and then she would begin cleaning up the mess she'd made, knowing that her mess of a marriage would soon be resolved.

Chapter 14

Cyrus

Cyrus leaned back in the leather chair, put his feet up on the lacquer white desk, interlocked his fingers, and rested his hands on his chest as he waited for his second wife, Noelle, to arrive. Thankfully, he knew her schedule and that she would be here soon. She'd better be because he couldn't stay long. He had to get home before Vanessa and their daughter Zoe arrived back from dance class, giving him a little more than an hour to get this done.

Noelle's office was more compact than he would have liked. As far as he was concerned, it was little more than a glorified storage closet; it didn't have nearly enough room for a big man like him to get comfortable. But Noelle seemed to like it enough. She had even added little, unique touches—picture frames, figurines, and a plaque on a wall with a motivational quote. She had decorated her office in all white and cream, like their living room back in Arlington. And she seemed to get plenty of work done in here. He could tell from all the tabbed file folders stacked neatly on her desk and the papers in binder clips with multicolored Post-it Notes on top. He shifted his feet and knocked those folders and papers to the floor, watching as they scattered on the hardwood. He chuckled.

Minutes later her office door swung open. Noelle stood in the doorway with her hands on her hips in all her beauty and fury.

Cy could remember muttering to himself the first day he'd spotted her walking on the stretch of sidewalk in Manhattan five years ago, "That is one gorgeous woman." As much as she'd pissed him off, he thought the same now, seeing her standing there in billowy, striped palazzo pants and a matching yellow halter top that accented her glowing, milk-chocolate skin.

"They told me you were back here and I didn't believe it! Cy, what do you think you're doing?" Noelle asked as she stepped into the room. She slammed the office door behind her, then glanced down at the floor. "And you're trashing my office, too? Have you lost your damn mind? This is my place of business, goddamnit! You have no right . . . *no right* to just roll up in here like—"

"*Like I own the place?*" he asked with raised brows as he lowered his feet from her desk back to the floor. "Is that what you were about to say? But you forget, baby, I *do* own the place. Half of it anyway. And I paid for all this shit. So I have just as much a right to be back here as you do."

He'd come here today to remind her of exactly that—and of everything else he had done for her as her husband and provider. Sure, he may have been married to two other women while he was married to her, but that didn't mean she had the right to behave the way she was behaving, to disrespect him like she'd been doing for the past two and a half months. She was obviously under that bastard Tariq's influence now, but Cy was about to break that spell. He had to take back control of Noelle and their relationship, especially because they were scheduled to have their annulment hearing next week. Just like with Diamond, it was time to remind her who was in charge.

"Don't you dare call me 'baby'! Not after what you've done. You don't have the right!" she shouted.

"No, I do have the right, *baby*," he repeated while smiling smugly up at her. "Because I'm your husband."

She crossed her arms over her chest. "No, you're not. You never were."

"I said my vows just like you did."

"Yeah, I said them—and I *meant* them! You said them knowing damn well you were already married to someone else. You were married to Vanessa for years before we even met." Her eyes now blazed bright as she pointed at him. "You knew that what you were doing was illegal and you had no intention of ever—"

"Even if it wasn't legal, that doesn't mean I didn't mean what I said that day," he argued, rising to his feet. "I pledged myself to you and I pledged that I would honor and take care of you from that day forth. And haven't I done that? When you needed me to write check after check after check for this place, didn't I do it? When you wanted to buy the house, the cars, and have that expensive furniture sent in from Italy, did I ever complain? You tried to stab me with a damn butcher knife—"

"How *dare* you bring that up! I was depressed and suicidal back then. You know that!"

"I didn't let the cops arrest you, did I?" he continued, undaunted. "I handled it. I took you to the doc and got you evaluated. I got you put on meds. I took care of you like I always did. I stood by you. Now the shoe is on the other foot and you won't stand by me! I saw that bullshit filing your lawyer sent. You're trying to bleed me dry!"

"'Bleed you dry'?" She screwed up her face. "I'm just asking for what I'm owed so I can keep a roof over my head and my business open! Besides, this isn't about what I'm asking for and you know it. You want me to call off the annulment. You want me to stay married to you!"

"No, I know we can't stay married." He reached out and grabbed her hand, holding it tight even as she tried to yank it away. "But that doesn't mean you can just toss aside the five years we had together, baby. If that love was real, it doesn't fade away that quickly. I know mine hasn't. We don't need lawyers and the court to get involved in this. You and I can work this out ourselves!"

" 'Work this out ourselves'?" She barked out a laugh. "You've got some goddamn nerve, Cyrus Grey. I get it now. You don't want me to be Vanessa and Diamond's sister wife anymore. You just want me to be your *side piece*!" This time, she did yank her hand back. "To hell with you! I deserve better. I deserve more! And I know for sure now that you aren't and never will be the man to give it to me." She pointed to her office door. "Now if you could do me a favor and get the hell out of my office and my store, I'd appreciate it."

Cyrus tilted his head. "Do you think Tariq is the man to give it to you? He's got you fooled real good, don't he?"

"Get out," she repeated firmly.

"You can't tell right from left or up from down anymore, can you? I gave you more credit than this, Noelle."

"I said get . . . *out*!"

"When are you gonna figure out that nigga doesn't give a shit about you? He's just trying to get back at me because he didn't succeed in taking me out! He tried to have me killed!"

"That's insane. You're just accusing him because you—"

"And he probably has you lined up next for a bullet when you're no longer useful to him," he pressed on. "When are you gonna figure that out?"

She closed her eyes and took a deep breath. "Cy, you sound deranged and paranoid. Tariq had nothing to do with what happened to you. Stop projecting your shit onto everybody else! Not everyone is as devious and deceitful as you are. Besides, what makes you think I would believe anything you say about him for one second after all the lies you've told me? After all you've done to me? *To Vanessa? To Diamond?* I have no reason to trust you!"

"Yes, you do! Because what we had was real. We had five years together, Noelle. Four of those years as man and wife. You barely know that nigga! You don't have with him what we had."

She opened her eyes and shook her head. "No, Cy, I have more. *A lot* more. He loves me. He is dedicated to me. He wants to take care of me . . . of our family. The family you couldn't give me, even though I begged you for it."

Cyrus squinted. "Oh, so he's making promises about giving you a family, too?"

Tariq really was working his magic. Cyrus could give him that.

"Let me guess . . . he's gonna marry you and you're gonna buy a big house with a white picket fence and a playground in the backyard for the three kids you were on my ass about for years. Maybe get a dog as well?" He smirked. "So when are you two supposed to get started on this family? After the annulment goes through?"

"We've already started." She seemed to hesitate. She loudly exhaled again. "I'm . . . I'm pregnant, Cy. Tariq and I are gonna have a baby."

Cyrus blinked in amazement. His smirk abruptly disappeared. He swore the air had been knocked out of him.

Pregnant, he thought. *We've been separated less than three months! How the fuck is she pregnant already?*

So Tariq had been working overtime to sink his hooks

deeper into her. A baby would surely do it—her heart's one desire. That bastard was always one step ahead, and Cyrus was once again left fumbling, caught off guard by his former protégé's next move.

"That's why I need you to let this go," she whispered, stepping forward holding her hands clasped in front of her as if she were in prayer. "Let's just go our separate ways. Let me lead my life. Let me be happy with my baby and the man that I love. Please, Cy! Just . . . just stop."

For the first time he was speechless. He didn't know what to say or how to respond.

"Cy?" she began softly, peering up at him, "did you hear me?" She took another step toward him. "This needs to stop. You have to stop—for everyone's sake."

Stop? She wants me to stop?

His shock quickly transformed into anger. His face hardened. He grabbed her shoulders, making her yell out in surprise.

"I'll be goddamned if I just roll over and let you have your little, weak ass fairy tale with that nigga. I'm comin' for you, and you can tell that motherfucka I'm comin' for him, too."

He then roughly shoved her back, making her yelp again. He swung open her office door and stalked across the store, slamming the boutique's door behind him, making the salesgirls and customers cower in his wake.

That evening Vanessa was late bringing up his dinner, but Cyrus barely noticed. Instead, he sat in bed in his pajamas, glaring absently at the flat-screen television mounted to his bedroom wall.

His wife Noelle was having a baby. She was having a baby with another man—the man whom he had once trusted. The same man who had tried to have him killed and sabotaged his entire life. The realization settled over him like a growing fever, making his temperature rise and his heartbeat quicken.

He could think of a thousand ways to take out his revenge. It could be as simple as showing up to his house in Virginia or Tariq's home in DC and shooting both Tariq and Noelle in bed to pay them back for what they had done to him, but he knew that would be stupid and reckless. He had already committed two murders on impulse. It wasn't smart to make it a habit. No, he had to be careful how he went about it this time around.

"Dinner's served," Vanessa announced as she shoved open his bedroom door.

She was carrying a serving tray. She set it down in front of him, and he could see that she had made spaghetti for dinner with garlic bread on the side. Cyrus muttered his thanks before shaking out his dinner napkin and tucking it into his pajamas. He glanced at her right hand and noticed that there was a cloth bandage wrapped around it.

"What happened to your hand?" he asked.

Her eyes snapped down to the bandage. She held her hand against her chest, cradling it protectively.

"Oh, nothing. I accidentally cut my hand making dinner. I nicked it slicing the garlic bread. No big deal."

He glanced at his night table. "And what happened to my old alarm clock?"

"Alarm clock?" She followed his gaze and shrugged. "I accidentally knocked it over when I was tidying up in here while you were in the bathroom. Do I need to get you another one?"

He shook his head and grunted again. He resumed eating his dinner.

"Don't you think it's time you try eating with the rest of us downstairs?" she ventured, lowering her hand back to her side. "Walking around might do you good."

He shook his head as he stabbed one of his meatballs with a fork. "Not ready yet. Still too weak. Give me a couple more weeks. I'll be ready then."

"*Really?* Because you're looking so much better already, Cy!" she exclaimed, crossing her arms over her chest as he shoved another forkful of food into his mouth. "*So* much healthier! I bet you could walk down the stairs with no problem now if you wanted to. Maybe even out of the house. You could maybe even take a quick trip or two."

At those words he stopped chewing. He gazed up at his wife in confusion, but her smile never budged.

Vanessa shrugged again. "Or not. It's just a suggestion, but I guess you would know best."

She then patted his shoulder, turned, and walked out of the bedroom.

Chapter 15

Noelle

Noelle strode through the courtroom doors on wobbly legs. She dropped a hand to her stomach and took a shaky breath, trying to steady her nerves.

"Good job," her lawyer whispered. The petite woman placed a hand on Noelle's shoulder and gave it a quick squeeze.

"Thank you," Noelle whispered back. "I was so nervous up there."

"You couldn't tell at all," her lawyer said. She then glanced at her wristwatch. "Look, I have to go, but I'll follow up with you tomorrow. Again . . . good job."

Noelle waved and watched as her lawyer walked down the corridor, juggling her suitcase, purse, and a stack of manila file folders in her arms.

They had just finished the hearing at which Noelle had to provide her formal testimony for her annulment before a judge. She'd had to sit on the stand and testify under oath. It had been a nerve-racking experience, but she was glad it was over.

"You did do a good job," a familiar voice said behind her, making her jump in surprise.

She turned to find Tariq striding toward her, grinning.

"Baby," she cried, stepping into his outstretched arms, "I didn't know you were here! Were you in the court-room? I didn't see you."

He embraced her, then gave her a quick kiss. "I snuck in about halfway through. I just sat in the balcony. I didn't want you to know I was there. Didn't want to make you nervous."

That was the reason she had given him for not wanting him to come with her to the hearing—that seeing him would make her anxious and tongue-tied. The truth was, she didn't know if Cyrus would show up and she didn't want the chance of any altercation happening between the two men.

The last time she had seen her husband, he'd been furi-ous at her and intent on coming after Tariq. She had no idea how they navigated still being in business together with so much anger between them. Maybe it was because they hadn't seen each other in person since Tariq and Noelle had hooked up. But she was convinced that if they were in the same room, the sparks would really fly.

Or more like explosions, she thought ruefully.

"I figured if I got here a little early I could watch some of it . . . make sure you were okay," Tariq now explained.

"Aww, thank you, baby," she said before giving him an-other kiss.

They then walked hand in hand down the corridor to the courthouse exit doors.

Noelle could use Tariq's support. Though her testimony had gone well according to her lawyer and Tariq, her hus-band had thrown her a last-minute curveball. She'd been shocked that Cyrus hadn't come to the hearing. She'd thought he wouldn't miss the chance to glower at her from his lawyer's table while she sat on the stand while she gave the oral testimony that would finally end their farce of a marriage. But he hadn't shown up—to her great relief. Of course Cyrus wouldn't let her off that easy.

"He wants full ownership of Azure," her lawyer had told her in the hallway while they waited for the hearing to begin. "Mr. Grey wants to continue to operate your boutique, but he no longer wants you as joint part owner or manager."

"*What?*" Noelle had cried, staring down at the court papers as her lawyer handed them to her.

She had braced herself for closing the shop down entirely, and maybe reopening it in the future when she'd saved enough money. But in no way had she anticipated that Cy would want the shop for himself, let alone keep the doors open without her. She had put her heart and soul into that boutique. She'd even come up with the name, basing it on one of her favorite Ella Fitzgerald ballads. She was the one who had designed it, promoted it, and hired the staff. She was on a first-name basis with many of her customers. Cyrus had no interest in the shop beyond its bottom line.

"Don't freak out. I told you to prepare for something like this," her lawyer had said.

"But what does he even know about women's clothing?" she'd asked, examining the letter from his lawyer. "Why . . . why would he even . . ."

Her words had drifted off as she struggled to grapple with what she'd been told.

"I have no idea why he wants your boutique," her lawyer had confessed, "but his lawyer gave me that today. And that's only one of your husband's stipulations. He also wants to retain your home in Arlington, the vehicles, your vacation condo in the Bahamas, and all other properties. He doesn't want to grant you any alimony either. His lawyer said that Mr. Grey believes that if it wasn't a real marriage, according to your annulment filing, then you shouldn't be granted any real assets."

Listening to her lawyer, Noelle had wanted to rip up the papers in her hands.

"Look, marital separation is rarely easy, and annulments can get particularly messy in the state of Virginia," her lawyer had explained.

"So what now? The judge has to decide whether I get Azure or Cy gets it?"

"In Virginia, judges only divide property in a divorce. Not in an annulment. I told you that was one of the risks of going this route."

"But I didn't have a choice! We weren't legally married."

"I know. He knows that as well, which is likely why he's doing this. You're either going to have to go through arbitration and hope Mr. Grey backs down, offer to buy him out, or . . ."

"Or what?"

"Forfeit the store."

Cyrus knew that when it came down to it, she was willing to lose the alimony or the house and the cars, but he was well aware he would hurt her by taking her business away and operating it without her. And he had only made this decision after she'd told him last week that she was pregnant with Tariq's baby, that she was happy and in love. Cy was upholding his vow to "come after" her. She just hadn't known when he'd said it, what he'd meant. His pettiness and vindictiveness still stunned her for some reason, even though she understood better the monster her husband really was.

But Noelle didn't tell Tariq any of that. She didn't want to ruin the moment. She was just happy to have him here, to have his arms wrapped around her. She needed the reassurance of his presence right now.

"I took the whole day off," she announced as they emerged from the courthouse into the warm sunshine. "Don't even have to go back to the shop. So this is my suggestion." She rubbed his arm through his suit jacket. "Why don't you and I sneak off together? Maybe grab a quick lunch. Then head back to my house, where I can model the new negligee for you that I picked up yesterday at Bite the Fruit," she whispered saucily. "I'll even let you do a little biting and nipping, too, if you're nice."

"Damn! That *does* sound like a perfect afternoon," he said with a laugh as they walked down the stone steps to the sidewalk. "And I would if I could, sweetheart, but I have a meeting with a lawyer over the border in Maryland that I've gotta get to in a couple of hours."

Her face fell. "Really?"

"Yeah, unfortunately. It's an important business meeting. I'm getting an update from him on something, and I can't get out of it."

"That's okay. I understand," she said, trying to mask her disappointment.

She'd hoped spending some time with Tariq would take her mind off the hearing and Cyrus's last-minute filing that now put her ownership of Azure in jeopardy.

"You sure?" Tariq persisted.

"Yeah! Of course! It's business. I get it."

Tariq paused on the sidewalk beside her. His eyes raked over her face.

"What?" she asked, laughing nervously. "Why are you looking at me like that?"

"Why don't you come with me?" he suddenly asked.

"With you where? *To your business meeting?*"

"No, come with me to Maryland. The business meeting shouldn't take long. We can grab lunch before. I know this nice bistro nearby that you'd really like. I'll do the meeting. You can stroll around and look at the shops while you wait, and then we can hang out together for the rest of the day."

Her brows drew together. "Do you really want me tagging along like that?"

"If it was my choice, I'd have you with me always." He kissed her cheek, making her smile again. "I'll just have to settle with having you with me today, though."

"But what about my car? I can't just—"

"It's in the courthouse parking garage, right? Is somebody gonna steal it from there? They ain't that crazy!"

He had a point. Though part of her knew she should say no anyway. Tariq was obviously changing his whole schedule around just to accommodate her, but she really did want to be with him—no matter how selfish it sounded. Things seemed a lot easier, and the world was a lot brighter whenever he was around.

"Okay, if you really don't mind my being there . . ."

"I don't. Trust. Now come on," he said, nudging her chin and giving her another quick peck. "Let's get going."

The drive to Maryland was a tranquil one, though Noelle did her normal wincing as Tariq zipped down the highway in his roadster, making him laugh at her squeamishness.

When they arrived at the French bistro near Main Street, it was as nice as Tariq had described. Little wooden tables sat around an airy room filled with fresh hydrangeas and roses. She and Tariq took one of the tables in the back, overlooking the street traffic. The serene setting and Tariq's company was just what she needed. She felt lighter. Cy and all his drama became a far more distant concern.

When the waiter arrived Noelle ordered the frisee salad with bacon, eggs, and French fries on the side, and Tariq ordered a smoked salmon tartine. As he set their food on the table, Noelle instantly reached for her French fries and dipped them into the petite bowl of mayo. Watching her, Tariq cringed.

"That looks disgusting."

She laughed as she took another bite after double-dipping her second fry. "I know. I tried it once in Paris and got too grossed out to finish, but I just started craving it for some reason. Blame the baby, not me."

"Well, I'm glad to see you smilin' either way."

Noelle paused mid chew. "What do you mean? I was smiling before."

He ate some of his tartine, lowered his fork and knife, and shook his head. "Nah, that wasn't a real smile. I know the difference. This is you happy. Before that was you pretending to be happy."

She inclined her head and sucked her teeth playfully. "You think you know me so damn well, don't you?"

"Every facial expression . . . every gesture . . . every mood," he said, sounding somber for the first time. "Nothin' gets past me."

"Next you'll be saying, I'll be watching you." Her eyes widened comically. "It all sounds creepy as hell."

"It's not creepy. You study and get invested in understanding what you love. It's as simple as that." He took a sip from his wineglass. "For example, if I didn't know you well, I wouldn't have known something was up back there at that courthouse. Something was wrong. What was it?"

She stopped chewing. "Huh? I don't know what you mean."

"Come on, Noelle. I can judge your moods, but I'm not a mind reader, baby. Somethin's up. You just aren't telling me what it is."

She shrugged, now feeling nervous under his watchful

gaze. He said you study what you loved, and he certainly was studying her right now.

"I just . . . I just finished testifying on the stand. I was a little rattled after it. That's probably it."

"You're not a good liar, because if that was the case, you wouldn't be rattled now by me asking you these questions."

"Okay, maybe . . . *maybe* I was a little upset, too, because of something else that happened. But it doesn't matter. My lawyer is working on it."

"What happened? What does she need to work on?"

Noelle raised her napkin to wipe her mouth, trying to steal some time as she contemplated her answer. She guessed she should just tell Tariq the truth, because his spidey senses obviously weren't going to stop tingling.

"Cy . . . Cy countered my terms for our annulment," she explained. "I was counting on him doing it. It wasn't a surprise. I knew he wasn't gonna just roll over and accept everything. But I hadn't planned for him to be so . . . so petty. I don't know why I hadn't. I keep forgetting the man I'm married to. Who he really is. But he reminded me today."

"What did he do?"

"He won't give me alimony. I'd anticipated that. He wants the house and the cars, too. Okay, I can accept that as well," she said with a shrug. "But he wants Azure, Tariq. He wants full ownership of my store and wants to keep operating it without me."

"That doesn't even make any sense! Why in the world would he want a women's dress store?"

"To hurt me. To hurt *us*. He can see I'm happy now. I'm moving on. I was willing to leave all the rest behind, but the one thing besides you and the baby that meant something to me, he had to come after it. But I've been thinking about it, and you know what? He can have the shop." She gave a dismissive wave. "Take it from me if you want. He can say and do whatever he wants, but I'm not going back to him! I keep telling him that. I even told him that a couple of days ago, and I meant it. I am not going back."

"You told him that a couple of days ago?"

She nodded sheepishly and lowered her eyes again. "He stopped by Azure. Just popped up out of the blue. I didn't even know he was coming or that he was walking around now. All the articles online said he was still on bed rest. And then, suddenly, there he was in the middle of my office. It was crazy!"

She raised her eyes to look at Tariq. He was leaning back in his chair. His face was passive.

Why wasn't he angry or irritated? She thought he would be if he'd found out that Cyrus had ambushed her like that, but he was taking it better than she'd anticipated.

"Well, anyway, I handled it," she said, batting away talk of her husband. She was tired of talking and thinking about Cy. She reached across the table to place her hand over Tariq's. She gave his hand a squeeze. "It's over. He didn't hurt me and—"

" 'Didn't hurt you'?" Tariq was squinting again. Now she saw the first flickers of anger in his dark eyes. "So did he touch you? Did he threaten you?"

Noelle hesitated. She didn't want to make a bad situation worse, to get Tariq more riled up than he already was, so she lied and shook her head. "No, he didn't. He didn't do anything. He just . . . like I said, it's over."

Tariq didn't respond for a long time after that. Finally he pulled back his hand and began to eat again. "Okay, well, I think based on everything you said that our next move should be getting you out of that house. You don't want to run the risk of him just popping up again, especially at your home."

"But why do I have to move? I can change the locks. I could—"

"You really think a lock on a door is gonna keep him out? That nigga stepped over a line when he just showed up at your office unannounced, Noelle. That means he's unstable. Unstable makes him dangerous. I don't like it. Besides, he's gonna get the house eventually. You said so yourself. You should move out now. Get a smaller place that you can afford on your own or . . ." His words drifted off.

"Or what?"

"Or move in with me. I've got plenty of room. Even got a spare guest room that would make a nice nursery."

It was a kind, sweet offer, but she didn't want to be like a hermit crab, moving from one man's seashell to another's. She opened her mouth to gracefully decline his offer, but stopped when Tariq held up his hand.

"Don't say yes or no right away. Ruminate on it for a little bit, okay? We got a little time."

She nodded and returned to eating her lunch.

Chapter 16

Noelle

An hour later they left the bistro, walking hand in hand.

"So I'll see you in a little bit," Tariq said. "It shouldn't take more than an hour at most. Walk around Main Street. Check out the shops. Then I'll meet you back here and we'll continue our day together."

"I think I can do that." She ran her hands over his lapels and tapped the knot in his silk tie. "Have a good meeting, baby."

She leaned forward and they kissed goodbye, long and hard. He grinned. "More of that later or I'm never gonna make it to this thing on time."

Noelle watched as he turned and walked away just as someone called out, "*Noelle?*"

Noelle glanced over her shoulder to find Diamond, Cyrus's third wife, standing on the sidewalk.

She hadn't seen the young woman in months, not since that night when they'd all eaten dinner together and tried to solve who was behind the shooting. It turned out that Diamond was behind it—according to the cops—but Noelle hadn't known it at the time.

She still found it hard to believe, though. The young woman had been solidly in Cyrus's corner, defending him to both Noelle and Vanessa, but maybe it had been just a façade to fool them into thinking she had nothing to do with it, to get them off her trail.

The young woman didn't look anything like when Noelle had last seen her. She had gotten rid of her braids and now wore her hair in a ponytail. She looked like she'd lost quite a bit of weight, too. Gone were the plump apple cheeks Noelle remembered from months earlier. They were now sunken and hollowed out.

"Uh, h-hi, Diamond," Noelle said.

She cursed under her breath as she did it. She wished Tariq would have stayed. It would have given her an excuse to avoid talking to Cyrus's other wife—a possible murderer.

Diamond's gaze followed Tariq's retreating back. "Wasn't . . . wasn't that Tariq Donahue, Cy's business partner?"

Noelle nodded. "Yes, it was."

"And you were kissing him?" Diamond asked, pointing after him.

Noelle didn't like the look of disgust on Diamond's face, or the tone of her voice. Why was she questioning her about this? What gave her the right?

"Yes, I was, though I don't see why that's any of your business."

Diamond slowly shook her head. "You said that night when all of us were together that you never cheated on Cy. We both said it! So *you're* the one having an affair with Cy's business partner behind his back this whole time?"

"We weren't together 'this whole time'. Tariq and I only got together after I left Cyrus. Besides, why am I even explaining myself to you? Again, how is this any business of yours?"

"It's my business because I'm the one being accused of cheating on him and planning his murder! I'm the one no one trusts!" she yelled, stepping toward Noelle, glaring up at her. "Meanwhile you're the one walking around Main Street, kissing up on his business partner. You're the one who probably wanted him out the way all along!"

"What are you saying?" Noelle pointed at her chest. Several people slowed down, watching as the two women argued. "That I tried to have Cyrus killed?"

"It makes sense! You don't want to be with him anymore, right? You're fucking Tariq Donahue! Why not pin it all on me?"

"I didn't pin it on you! I never told the cops I thought you did it. That guy . . . your pimp . . . your boyfriend confessed, remember? I read the stories, Diamond! He told them what happened and what you did. I never—"

"He's lying!" Diamond shouted. "He is lying! Why won't anyone believe me? I would never want to kill Cy! He's . . . he's . . ."

She didn't finish. She broke down into tears before she could, and Noelle stared at her dumbfounded.

"Ladies, you're gonna have to take this elsewhere," a cop said, suddenly appearing beside them. His stern eyes shifted between them. "You're in front of a private business and the owner doesn't want any—"

"Yes, Officer, we understand. Sorry for the disturbance. We're leaving now. Thank you," Noelle said, wrapping an arm around Diamond's trembling shoulders. She then guided her away. The young woman didn't argue. She was still too busy weeping. She remained docile as Noelle steered her along.

They walked for several yards until Noelle spotted a small park with stone benches where a few people were eating lunches and talking. Noelle noticed an empty bench.

"Over here," she whispered to Diamond. She sat down first. The young woman plopped onto the bench beside her. Noelle handed her a tissue from her purse and watched as Diamond wiped her eyes and blew her nose.

Noelle was once again struck by how young Diamond was—only twenty-three. What had Noelle been like at that age?

Probably just as vulnerable, Noelle conceded.

Probably just as lost, too, though her success at modeling had offered something to run after and focus on to keep the sadness and loneliness at bay.

"I'm . . . I'm sorry," Diamond finally said, giving a loud sniff. "I'm so tired of crying. Feels like that's all I do nowadays. I'm so damn tired of crying!"

"It's okay," Noelle whispered.

"No, it's not. And I didn't mean to flip out on you like that. To accuse you. You were nice to me. You've always been nice to me. I've just been . . . I've been going through a lot lately."

"I can imagine," Noelle answered softly.

"Everyone thinks I did it. I mean, I get why." She lowered her gaze to her lap where she was wringing her tissue. "I'm the stereotypical conniving killer, right? I used to do sex work. I fell in love with Julian a while back and I was dumb enough to trust him, even lie for him . . . but I'm not that dumb anymore. I would never lie about something like this!"

"I believe you," Noelle said.

"You do?"

Noelle nodded. "I do."

She didn't know why she believed Diamond, but she did. Maybe it was because she had also fallen in love with a man who had lied to her and betrayed her. Cyrus was *still* betraying her, twisting the knife slowly, drawing pleasure from her pain. Diamond had obviously fallen into the same trap.

"My lawyer is hoping he can get me off," Diamond continued. "That's why I was here today. To talk about my case yet again, but it just feels like a waste of time. No one is going to believe me. Well, besides you and Cy. But even Cy has been acting . . . well, different lately." She winced. "I don't even recognize him anymore."

Noelle took a deep breath. "You shouldn't depend on Cy, Diamond. I said so that night long ago and I meant it. Cy will always put himself first. He doesn't have your back. Focus on yourself and your case. Because you have to. If you know you didn't do this, you shouldn't go to jail for it."

"I shouldn't, but I am," Diamond said, raising her gaze from her lap and staring off into space. "The cops think I'm making this all up, but I wish I *was* making it up some-times. Maybe then I wouldn't remember what happened that day." She turned to look at Noelle again. "You know I still have dreams about it? I guess you could call them nightmares. It always happens in slow motion, too. I'll see that guy coming out of the stairwell in our building. I see him coming toward Cy and me, pointing his gun at us. I remember the look in his eyes. The 'nine' tattoo on his arm," she said, making Noelle frown again. "I want to run. I want to shout to Cy to run, too . . . that this bastard is gonna kill us, but nothing comes out. I'm just . . . just frozen. And then the gun fires, but this time the bullets don't hit Cy. They hit me. And then I-I wake up."

Noelle didn't know what to say, too embarrassed to admit that she had stopped listening to Diamond's retelling of her dream. She was still stuck on the "nine" tattoo Diamond had mentioned had been on the shooter's arm. It sounded very similar to the tattoo Tariq had on his chest and had also been on the forearm of Tariq's friend, Big El. Tariq had confessed that he and Big El had been in the same gang together long ago. That's where they had gotten the tattoos. The revelation had shocked Noelle, but she'd let it go, agreeing with Tariq that crimes he'd committed back in his teens shouldn't be held against him now. She couldn't judge him by the guy he was more than fifteen years ago.

But Noelle hadn't known the man who had shot Cy had worn the same tattoo. It was an eerie coincidence that didn't sit well with her, listening to Diamond's story. Had Tariq once crossed paths with the shooter? Might he have known him?

"I'm . . . I'm sorry for . . . for what happened to you," Noelle said weakly, now knocked off-kilter.

"Thank you." Diamond gave a pained smile before rising to her feet. "And thank you for the Kleenex . . . and for listening to me."

"Of course! I just wish there was something I could do to help," she said, standing up as well.

"I appreciate that, but there's nothing anyone can do. It is what it is."

The two women walked in silence. Noelle didn't know where they were headed, but she didn't want to leave Diamond alone right now. She seemed so sad, almost desolate. She realized belatedly that they were walking to a nearby parking lot. As they neared Diamond's Volkswagen, Noelle placed a hand on the other woman's arm.

"Please keep in touch. Let me know how you're doing. You still have my cell number, right?"

Diamond nodded. "Yeah."

"I mean it! I know that how we met each other wasn't under the best of circumstances, and all that's happened since . . ." She sighed heavily. "It hasn't been easy for any of us, but it's been really hard for you. I will never know what it's like to be in your shoes. I get that. But if you need to commiserate . . . if you need someone to talk to, I—"

"I'll call you. I will." Diamond smiled again. This smile didn't look as pained as the last.

Noelle squeezed Diamond's arm reassuringly and watched as the other woman turned, opened her car door, and climbed inside. She stood on the curb and waved goodbye when she pulled off, unable to shake her new sense of unease.

Chapter 17

Diamond

"Mrs. Grey, are you saying that you did not purchase a five-thousand-dollar gold chain for Mr. Mason in exchange for the attempted murder of your husband?" Darius asked while pacing back and forth.

"No, I did not," Diamond answered from her perch on the sofa, keeping her answers brief and straight, to the point, like he'd told her.

They were in her living room, rehearsing her testimony for her murder trial in a few months. This would be the third time doing it; they'd done another practice session at his office almost a week ago—the same day that she'd stumbled upon Noelle on Main Street.

After Darius had reluctantly agreed to put Diamond on the stand, he'd insisted that it was important that she paint herself in a good light. She guessed him grilling her over and over again was the best way he thought she could do it. But these practice sessions didn't seem to be getting any easier. They weren't making her more confident, either.

Even though she tried to keep her answers short, she kept getting tongue-tied. Having Darius here alone with her in her cramped apartment didn't make her any less nervous. He'd already loosened his tie and rolled up his sleeves. Her gaze kept drifting to the arms that had held her in the alleyway near her job when she'd broken down into tears a couple of weeks ago. She wouldn't mind him holding her again right now to reassure her that everything was going to be okay.

"So why did you purchase the gold chain?"

She snapped her gaze from his arms and returned her focus to the face. It didn't make her ordeal any easier. She kept zeroing in on his lips. "Huh?"

"I said, if you didn't buy it in exchange for Mr. Mason trying to murder your husband, why did you purchase the chain, Mrs. Grey?"

She gnawed her bottom lip. She began to wring her hands in her lap. "Umm, well . . . because he told me that he would tell me who shot Cy . . . I mean, he promised he'd tell me if he did it only if I bought him the chain. That's . . . that's the only reason why I did it."

Darius stopped his pacing to stare down at her over the top of his glasses. "So you were waiting for confirmation that he shot your husband? Is that what you're saying?"

She quickly shook her head, making her hair whip around her shoulders. "No! No, I wasn't waiting for anything. I just wanted to know if he did it."

Darius loudly grumbled, closing his eyes and pinching the bridge of his nose. "Diamond, that is not a good answer."

"But it's the truth!"

"But you're making it sound like you really *did* believe Julian shot your husband. That he could've killed him."

"I didn't know either way! I just wanted a straight answer, and that piece of shit wouldn't give me one. I was scared! I didn't know what else to do."

"And yet you went gallivanting around town with him

in your Aston Martin and bought him a gold chain. That doesn't sound like a woman who's scared."

"I wasn't 'gallivanting.' What the fuck does that even mean? I was only trying to—"

He tilted his head and opened his eyes. "And could you stop cursing, please?"

"I cuss when I'm mad, Darius! Like a *normal* human being."

He dropped his hands to his hips. "I get that. I also get that you're gonna have to be very careful how you phrase things while you're on that stand. If you want to get the jurors on your side, watch your language."

"Why? Because they all believe I'm a conniving whore who tried to kill my husband?"

"That's not what I said."

"You didn't have to say it."

"Jesus," he murmured tiredly, closing his eyes again.

"Look, we've been through this. I'm no angel. And no matter what I do or say, or what phrasing I use, no juror is gonna believe that I am. I'm not proud of everything I've done in the past, but I'm not going to beat myself up for it, either. I was naïve. I was even stupid sometimes. But what I did was the best I could do!"

Darius lowered his head and rubbed the back of his neck, like he was trying to massage out a knot. "I can't believe we're on this again."

"You're damn right we're on this again! I had to pay for rent. I had to pay for food and my tuition. I needed money fast, and porn and turning tricks was the way to do it. I mean . . . damn, it wasn't like I was robbing anyone! I wasn't selling crack! I did what I had to do, and I'm sorry I'm not willing to drop to my knees, whip my back, call myself a dirty whore, and beg the jurors for their forgiveness! I'm sorry that I'm not a perfect, law-abiding citizen like you, but—"

"Goddamnit, I'm not perfect!" he shouted, wrenching off his glasses, tossing them onto her coffee table and glaring down at her. "You think you're the only one who's suffered? You think you're the only one who's been through shit? Huh?"

Diamond went quiet and stared up at Darius in shock. Didn't he just lecture her about cursing?

"Well, you're not! Stop fuckin' assuming shit about me . . . that my life is or has been perfect! *Okay?* Just because I'm not facing a murder charge and my face hasn't been plastered on the evening news doesn't mean I haven't fucked up or been through my own shit, because I have!"

He flopped back onto the couch beside her. Her living room was achingly silent after that.

"Well, look at you," she said. "I really got you fired up, didn't I?"

She watched as he blew air through his inflated cheeks, rolled his eyes, and laughed ruefully. Without his glasses and now furious, he looked kind of sexy. With the top buttons of his shirt open and his sleeves rolled up exposing his neck, wiry arms, and wispy dark hairs on his chest, he was more than a little sexy. He was downright irresistible.

But she had to resist. She was a married woman, after all.

Married to a man who's also married to two other women, a voice in her head countered. *Married to a man who dangled you over the side of a bridge!*

That all was true, but more importantly, she was certain a straitlaced man like Darius had no interest in a "tainted" woman like her despite how imperfect he claimed to be.

"I'm sorry," he mumbled, turning to look at her. "I shouldn't have . . . I shouldn't have shouted at you like that."

"No, I'm sorry for setting you off in the first place. Well, not really," she conceded with a laugh. "Seeing you like this is kinda refreshing. You come off less stuck-up when you're pissed off."

He eyed her. "You know, for someone who hates being judged, you sure don't have a problem judging other people. You've made a lot of assumptions about me, and none of them are right."

"Then tell me what I got wrong." She gestured to him. "Tell me something about you that would surprise me."

"Are you serious?"

"Yes, I'm serious! You know I did online porn . . . that I had sex for money. Whatever you tell me about yourself couldn't be nearly as eyebrow-raising. This is a no-judgment zone."

To be honest, she'd be relieved to hear something about him that made him seem more human.

"Okay, umm . . ." He looked up at her ceiling and seemed to think for a bit. "I haven't done my laundry in almost two weeks. Haven't had the time. I haven't done the dishes, either. They're piling up in my sink and starting to smell a little."

She burst into laughter. "Oh, wow! I'm about to call the cops!" She beckoned him again. "Come on, you're gonna have to try harder than that."

She watched as he rubbed his hands together, like he was trying to warm them. He seemed to be considering something. She wondered what he would tell her next. Maybe that he had an overdue parking ticket or he once parked in a handicapped space. Or maybe that he secretly cut off the "do not remove" labels from some pillowcases.

"I'm . . . I'm an addict," he said.

She frowned, wondering if she had heard him correctly.

"Well, a *recovering* addict," he clarified. "I haven't used in more than six years. But they teach you in AA that whether you're actually using or not is irrelevant. You will *always* be an addict."

"Addicted to what? *To drugs?*"

"No, I was addicted to cereal. Of course I was addicted to drugs!" He looked more amused than annoyed by her question. "Uppers were my drug of choice. In college I took Adderall so I could pull those all-nighters and study for exams. Then I started crushing the Adderall and sniffing it. I moved on to coke for a while . . . then speed. By my second year of law school, my habit was pretty bad. I was using my student loan money to pay for it. Then my mom got sick. It was lymphoma. She'd been a smoker her whole life. She went into the hospital. When she died, I spiraled. Things got really dark. I don't think I would've made it if it wasn't for my brother." He dropped his gaze. "He saved my ass. Who would've thought it, considering how he was back then."

"What do you mean?"

"I was the good son. He was the bad son. He was the crazy, fun dude who everybody liked. I was the nerd up in my bedroom, all alone with my head in my books. Those were our roles. I was supposed to be the one with promise. Our mother had pinned all her hopes on me. My big brother, T. J., had broken her heart when he started running with the wrong crowd, when he ran away from home and got into trouble. She said she didn't recognize him anymore . . . that he turned out just like his no-good daddy." Darius paused. "We had different fathers," he explained.

Diamond nodded, still stunned by the story Darius was telling. He had been a drug addict? Her eyes scanned over him. She still found it hard to believe.

"Mama told me to stay away from my brother and focus on school so I wouldn't go down the same path, and I did. Besides, he barely came around anymore. His friends were his family. Not us. He did his own thing and I did mine. But I felt isolated without T. J. there. The house wasn't the same without him. I still graduated first in my high school class, though. I went to college on a full scholarship. But I think after a while I started to buckle under the pressure, you know? I didn't want to always be at the top of my class. I didn't want to always be the 'good son.' That's around the time I started using. Maybe the two are related. Maybe not." He shrugged. "But either way, my habit got so out of hand that I was high almost constantly. I was failing my classes. I dropped out of law school. I owed my dealers money. One was threatening to kill me if I didn't pay up."

"Oh my God! You had to be scared out of your mind!"

She rested a consoling hand on his shoulder. He reached up and grasped it within his own, making her hand tingle. Her entire body seemed to radiate warmth now, just from his touch. He raised his gaze and turned to look at her. Their eyes met.

Diamond wanted to hold him, to comfort him and tell him she was sorry for seeing his glasses and the lack of swagger and assuming he'd led an easy, boring life. She hadn't known about his mother or his brother. She hadn't known that he'd been an addict and had to drop out of school. He was broken just like her, but she'd been too blind to realize it.

She wanted to kiss his pain away. But she didn't. Instead, she broke their gaze. He released her hand and she removed it from his shoulder, deciding it was better to keep her hands in her lap. She shifted on the sofa, putting a little more distance between them, hoping that would be enough to stave off the desire she felt flaring up inside her.

"I didn't know what to do, so I looked up my brother to see if he could help me," Darius continued. "He had money by then. A nice place and a car. Mama thought he would never amount to anything . . . that he would be nothin' more than a street thug for the rest of his life. But he turned out a lot better than she'd expected. I guess a life of crime ain't all bad, huh?" he asked wryly. "Anyway, he paid off my dealers, and when one refused to take the money I owed and tried to strong-arm him for more, T. J. made him go away."

"Made him go away? What . . . what does that mean?"

"I don't know. And honestly, I didn't want to know. I still don't. I know who my brother is. I knew how he made his way . . . how he handled things. He fixed the problem for me and I was grateful. He put me in rehab. That was his condition for paying off my debts. I had to get clean—and stay that way. 'Or I'mma take what you owe me out of your ass,' T. J. told me. When I got myself together, I reenrolled in law school to finish my third year. He paid for that, too."

"Whoa! He really did *all that*?"

Darius nodded. "And he won't let me forget it. Every once in a blue moon he'll call in a favor. He'll remind me of how he helped me and what I owe him."

"Has he asked you to do anything crazy?"

"Nothing illegal if that's what you mean. At least not so far. But his latest request hasn't been an easy one." Darius smacked his lips. "Man, my throat is dry. Can I have some water?"

She nodded, and tilted her head toward her kitchen. "Sure, it's in the fridge. Glasses are in the cabinet overhead."

Darius rose to his feet and crossed the short expanse of her living room before opening the refrigerator and removing the plastic pitcher filled with ice-cold water. With him across the room, she didn't feel as much tension. It was easier to breathe.

"So are you and your brother closer now than you were when you were younger?" she asked casually, clearing her throat. "Do you still see him?"

"Yeah," Darius said as he opened one of her cabinets and took out a water glass. "I . . . uh . . . I saw him just last week. He stopped by my office."

"Just for a visit or to ask for another favor?"

"A little bit of both," he mumbled.

"What? What's wrong?"

He closed the cabinet and turned to her. "What do you mean, what's wrong?"

"You looked . . . I don't know . . . weird all of a sudden."

"I just don't like to talk about my brother."

"Umm, we just spent the past fifteen minutes talking about your brother."

Darius nodded before pouring some water into his glass and taking a sip. "I know, and I shouldn't have. He asked me not to, and I don't know why the hell I went blabbing about that shit to you now. He'd kill me if he knew I had."

"Why?" She searched his face. "Why doesn't he want you talking about him?"

Darius hesitated.

"What? What is it?"

He lowered the glass from his lips.

"Just say it, Darius!"

And he did. He told her everything.

Chapter 18

Vanessa

"I'm heading to Janeiro now, Cy!" Vanessa called over her shoulder as she strolled down the hall. "I'll be gone for a couple of hours at most. If you need me, call my cell!"

For the past few days she had mentioned casually that her girlfriends wanted to meet her for lunch.

"They just miss me *so* much," she had told her husband, trying to sound forlorn and put upon. "We haven't met up in ages. I guess they're getting impatient. I told them I could hang out with them for an hour or two . . . maybe. That is if you can stand me being gone that long."

"Sure," he'd said as he typed on his laptop, which was perched in front of him while he reclined in bed. "Whatever! Do your thing."

Of course it was all fictitious. Her girlfriends hadn't called her begging for lunch. She wasn't heading to Rio de Janeiro Grill, a Brazilian steakhouse about fifteen miles from her house, where the servers made a big production of cutting the meat skewered on swords at the diners' tables. Instead, she was headed to meet Bilal. They were finally putting their plan into motion. They were finally going to kill Cy today.

And it's about damn time, she thought.

If he followed his normal behavior pattern, he would leave the house soon after she did. Bilal and she would trail him in a rented vehicle, and when Cyrus climbed out of his BMW Bilal would shoot him. He'd hop back into the car while she waited in the driver's seat and they'd drive away.

It was admittedly a perilous tactic, but if they did it fast enough, no one would recognize either of them before they got away.

"Did you hear me, Cy?" Vanessa now shouted again. "I'm leaving!"

She wanted to make certain he believed she was no longer home.

"Got it!" Cyrus called back. "Just make sure you don't take all damn day this time!"

"Just make sure you really *die* this time," she muttered under her breath before striding to the stairs.

Certain of their success and the end of her drudgery and agony, Vanessa hopped down the stairs to the first floor and sailed toward the front door. She crossed the marble tile of the foyer and swung the door open, only to stop in her tracks when she saw her eldest son, Cy Jr., standing on their welcome mat. She watched him tug off his headphones and adjust the skateboard in his arms.

"Junior! What . . . what are you doing back home, baby?" she cried, trying to hide her panic.

She had purposely made sure her children would not be anywhere near home today so Cyrus would have no reason to keep up his invalid charade. Bryson and Zoe were on an outing with their grandmother, who Vanessa had given express instructions to keep them busy for the next two hours—at *minimum*. Cy Jr. was supposed to be at the nearby skate park with his friends. He'd left more than a half hour ago. So why was he back here already?

"It's too hot and the skate park is too crowded today, so I just came back home," he lamented with a shrug of his lanky, brown shoulders. "I was gonna grab a Gatorade and play video games." He stepped forward, as if to walk back into the house, but she blocked his path in the doorway.

"It's n-n-not too hot!" she stuttered. "Why don't you try the basketball court next to it? There's always the neighborhood boys over there to play with!"

"But you know I'm not that good at basketball, Mom. And I don't have a—"

"Nonsense!" she exclaimed, shutting the front door behind her. She firmly held his arm and steered him back to their stone walkway, guiding him away from the house. "You'll play just fine. Now go have fun with your friends!"

He puffed beside her, pulling his arm out of her grasp. "But I don't wanna, Mom!"

"Junior," she said tightly, "your father needs some rest and quiet. It's hard for him to recover with all the noise and you, your brother, and your sister running around the house. Don't you want Daddy to get better?"

Cy Jr. went silent. He grimaced.

Vanessa hated guilt-tripping him, but she needed to get him away from the house. She needed to be on her way, too. Bilal was waiting for her.

"Don't you, Junior?" she persisted.

The eleven-year-old finally raised his gaze to look at his mother. "Why should I care about him when he didn't care about us?"

There was a hard edge to his voice. She recognized the hatred in his eyes.

She'd seen it flare up during her own unguarded moments, when she caught herself in a mirror or another reflective surface. Cyrus didn't even have to be around for it to happen; the fury was always with her. It was like a fire was raging inside her, burning at her skin, begging to be let out with all its force and intensity.

Vanessa had suspected Cy Jr. was battling a similar rage. He was furious at his father for everything that had happened, that had been brought to light. He'd refused to talk to her about it, but she knew instinctively that something was wrong with her baby; he didn't need to tell her. She now raised her hand to his cheek.

"Junior, I know that you're mad at Daddy, but—"

"He lied to us. He lied to *you*!" Cy Jr. argued. "He cheated on you, Mom!"

"I know. I *know*. But that's between your dad and me. I've got this. Okay?" she assured him. "You don't have to worry about any of that. Go to the basketball court. Have fun with your friends. Worry about anything but this, baby. Mama will handle it."

Of course she couldn't tell her son *how* she was handling it, but she wasn't lying. She would fix this. She would finally fix this mess once and for all, and she and her children would be happy again.

Once that son of a bitch is gone, she thought.

Cy Jr. still hesitated, like he still wasn't sure, like he didn't want to leave, but he reluctantly nodded. "Okay," he mumbled.

She walked with him to their driveway, where her car already sat idle with the engine running, thanks to her remote.

"Here's some money, too," she said, digging into her purse. She handed Cy Jr. a twenty-dollar bill. "Buy some lunch. I mean real food, Junior! Not just junk."

He nodded absently before tucking the bill into the back pocket of his jeans. She kissed his cheek and whispered goodbye. He strolled back to the neighborhood sidewalk. Vanessa opened the door to her SUV, but paused to watch her son hop onto his skateboard and roll away. When he disappeared around the corner she finally climbed inside and drove off.

"Where were you, bae?" Bilal exclaimed as he opened the car door and hopped out. She switched places with him and sat in the driver's seat. "You said you were gonna be here fifteen minutes ago!"

"I got held up," she muttered before slamming the door shut behind her. She adjusted her sunglasses and the long, blond wig she'd carried in her handbag and had thrown on her head on the way there. She watched through the windshield as Bilal raced to the other side of the car and climbed onto the passenger seat.

"Held up by what?" he asked.

"Nothin'. It doesn't matter! I'm here now. I'm ready."

After she'd left the house she'd driven directly to the parking lot of an industrial park complex full of concrete buildings and tractor-trailer cabs that was a five-minute drive from her neighborhood. She and Bilal had agreed to meet there. They decided they would tail Cyrus together in the navy-blue Ford Taurus with dark-tinted windows that Bilal had rented.

"Did you bring the gun?" she asked, settling into the seat and buckling her seat belt.

He nodded. "Yeah, it's the glove compartment." He patted the dusty dashboard. "Has he left the house yet?"

She removed her cell from her purse and pulled up a phone app. It was connected to a small Bluetooth camera she'd set up in her foyer. In it, she could see her husband plodding down the stairs to the first floor. He paused in the foyer mirror to examine his reflection, to run a finger over his mustache.

"He looks like he's about to leave," she said, tossing her cell to Bilal. He scrambled to catch it. "Let's go!"

She threw the car into drive and floored the accelerator. Bilal lurched back in his seat as they pulled out of the industrial park's parking lot with a squeal of tires and the gunning of the engine.

"Why are you driving so fast?" he asked as she made a hard right at a corner.

"Because we want to catch him before he leaves. If he drives off before we get there, we won't know where the hell he went," she replied, keeping her focus on the roadway.

"But if you drive too fast, the cops could pull us over, bae! I have a Glock in the glove compartment and I don't have a gun permit. If a cop searched the car, we could—"

"Calm down. No cops are gonna pull us over," she said, making a hard left, whipping him in his seat.

They were about half a mile from the house. She could see the brick sign leading to their development in the distance.

"What if it doesn't work?" Bilal ventured.

"What if *what* doesn't work?" she asked, barely paying attention, so focused on getting back to her house.

"What if he drives to a place where I can't get to him? What if he . . . he recognizes me?" Bilal asked, his voice rising with panic. "What if . . . what if I can't do this shit, bae? I mean . . . I'm really supposed to kill him? I've never killed anybody before!"

She drew to a stop at the end of the block, pulling in front of one of her neighbors' houses. She turned to stare at her lover, whipping off her sunglasses. "Are you backing out of this?"

He fidgeted in the seat beside her but didn't respond.

"You're gonna leave me and our baby to that . . . *that monster*? You know what he's gonna do to me when he finds out that I'm pregnant, right? You know what he's gonna make me do to it?"

Bilal cringed.

"I thought you were my man! My protector! You swore you would take care of me!"

"I know. I *know*! And I will! But maybe we should—"

"There is no maybe! We *have* to do this," she said, gazing into his dark eyes. "You have to do this—or we are done. You hear me? If you won't help me, I don't fucking need you!"

His jaw tightened at her words, but he didn't argue with her. He didn't hop out of the car, either. Gradually, he nodded.

"Fine," he muttered. "Fine. I'll do it."

She shifted in her seat, prepared to accelerate down the block, but stopped short when she saw the door to her garage slowly open.

"There he is. He's heading out!" she yelled.

They watched as the door rolled to the stop. Her husband began to back out of their garage in his BMW sedan.

"Keep your eye on him, but make sure you keep your distance, too, bae," Bilal whispered. "We don't want him to know we're following him."

"I know," she snapped.

Mr. Cold Feet suddenly wanted to take the lead and give out orders?

That's rich, she thought.

Vanessa eased the car forward, ducking slightly lower behind the steering wheel, but she braked again when another car whipped in front of her, barely missing her front bumper.

"What the hell?" she said, watching as the Porsche Boxster came at full speed down the road, then skidded to a halt at the end of her driveway, blocking Cyrus's exit and ruining her and Bilal's carefully constructed plans.

"Who is that?" Bilal asked.

They both watched in dismay as the driver's side door to the Porsche opened and a man stepped outside. Her mouth fell open in shock. She recognized the driver instantly. "What is he doing here?"

"*He?* He *who?*" Bilal asked.

"Tariq. My . . . my husband's business partner."

Chapter 19

Cyrus

When Cyrus saw in his rearview mirror the familiar black Porsche Boxster blocking his path, he slammed on his brakes. As he watched Tariq throw open the driver's side door and step out, casually buttoning his suit jacket while he rose to his feet, Cyrus's balls clenched. They damn near rose into his gut.

It wasn't fear that made him respond this way. At least that's what he told himself.

I'm not afraid of that motherfucka, he thought, even as Tariq strolled up the driveway toward his car.

Tariq had caught him off guard. That's all. He hadn't expected him to just show up here. But Cyrus should've known that snake would always be somewhere lying around, waiting to strike. And to make matters worse, Tariq was ruining one of the few chances Cyrus had to leave the house on his own, now that his lying, cheating bitch of a wife Vanessa was off doing God knows what with her lover.

The latest recording from her room hadn't revealed the

details, but he knew those two were up to something, and he was on his way to find out. He'd put a tracker on her car two days ago. The last he'd seen, she'd stopped at a nearby industrial park—nowhere near the Brazilian restaurant she'd claimed to be headed to. So she'd gone from screwing her lover in public parks to an industrial park. He didn't know if that counted as an upgrade. Either way, he didn't have time for whatever this was with Tariq.

Cy's cautious gaze tracked his adversary as the other man drew closer to his BMW. He watched Tariq's hands, anticipating the moment when the bastard reached for a weapon.

Well, unlike back in Baltimore three months ago, Cyrus had a weapon of his own, and he was more than willing to use it.

Cyrus started to reach behind him for his gun but stopped short and jumped in his seat when Tariq rapped his knuckles on the trunk of the BMW.

"Get out of the car, Cy!" Tariq ordered. "Can't sit in there all day, nigga. Hop out!"

Cyrus narrowed his eyes at the other man's image in his rearview mirror, annoyed by his tone and his demand. He removed his seat belt, turned off the engine, and climbed out of the car.

"Hiya doin'?" Tariq looked him up and down. "You look good. Put on a little weight, though."

"Yeah, well, I don't mind." He glanced down at himself. "I'd rather be fat and *alive* than dead."

"You raise a good point. You know most men who dodged death," Tariq began as he leaned back against the car hood, "would see it as chance to enjoy life, embrace change, make amends, and make things right—but not you." He slowly shook his head. "You still on your same ol' bullshit. You just won't learn your lesson, will you, Cy? You keep makin' me have to explain this shit to you."

"So you really came all the way here just to give me a lecture?" Cyrus asked, slamming his car door closed behind him. "You really expect me to believe that?"

"Oh, were you expecting me to do something else? Is that why you keep hidin' in your house behind your wife and kids like some bitch?" Tariq sneered, adjusting his necktie.

"Fuck you! You've got some goddamn nerve talkin' to me like that, let alone showin' your face around here. The cops could be here at any moment and you won't be so smug when—"

"The cops ain't comin' because you and I both know you ain't gonna call them. And *you're* the one with some goddamn nerve showing up at Noelle's dress shop!" He pointed up at Cy. "I knew your dumb ass would end up begging her to take you back. Your ego can't handle seeing her happy and movin' on without you. But I didn't think you were dumb enough to threaten her, let alone put your fuckin' hands on her. Not after what I said to you the last time we saw each other." His eyes went glacial. "Nobody could be that fuckin' stupid."

"She went runnin' to you, telling you everything, huh?" Cyrus shrugged. "I'm not surprised since she thinks you're her knight in shining armor now. Like your dick is made of gold."

"No, she didn't. She lied and said you didn't lay a finger on her, but I figured it out. I know her better than—"

"You don't know her!"

"And you don't love her! You just saw her as something you owned. You didn't even want her anymore. You just want her now because someone else has her."

"You think cuz she's dumb enough to let you raw dawg her and put a bastard in her belly that you've become an expert on love and my wife? If you do, you're as dumb as she is."

Tariq didn't immediately respond, but Cyrus wanted to see him lose it, to fly into a rage and show his neighbors and all the world that he was no better than Cyrus. Instead, Tariq maintained his cool. Cyrus watched as he pushed himself away from the hood and took a deep breath.

"Cy, I told you before not to call her stupid," he began in a measured voice. He then took another threatening step toward him. "And if you ever . . . *ever* speak about our baby again, I will—"

"*What?* Shoot me again? You really wanna take that chance?"

Tariq inclined his head. "I already told you. I don't know anything about that, but I *do* know where you were a little over three weeks ago. I can make a call to the DC cops and tell them to check out the roadway and stoplight cameras near Ray's Bar & Lounge from that day."

When Cyrus heard those words, his confident smirk disappeared. He swore his stomach did a backflip. He almost upchucked his lunch right there on his driveway asphalt.

Tariq grinned. "I heard there were two murders there. One was the poor bartender. The other was an old acquaintance of mine by the name of Big El, who had gotten to be such a damn nuisance. He kept trying to hit me up for more money because of a favor I asked him to do for me a while back. A favor that he didn't do well. But whoever shot him took away that headache for me. I guess I should thank them."

Cyrus's breathing became more labored. He could have sworn his collar was choking him.

"I could ask the cops if any of those cameras caught a silver BMW racing away from the scene of the crime. Maybe they could even zoom in on the license plate."

"How the fuck do you know all this?" Cyrus asked in a hoarse whisper. "You've been following me?"

"I've got a full-time job, Cy, and a pregnant girlfriend. I ain't got time to be following your ass around! Besides, I don't need to follow you to keep an eye on you. I have my ways. Trust."

He had his ways? Cyrus took a frantic glance around him, in search of an unfamiliar car or person lurking nearby.

He'd thought since that lying motherfucka he now knew was "Big El" had snuck up on him and shot him at his condo in Baltimore, he'd gotten a lot savvier and more aware of his surroundings. But had Tariq had someone trailing him this whole time and he hadn't even noticed?

Once again, Tariq was two moves ahead on the chessboard. Once again, it pissed Cyrus off.

"So keep testing me," Tariq said. "Come after Noelle again. Lay one fuckin' finger on her and see what happens. I know all your dirt. You keep forgetting that. And you're too big of a slob to clean up behind yourself. I will expose you. I will ruin you. Stop . . . testing . . . *me*."

Tariq then turned and walked back toward his car. As he tugged the door open and climbed inside, Cyrus was gritting his teeth again so much that his jaw hurt. Once again he reached for his gun but stopped short when Tariq said over his shoulder, "And don't think about shooting me in the back. Wouldn't want the neighbors to see."

Cyrus lowered his hand. Did Tariq have eyes in the back of his head as well?

His plans to spy on his wife Vanessa were now forgotten. He realized that if he wanted to finally stomp Tariq into the dust, he had to narrow his focus and be much more careful. He had to have more stealth to beat Tariq at his own game.

Come hell or high water, he would finally get his revenge.

Chapter 20

Noelle

Noelle looked up from her menu when she heard someone walking toward her table. She expected to see Diamond, looking frazzled, rushing toward her while apologizing for being fifteen minutes late. Instead, she saw her smiling waitress.

"Ready to order yet? Had enough time to look over the menu?" the young woman asked, taking a notepad out of the black apron cinched around her slim waist.

Noelle shook her head. "No, not yet."

Her focus, unfortunately, wasn't on whether to get the chicken wrap or the beer-battered fish tacos, though, truth be told, thanks to the pregnancy she was having a hard time keeping her food down anyway.

"I'm still waiting for my guest," she explained to the waitress. "When she comes, I'll order then."

"Gotcha," the waitress said before walking off.

Noelle turned to the bistro's floor-to-ceiling windows, on the lookout for Diamond.

Cy's other wife had called her out of the blue a few days ago, asking if they could meet up for a quick lunch and chat. Noelle had been surprised by the invite but didn't want to tell her no. She'd remembered Diamond's tears the last time she'd seen her, how desperate the young woman had seemed. Diamond also seemed like she could use a friend. Noelle wasn't sure if she was the right person for the job, but she remembered what it was like years ago, when she was severely depressed and at an all-time low. It had gotten so bad that she was suicidal, and she wasn't even facing something as desperate as a murder charge. She could have used someone to talk to, someone to make her feel a little less crazy and alone.

She finally spotted Diamond scurrying to the bistro's doors, shaking off water from her umbrella. The rain had stopped a half an hour earlier, leaving puddles along the sidewalk and in potholes on the street, making a rainbow appear in the purple and orange sky beyond the office buildings in the distance.

"Hey!" Diamond said, striding to the table. "The traffic from Baltimore was a pain in the butt! Sorry I'm a little late."

"It's okay!" Noelle watched as Diamond took the seat opposite her at the table. "Sorry the traffic was so bad."

"You know how it is with the rain and the beltway. Traffic sucks normally, but it only gets worse in bad weather. Can't get away from it!"

The two women gazed at each other awkwardly as silence fell over their table. They'd talked about traffic and the weather, covering all polite, inconsequential conversation. So what else should they talk about?

Their husbands?

Unfortunately, they had the same one.

Diamond's murder trial?

She didn't want to make Diamond burst into tears again.

"Hi! Welcome to the Blue Bistro! Can I get you some-

thing to drink?" the waitress asked while walking up behind Noelle, breaking into the silence.

"Uh, water is fine for me," Diamond said, "with a
lemon. Thanks."

The waitress nodded and walked off, and Diamond and
Noelle stared at each other again.

"So you're probably wondering why I called you . . .
why I asked you to meet me here today," Diamond finally
began, leaning forward in her chair.

"A little. But I told you to call me if you needed anything. If you needed someone to talk to." Noelle shrugged
after taking a quick sip of water from her glass. "I figured
you were taking me up on my offer."

"I was. I mean I am! There's just . . . there's just something else I wanted to ask you. Something that I wanted to
talk to you about, because you seem nice . . . like a good
person, Noelle. I can't believe I'm saying this to the
woman who's married to my husband, but you do. You in-
vited me to that dinner months ago to warn me and
Vanessa that our lives could be in danger because of Cy.
You didn't have to do that. You took a big risk, so I figured I should . . . you know . . . reciprocate by taking one,
too. I mean, if I knew something . . . if I knew something
about someone around you that was important, it would
be wrong to not tell you, right?"

Noelle lowered her glass back to the table. "I don't
know what you mean."

"I mean you're dating Tariq, Cy's business partner now.
You told me that. But how . . . how well do you know him?"

Noelle cocked her head, taken aback by the question.
Why was she asking her this? What was this woman's ob-
session with her and Tariq?

"I mean, there's casual dating," Diamond continued.
"Maybe you guys are like that and you wouldn't care one
way or the other if there was something about him that

you didn't know. But you could be more serious than that. It's just . . . I found out something big about him—"

"You found out something big about *Tariq?*"

Diamond nodded. "And I wasn't sure if maybe you should know. If you guys were close enough that—"

"I'd say we're pretty close. He asked me to move in with him." Her hand instinctively dropped to her stomach beneath the table. She clutched it protectively. "We're . . . we're having a baby together."

Diamond blinked. "Oh, man, that *is* serious."

"I'd say so. So if you know something about Tariq, I want to know. I *should* know," Noelle said grimly, feeling her stomach tighten again, and not because of the baby this time.

She had already endured so much with Cyrus. She didn't want her relationship with Tariq to turn out to be one big fat lie, too. Not after she took such a big chance. Not after she put so much faith in him even though almost every impulse told her not to. Finding out it was just another con might break her.

"But how do I know if I tell you, you aren't gonna go running back to him?" Diamond asked. "I mean . . . you're having a baby with him."

"Because I give you my word that I won't. I wouldn't—"

"All right! Here's your glass of water," the waitress said, setting a glass in front of Diamond, interrupting their conversation. She certainly was an overeager beaver. She pulled out her notepad again. "Are you ladies ready to order?"

Noelle settled on a cranberry salad, while Diamond ordered a BLT. When the waitress left, Diamond leaned forward and rested her elbows on the tabletop. Noelle held her breath, bracing herself for what the young woman was about to tell her.

"My lawyer . . . Darius . . . he works for Tariq," Diamond whispered.

When she did, Noelle exhaled—now relieved. The rigid muscles in her back and shoulders relaxed.

So *that* was Diamond's great revelation? Noelle had thought it was something serious.

"Okay," Noelle said, nodding, waiting for her to continue.

"Tariq hired Darius to be my lawyer. He told him to represent me for my attempted murder case."

"*What?*"

"Yeah, I was shocked, too. I thought Darius was working pro bono. That's what he told me—at first. I didn't know that anyone hired him, let alone that it was Tariq." Diamond paused. "And it's not just that. Darius . . . Darius and Tariq are brothers, Noelle. Did you know that?"

Noelle slumped back in her chair, now stunned. She didn't even know Tariq had a brother.

"Well, half brothers," Diamond explained. "Different fathers, but either way, Tariq is Darius's big brother. His big brother T. J. Darius said Tariq called him one day and said he needed a favor. He asked him to represent me. He told him that it was very important that he get the jury to find me not guilty. He said he wouldn't accept any other alternative. Darius doesn't know why Tariq did it, but he thinks his brother may know who really shot Cy. That's why he doesn't want me to go to jail for this. He knows I didn't do it!"

Noelle took several deep breaths, telling herself not to freak out, but she could feel herself unraveling. She was getting flashbacks to when she arrived at the hospital in Baltimore and found out that her husband was not the man he claimed to be.

But there could still be a valid explanation for every-

thing, a panicked voice in her head argued. *There could be a good reason why Tariq didn't tell you any of this.*

"Maybe . . . maybe Tariq didn't want you to know that he was footing the bill for your lawyer because he just didn't want to complicate things," Noelle argued. "Because of me, he and Cy are feuding now, and—"

"But why not tell *you*? Why did he tell Darius not to tell *anybody*? And it's not just that."

Jesus, what next? Noelle thought.

"Tariq isn't just Cy's business partner, Noelle. He's done things. Do you understand me? Really bad shit. Darius said his brother is a man most people learn not to fuck with," Diamond whispered. "And he's taken care of people who weren't smart enough to figure that out."

It was happening all over again. Someone was pulling the string on the elaborate shroud that a man she deeply loved had created for her, and she was watching the garment slowly unravel, showing her how shoddy the thing had been to begin with.

She felt so naked, listening to Diamond tell her the truth about Tariq. And absolutely terrified. She almost started shaking in her chair. She wanted to deny it and tell Diamond that either she or Darius were goddamn liars, but the pieces Diamond was handing her were starting to fit the jigsaw puzzle of unanswered questions Noelle had pushed to the back of her mind for weeks . . . for months.

"The man with the 'nine' tattoo on his arm that you said shot Cy," Noelle now whispered, feeling tears prick her eyes. "What did he look like?"

Diamond squinted at her, probably confused by the seemingly random question. "Huh?"

"The man with the tattoo who shot Cy, tell me what he looked like!" When Diamond hesitated, Noelle gritted her teeth with impatience. "Just tell me!" She opened her eyes, and one lone tear spilled onto her cheek. "What did he look like?"

"He had a mask on when I saw him, but the guard in our building said he saw him, too. He said he was light-skinned, and he had cornrows, I think. He said he had tat-toos all over. On his face. His neck." She eyed Noelle, noticing how the other woman's expression had changed as she spoke. "Why? Have you seen him?"

"Big El," Noelle murmured.

He had to have been the one who'd done it. Tariq's friend and former gang member had pulled the trigger, but had he done it at Tariq's behest?

Darius said his brother is a man most learn not to fuck with. . . . And he's taken care of people who weren't smart enough to figure that out, Diamond had said.

Perhaps Cy had been one of those people.

"*Big El?* Who's that? Is . . . is he the guy?" Diamond now asked eagerly. "Do you know who he is? Do you know his name?"

"I don't know. I don't know anything. I'm sorry, but . . . but I have to go," she said, rising from the table.

"What?"

"I'm sorry, Diamond," she said, gathering her purse and placing money on the table. "I have to go, but I swear I'll call you, and I won't tell Tariq any of this! Don't worry."

She then rushed to the bistro's door.

When Noelle left she didn't drive to Azure or back home to cry her eyes out. She went straight to Tariq's house. She noticed that his car wasn't parallel parked in its reserved spot. It was still early afternoon. He shouldn't be home from work for another few hours anyway, and that was a good thing, she resolved. It would give her enough time to do what she needed to do.

"Trust me," she muttered angrily between sniffs as she climbed the metal stairs and unlocked his front door with the keys he'd given her. "That son of a bitch told me to trust him and he was lying to me this whole goddamn time! Making me his puppet."

But she wouldn't give way to tears and frustration this time around, as she had with Cy.

Fool me once, shame on you. Fool me twice, shame on me, she thought.

She would take back control of the situation and no longer be manipulated. Her life and her baby's life depended on it. She would find out the full truth, and when she did she would take the evidence to the cops.

Noelle slammed the door behind her and marched straight to his home office first, saving his bedroom for last. She was in search of anything she could find, any new evidence revealing the lies that Tariq might have told her, the secrets he'd kept from her. She rummaged through his file cabinets and desk and bedroom drawers. She dug through his closet, storage boxes, and even his bathroom cabinets, but didn't find anything. After a couple of hours of searching, she had to give up. Tariq would be home soon.

She began to put everything back in its proper place, trying to remember exactly how everything had been arranged.

Tariq was fastidiously neat. He would notice little details like that.

As she stood in his walk-in closet, placing shoeboxes back on their shelves, she noticed a false panel in the wall behind a row of suits and slacks she hadn't spotted before. It was maybe a foot above the floorboards. It looked like one of those panels plumbers or electricians use to get to pipes or wires in a wall. She dropped to her knees, feeling wool and cotton slap her face as she tapped the panel, then nudged it. She saw it give a little. She began to gently shift it aside and discovered not pipes or wires behind it but a black, polycarbonate suitcase.

"What in the . . ." she whispered.

Noelle dragged it out and set it on the closet's hardwood floor. She didn't know what was inside, but it certainly was heavy. She unhooked the clamps on the side and tried to raise the lid, expecting it to be locked. But it wasn't. She quickly spotted the grip of a handgun and then another as she opened the suitcase. She breathed in audibly and started shaking all over again when she saw there were at least five handguns inside, nestled among the gray padding. There were also several magazines filled with bullets.

"Oh, God. Oh my God," she whispered, feeling short of breath.

What was Tariq doing with all these weapons? This wasn't just a homeowner trying to protect himself. What normal person needed this much firepower?

Cyrus had told her that Tariq was a ruthless killer. But she'd just dismissed it as more of Cyrus's lies. She'd thought Cy was, like all the other times, being vengeful and spiteful and wanted to ruin one of the few good things in her life. But Diamond had told her the same thing. And now she'd found this?

Maybe this time was one of the few times Noelle should have listened to Cy from the beginning.

She felt the bile rise in the back of her throat. She slammed the lid of the suitcase shut and shot to her feet. Noelle barely made it out of the closet and to Tariq's master bath before she threw up. Half of it landed in the toilet, the rest on the marble-tiled floor.

By the time Tariq arrived home from work more than an hour later, Noelle and the bathroom were clean. The suitcase had been returned to its wall panel in his closet. Tariq's dresser, drawers, shelves, and office were back to their normal state. She'd finished it all with only a few minutes to spare.

Tariq walked upstairs and found her lying on his bedspread in one of his bathrobes, like she'd been lying there the whole time, waiting for him. Noelle was flipping channels on his wall-mounted, flat-screen television when he walked in.

"Well, this is a nice surprise!" He leaned against the doorframe. "I didn't think you were coming over tonight." He began to undo his tie as he strolled farther into the bedroom. "I thought you had work to do at the boutique."

"I decided it could wait for another day," she said, pushing herself up from the bed.

"Did you now?" He took off his necktie and undid a couple of buttons of his dress shirt. He then cupped her face, leaned down, and kissed her.

Noelle tried not to flinch or pull away as he pushed the robe off her shoulders, as he eased her back onto his bed. She couldn't let him know everything had changed between them. What she'd discovered in his closet wasn't strong enough to take to the cops so she had to be careful. She still didn't know the man that Tariq really was, what he was capable of. But as he kissed her and peeled off his own clothes, he must have felt *something* was different.

Maybe it was how she kissed him back. Maybe her moans and whimpers sounded strange—more forced. Either way, he abruptly tugged his mouth away from hers.

"What's wrong?" she asked breathlessly.

He licked his lips. "Something's off." His eyes trailed over her. "I can't put my finger on what, though."

"Nothing's off, baby. You're just being paranoid." She wrapped her hand around the base of his neck and tugged him close. "Now stop talkin' and make love to me. I've been waiting all day for this."

He kissed her again, and pretty soon he stopped asking questions.

Chapter 21

Diamond

"Diamond? Diamond?"

Diamond turned away from the office window, where she'd been staring at the pouring rain. They'd had showers all week and she was already tired of it. She looked at Darius, who was sitting behind his desk, staring at her expectantly.

"I'm sorry. What did you say?" she asked.

"I asked you to recount again what happened the day of the shooting, but if you need to take a break—we can."

"No, I'm okay."

"Really? I know I've been asking a lot of you lately and—"

"No. No, you haven't." She shook her head and forced a smile to reassure him. "I know you're just trying to help. I just . . . I just have a lot on my mind. More than usual, if you can believe it."

Darius closed the manila folder he'd been holding and slowly set it on his desk. "Did something happen? Something else, I mean?"

Did something happen?

She laughed sadly to herself.

Where should she begin? She'd met up with Noelle a few days ago to tell her the truth about Tariq, Darius's older brother. She'd done it with good intentions, to pay back a favor that Noelle had done for her months ago. But seeing Noelle's reaction and how heartbroken she had been at hearing the news, Diamond now wondered if she'd done the right thing. The information she'd shared was bound to bring about the end of their relationship.

Good Lord, she's pregnant by him, Diamond now thought.

Maybe she should have minded her damn business and let Noelle discover the truth about Tariq on her own.

It didn't help, either, that she'd betrayed Darius's confidence in the process. And he was someone she didn't want to disappoint, not anymore. She liked Darius—a lot. Part of her suspected she was even falling for him.

No, there's no suspect. I am falling for him.

She'd tried to convince herself that it was because she was lonely. The marriage she'd thought she had with Cyrus was all an illusion and she didn't recognize her husband anymore. She could no longer count on him for comfort or support, and here came Darius, offering to do both. Yes, Darius's brother, Tariq, was paying him to represent her, but Darius didn't need to hug her the way he did, or hold her hand. He didn't have to reveal his past to her to show he wasn't perfect and make her feel more at ease around him. It had made her like him even more.

"It's . . . it's nothin'," she finally mumbled, shaking her head. "Don't worry about it. I'll work it out."

He leaned forward and rested his elbows on his desk. His brows furrowed. "It doesn't have anything to do with what happened last week, does it?"

"Why would it have anything to do with last week?"

Darius shrugged his broad shoulders. "Well, I kinda feel like I crossed some professional line with you that day. Like I said too much. Acted inappropriately. I spilled my guts. That's why I suggested we have our next meeting here in my office instead of your apartment. I guess it was my half-assed attempt to salvage the situation."

She glanced around her. He was right. There was no mistaking this was a business meeting in a lawyer's office. His law degree hung in a gilded frame on the wall, along with a plaque for legal excellence from the Maryland Bar Association. Two large, metal file cabinets sat in the left-hand corner. His desk, to his credit, was surprisingly neat, with his laptop and file folders. But she noticed that there were no pictures anywhere. Not of family, a girlfriend, or even his dog—if he had one. The walls were painted stark white. His office looked as reserved as the man himself.

"There's nothing to salvage. You didn't cross any line. And if anybody should apologize . . ." She hesitated. "It should be me, Darius."

His furrow deepened. "Why do you need to apologize? *I'm* the one who spilled my guts."

"I . . . I knew your brother was dating Noelle, Cy's other wife. So I told her what you told me about . . . about him."

Darius blanched.

"I know you trust him," she rushed out. "I know he's protected you since you were kids, but I didn't know what his intentions were with her. I mean, he tried to kill our husband!"

"I never said that! I don't know that for sure."

"But you suspect it, which is why I wanted to give her the heads-up. I wanted her to know the truth so she could make her own decision."

He closed his eyes, took a deep breath, and licked his lips. "When did you tell her?"

"A few days ago."

Darius slowly opened his eyes and sat back in his chair. "Well, it must not have gotten back to T. J. yet. If he found out I told someone the truth, I would've heard about it by now. If he found out about even half of this, he would have been blowin' up my phone, asking where I'm at so he could come and kick my ass from here to Annapolis."

"Is he gonna hurt you?" she asked, now sincerely worried for his safety, regretting her bad decision even more. "Is he gonna—"

"*Kill me?* No," Darius said, shaking his head. "He's still my brother. He has a lot of bark, but he would never do me any harm. Even for something like this."

"Are you sure?"

He nodded. "I know my brother."

"She won't tell him. She promised she wouldn't."

"And you believe her?"

Diamond gnawed her lower lip. She hesitated again. "Yes?"

He barked out a laugh and rubbed his hand over his face. "Oh, man. Oh, man. Oh, man! I am so screwed."

"I'm sorry." She frowned when he kept laughing. His reaction confused her. He wasn't having a mental breakdown, was he? "Are you all right?"

He nodded, still chuckling.

"Aren't . . . aren't you pissed?"

His laughter tapered off. "More pissed at myself than at you. I shouldn't have said anything. I shouldn't have told you that stuff that night but . . ." His words faded.

"But what?"

"But I did."

"Are you gonna tell your brother what I did?"

"Absolutely not!" he said with widened eyes. "Besides, T. J. always thinks he's so smooth. He always has some con going. I figured his lies would catch up to him eventually. He'd mentioned Noelle a couple of times, but I didn't know he was running a con on her, too."

"You think it's a con? So you don't think he really cares about her?"

He shrugged. "I don't know. You can never tell with T. J. Maybe it was just a con at first . . . maybe he was just pretending and thought he had it all under control, but things got real and the situation just got away from him. I know what that's like." He cringed. "The morning after our last meeting, I woke up and I thought, *What the hell got into your head, Darius? Why did you say all that shit?* I mean . . . I told you about T. J. and my drug addiction. Hell, I even told you that I never felt like I could live up to my mom's expectations!" He shook his head again, looking almost mystified. "And I still have no idea why."

"I guess I have the kinda face that makes people confess things."

"Maybe." He scanned his eyes over her. "Or maybe there's something about you that messes with my head."

She stilled. Her heart skipped a beat. She saw something in his eyes then, a hunger and a need that she hadn't noticed before. Had he been hiding it this whole time?

"I . . . I mess with your head?"

He sighed gruffly. "I'm gonna be honest with you. This case hasn't . . . it hasn't been easy for me, and not just because the odds are stacked against us or because you've been a pain in the ass sometimes."

"Did you just call me a pain in the ass?"

"Combative, too," he continued. "There are plenty of times I wanted to quit, but I knew I couldn't because you don't deserve to go back to jail. You didn't do this."

"Look, I realize I haven't been easy to work with, but I wasn't always like this! I wish you could've met me before all this happened. I was a lot more kind. A lot less defensive. I was much . . . nicer."

He held up his hand. "You don't have to explain. I get what you're going through. Besides, those things aren't the real reason why it's been so hard for me. You're fine. You're more than fine." The need in his eyes bubbled to the surface again. "There's just something about you. How you're so honest and vulnerable. You're smart and insightful. You're—"

"Cute?" she asked with a smile, leaning forward in her chair again to gaze at him, entranced by his words, wanting to make the need in him flare even stronger. "Don't forget cute."

"That's not funny, Diamond."

"I wasn't joking. A woman likes to hear nice things about herself every now and then, and I haven't heard any in quite a while."

"Even from your husband?" he asked, raising his brows.

"*Especially* from him. It's not the same between us anymore. I can tell. And I miss feeling good, Darius. Getting a compliment. I like it. I like it a lot. When you're done, I can tell you some nice things about you, too, if it makes you feel any better."

"See what I mean." He gestured to her. "This isn't appropriate."

"So what if it isn't? Why does it have to be?"

"Because I'm your lawyer, Diamond."

"I know that. You know that."

"And you're married."

"You and I both know that isn't true. It never was."

"And, like I said, I have to maintain a certain level of

professionalism." He was starting to look uncomfortable again.

But she didn't want him to be professional. She wanted him to hold her, to kiss her. And she wanted it even more now that she suspected he wanted it just as badly as she did. But they both had been fighting their desire this whole time.

He stood from his chair. "Maybe we should cut this short. Reconvene on another day." He walked around his desk like he was heading to the door to flee. But she didn't know where he planned to run away because this was *his* office. "You did a good job," he rambled. "But we can pick this up on Mon—"

He stopped short when she reached up and grabbed his hand. She instantly felt a charge when she did it—the same charge she'd felt at her apartment when she'd touched him. The same one she'd felt in the alleyway next to the Tavern when he wrapped his arms around her. Darius stared down into her eyes as she rose from her chair.

"I don't wanna leave," she said.

He loudly swallowed. "We're about to cross a line again, aren't we?" he asked as she linked her arms around his neck and stood on the balls of her feet.

"Only if you want to," she whispered up to him just as thunder cracked overhead and the sky beyond his office window suddenly went bright. "Do you want to, Darius?"

In reply, he wrapped his arm around her waist and pulled her close. Then he brought his lips to hers.

Diamond didn't know what to expect. Would he be an awkward kisser or a good one? Would he be overeager or would she have to take the lead? Diamond often went through this guessing game with clients back in the old days. The big, strong dude with the most talk and swagger would kiss like a lizard and hump like he was doing push-ups. The short, balding accountant would have the most tender touch and bestow her with butterfly kisses that could leave a girl whimpering and begging for more.

Darius turned out to be hesitant only for the first few seconds, then something broke free in him. She didn't know if it was her hands running up and down his back or her tongue sliding into his mouth, but he let out a groan and tugged her even closer. He tilted her head back so the kiss could deepen, and she damn near purred with delight. As their tongues danced, Diamond felt more alive than she had in months. The pain, sadness, and fear all melted away and she became pure, burning-hot lust that longed to be quenched. She didn't want this to stop at kissing. She wanted him to do a lot more than hold her close.

She stepped out of his embrace and, once again, he gazed down at her in confusion. "Too much?"

Diamond began to undo his necktie and shook her head. She tossed the tie aside. "No, not enough."

"What are you doing?"

"What do you think I'm doing?" she asked with a grin as she unbuttoned his shirt. But then she looked up when he abruptly grabbed her hands. "What? Is something wrong?"

Again, he didn't respond. Instead, he turned to walk across his office to his door, and her heart fell.

I pushed him too far, she thought sadly. She was asking for too much, and now he'd gone skittish. She'd scared him off.

But Darius surprised her when he slowly closed the door, revealing her raincoat hanging on its coat hook, dripping water onto his doormat. Then he locked the door.

"I get walk-ins all the time," he whispered. He walked back to her, pausing to close the blinds as well.

She could no longer see the rain but could hear it hitting the window. This time, Diamond wasn't the only one removing buttons. He slipped her T-shirt over her head and kissed her again, unhooking her bra as he did it. When she slipped the straps off her shoulders he stood back and stared down at her.

"What?" she asked nervously.

She had lost weight. Her body wasn't as voluptuous as it used to be and she didn't feel quite as womanly anymore.

"Damn, you're so sexy." He then reached out and held one of her breasts in his hands, and she shuddered all over. Her skin pricked with goose bumps. He kissed her again, and she fell back against his desk, dragging him along with her. His lips shifted from her mouth to her neck to her breast, making her breathe in sharply. He tugged one of the nipples between his teeth and she moaned.

When he pulled her jeans over her hips and down her thighs, she was almost relieved. Having his hands and mouth on her wasn't enough. She wanted more. A lot more. She pulled eagerly at his belt and then his pants zipper. She let her fingers follow the happy trail from his stomach and past the waistband of his boxers to his groin. When she held him in her hands he grunted. He was as ready as she was. More than ready?

"Condoms?" she whispered.

He nodded wordlessly, opened a desk drawer, and pulled out his wallet.

Everything after that seemed to speed up. He shoved down his boxers and put on the condom. She tried to do the same with her panties, but his mouth was back on hers. His hands returned to her breasts. Before she knew it, she was lying back against the desk with him between her thighs. He shifted her panties aside and slid a finger inside, testing her first. She moaned again. When he centered himself and thrust inside her, she cried out. He plunged over and over again, and she raised her hips to meet him thrust for thrust, spreading her legs to accept him. His mouth returned to hers, swallowing her cries and moans.

After a few minutes Diamond could feel herself drawing close. She gripped his shoulders, digging her nails into his skin. She closed her eyes. When the wave crested over her she bucked her hips. Her back arched and her legs fell akimbo. Her toes curled. She tried to cry out his name, but it came out in unintelligible syllables. He convulsed on top of her seconds later, shouting and groaning as he did it. They both fell back against his desk when it was all over, listening to the sound of their heavy breaths and the pounding rain.

Chapter 22

Vanessa

"Good night, sweetheart," Vanessa cooed to her daughter as she tucked her under her covers. She leaned down and kissed Zoe's pecan-colored cheek.

" 'Night, Mommy," Zoe murmured drowsily, smacking her lips. The little girl turned on her side and closed her eyes.

Vanessa crept across her daughter's pink-colored bedroom while listening to Zoe's soft breaths, stepping over a pile of Barbie dolls and dodging a giant stuffed unicorn as she did it. When she reached the door, she turned off the lights. A rainbow night-light burned bright near Zoe's bed. Vanessa blew a kiss and quietly shut the door behind her.

She then strolled down the hall, cracking open the door to her other children's bedrooms. She found Bryson snoring loudly on his Spider-Man sheets, clutching one of his action figures. She found Cy Jr. reclining in an armchair, wearing a headset and playing one of his video games.

"Behind you! Look behind you!" Cy Jr. shouted while

tapping the keys furiously on his controller. "Damn, I need more ammo!"

"Junior! Junior!" she called to him, making him yank off his headset. "Game off and lights off in an hour. You hear me?"

Her son absently nodded before returning his attention to the game on-screen.

"Sorry, it was my mom. Where are you?" he said to whoever he was playing with remotely.

Vanessa shut his bedroom door and continued down the hallway to their guest room. She yawned and stretched, ready to retire for the evening and relax.

"Nessa!" she heard Cyrus shout as she passed their bedroom doorway, stopping her in her tracks, making her flinch. "Nessa, you out there?"

She still hadn't recovered from her and Bilal's failed attempt to murder her husband four days ago. It was demoralizing to keep making plans, only to watch them crumble because something unexpected happened. The man seemed to be protected by some divine light.

"Or Satan himself," she mumbled.

"Nessa, did you hear me?" he called again.

Vanessa grumbled and strode to their bedroom. She shoved open the door and found her husband sitting in his usual spot on their bed with his laptop open, typing away.

"What?" she asked through gritted teeth.

"I was done with dinner more than two hours ago." He gestured to the pile of dirty plates, glass, and utensils beside him. "You never came to get my tray."

So he was still pretending to be an invalid? He was still making her cater to his lazy ass like some slave?

She began to walk around the bed to retrieve his tray, trying her best to keep her anger at a low simmer.

He snapped his fingers and pointed over his shoulder. "I need you to fix my backrest first."

Vanessa halted and glowered at her husband. She stomped toward him and yanked at the suede backrest, lifting it higher.

He nodded. "That's better. Thanks."

Her jaw clenched as she walked around the bed again and retrieved the tray of dishes. She started to walk back toward the bedroom door. The dishes rang and clanged in her arms like bells because her hands shook so much. Her eyes kept drifting to the steak knife smeared in Worcestershire sauce that sat on his plate. It was like the knife was calling her name. All she had to do was pick it up.

Pick it up and stab him.

"And next time," he called to her, making her stop again, "don't cook the meat for so long, will you? You know I like my steaks rare to medium rare. I want a little blood on the plate. This one was dry as hell, almost rubbery."

At those words, she almost hurled the tray to the floor. She almost grabbed the steak knife, turned around, charged at the bed, and plunged it into his chest over and over again.

"Is this enough blood for you?" she'd scream. "Huh, Cy? Is this bloody enough?"

But Vanessa closed her eyes and took several deep breaths instead. She forced herself to put one foot in front of the other and carried the tray out of the room.

By the time she'd entered the guest room five minutes later, she was almost blubbering. She slammed the door closed, collapsed onto the small bench at her makeup table, grabbed her cell, and dialed Bilal's number. He answered on the second ring.

"Hey, bae," he said over pounding bass music. "What's up?"

"I can't do this," she sobbed. "I can't do this anymore!"

"Do what? What are you talking about?" he asked, turning down the music that was playing in the background.

"What the hell do you think I'm talking about?" she whispered shrilly. "I'm talking about *him* . . . Cyrus! I can't take living with him anymore and catering to him. It's like chewing fucking glass! I hate him. I want him gone, Bilal!"

"But we already tried that, bae."

"So we'll try it again! We have to!"

"Well, when do you want to do it? When can we get him out of the house? Maybe we can—"

"No! No, every time we try to do it away from the house, something goes wrong!" She recoiled at what she was about to say. "It might . . . it might be better just to do it here."

"But I thought you didn't want to do it at your home. You said it could get messy and you didn't want your kids hearing or seeing—"

"I know what I said! You don't have to repeat it back to me. I didn't want to do it here for those reasons, but . . . but I don't see what other choice we have at this point." She glanced at her closed door. "Maybe we can do it in a way where the kids won't know. Do it while they're all asleep. They won't find out until it's over . . . when they wake up. I'll . . . I'll keep them out of the room."

Bilal went silent on the other end for a long time. Finally, he cleared his throat. "Okay, what do you need me to do?"

Two nights later, a little after three A.M., Vanessa crept down the hall back to her bedroom after making sure that everyone in the household was sound asleep, though she already knew they would be. At dinner, she'd spiked each of her children's glasses of juice with a sizable dose of grape Benadryl to assure they would doze throughout the night. She'd given Cyrus a hefty sample of crushed sleeping pills in his meal. When she'd peeked inside his bedroom to check on him only seconds earlier, he'd been snoring so loudly that she could've sworn the painting hanging over their headboard was rattling from the sound waves. In his condition, he wouldn't be able to put up much of a fight, if any, when Bilal entered their bedroom.

If all went as planned, Bilal would "break in" through the French doors leading to their deck. He'd climb the stairs while everyone else slept, tiptoe down the hall, place a pillow over Cy's head, fire off a couple of bullets at close range, and be in and out of the house in less than five minutes. She'd "wake up" a few hours later, just after dawn, and walk down the hall to rouse her husband, only to discover his cold, limp, bloody body. Tearful and grieving, Vanessa would lock the bedroom door and bar her children from going inside to see their dead father. She'd then call the police and tell them about the discovery.

Vanessa now stepped into the guest room, softly shutting her door behind her. She rushed to her night table to send one last text to Bilal.

"Is soccer practice tomorrow?" she typed.

It was their code that the coast was clear and they could proceed with their plan. After she typed the message she set down her phone. Vanessa climbed into bed. She stared at the glowing numbers on her alarm clock. It was 3:08 A.M.

Five minutes, she told herself. Five minutes and it all would be over. She'd finally be free. By 3:13 A.M. her whole life would change.

She watched as the minutes ticked by, imagining the

route Bilal was taking to her old bedroom. Time seemed to progress at almost a snail's pace. She tried to listen to what was happening but heard nothing.

Good, she thought. Then no one else in her family could hear anything, either.

Finally 3:13 A.M. arrived. She bit her lower lip. Had Bilal done it? Was Cy dead?

She heard a loud pop, making her raise her head from her pillow. Was that a gunshot?

She didn't know it would sound so loud. Something like that could easily have woken up one of the children.

She heard a second pop, even louder than the first. She heard a third and a fourth. She sat up in her bed and threw back the sheets. What the hell was Bilal doing in there? She'd told him to be stealthy and to keep quiet. She didn't want it to sound like a mob hit that even the neighbors could hear.

More gunfire, making her clap her hands over her ears. Then she heard someone yell, "Stop! Shit, stop! Please, don't kill me!"

The voice sounded an awful lot like Bilal's.

"Oh, damn," she whispered, feeling her blood go cold. She then hopped off the bed and rushed to the guest-room door.

Chapter 23

Cyrus

Cy heard his door creak open for the second time that night. The first visitor had been his wife Vanessa, no doubt checking to see if he was fast asleep.

The conniving bitch, he now thought.

Now her dumbass lover was creeping into his bedroom on a mission to kill him under her orders.

Cyrus had gotten wind of their plan about a day ago, when he'd listened to the recording from the guest room thanks to the device hidden under her makeup table. He knew tonight was the night she was supposed to drug everyone's dinner to keep him and all their children slumbering while her boy toy put a bullet in his head. But Cyrus was ready for her *and* him.

He'd dumped his drink down the sink and flushed his food down the toilet. He also had his Magnum under his pillow, loaded and ready. His hand was wrapped around the grip. His finger rested on the trigger.

He kept his eyes closed, but he could feel a looming presence drawing closer and closer to the bed.

That's close enough, motherfucka, he thought.

His eyes flew open and he found the young man standing about three feet in front of him. Cyrus couldn't see well in the dark, but he could see the whites of the young man's eyes as they widened to the size of saucers when he saw Cyrus was awake. He could see him take a step back.

"Fuck," Vanessa's lover whispered. It came out in a desperate squeak. He raised his handgun to fire, but he wasn't fast enough. Cyrus pulled out his Magnum, firing first. He just missed the young man's shoulder. Her lover fired back, but he did it facing the other direction and running at the same time. The shots went cockeyed. One bullet landed in the leather padded headboard. The other went in the ceiling. A third lodged in one of the bed's newel posts. Cyrus fired again and again. The young man grabbed for the door, but Cyrus caught him in the leg, making him shout out and crumple to the floor.

Cy stood over him, ready to fire another shot—this time, into his chest.

"Stop! Shit, stop!" her lover wailed, dropping his gun to the floor. He held up one hand in surrender while the other clutched his bloody shin. "Please don't kill me!"

Cyrus lowered his gun in disgust.

"Cy! Cyrus, what's happening? Are you all right?" Vanessa yelled, opening the door to their bedroom.

Cyrus reached down and grabbed her lover's weapon. He glared at his wife just as she flicked a switch, turning on the overhead lights.

"So this was the man you sent to take me out?" he shouted, pointing down at her lover, who was now groaning and weeping openly on the bedroom floor. "This sniveling piece of shit? Huh?"

Vanessa glanced at Bilal, then stared at Cyrus. She opened her mouth and closed it. "I-I don't know what—"

"Shut up!" Cyrus barked, making them both cower. "Not one more fuckin' word, you lyin' bitch!"

"Mommy!" Bryson yelled. "Mommy!"

"What's happening?" Zoe wailed down the hall.

"Go take care of the kids." Cyrus pointed his gun to the open doorway and tucked the other in the back of his pajama pants. "I'll handle this."

"What . . . what are you gonna do to him?" she asked, looking horrified.

"Don't worry about that. Take care of the kids and call the police."

She didn't budge at first. Instead, her gaze went back to her lover, who was still moaning and crying and making a big, bloody mess on their hardwood floor and Afghan rug.

"Don't leave! Don't leave me, bae!" her lover begged, reaching out for her. "He's gonna kill me!"

"I said *go*, Nessa." Cyrus pointed his gun at her, putting his finger back on the trigger.

She blinked and slowly backed out of the bedroom into the hall. "C-c-coming, babies!" she stuttered to their children as tears streamed down her cheeks. "Everything's fine. Mama's coming!"

She shut the door behind her.

Cyrus gazed down at the young man who had rolled onto his back and closed his eyes, as if accepting his fate.

"You see that. She turned on you, didn't she? She deserted you." Cy pressed his foot into his chest, making him cry out. Cyrus grinned. "But don't worry. I ain't gonna kill you."

The young man's eyes slowly opened. "You're . . . you're not?"

"No, I'm not. You can't help being dumb. You let my wife talk you into doing a very stupid thing tonight," Cyrus continued, pointing his gun down at him again. "You know that, right?"

The young man sniffed and gradually nodded.

"And you learned a hard lesson. Number one, don't carry a gun unless you know how to shoot it. Number two, if you're gonna ambush somebody, make damn sure they don't see you comin'. And number three . . . most important . . . don't ever steal from me."

The young man frowned. He slowly shook his head.

"No, don't shake your head! Because that's exactly what you tried to do. You tried to steal my life and my wife, and I won't stand for it. She ain't goin' nowhere." Cyrus pressed his weight onto her lover's chest. The younger man cried out again in pain. "You hear me? When you're in prison suckin' dick in the group showers, she'll still be here with me, and then it'll really settle in the big mistake you made tonight." He then took his foot off his chest. "How you just ruined your life."

The police and ambulance arrived less than fifteen minutes later. Their entire block now lit up with flashing lights. Their neighbors stood on their front lawns in their robes and slippers to watch the show as they carted away Vanessa's lover on a stretcher and rolled him through the ambulance's double doors.

"Can you tell me what happened here?" one of the state troopers asked Cyrus.

They were all in the kitchen. A few officers were examining their bedroom upstairs. Vanessa had sent their children to their rooms while she and Cyrus were being questioned.

"It's pretty simple, Officer. The man you all arrested broke into our house and tried to shoot me, but I woke up when he came into my room. I shot him first," Cyrus explained, sitting down in one of the kitchen chairs.

Vanessa stood awkwardly behind him. She radiated nervous energy. He knew his wife was probably wondering if he would tell the truth about how she was involved in this. She was terrified that he would turn her over to the cops. He secretly enjoyed watching her squirm.

"We understand that you knew the assailant." The trooper paused to flip a page in his notepad. "A Bilal Cullen. Yes, that's his name. You knew him. Is that correct?"

Cyrus nodded. "He's my oldest son's soccer coach."

"*His soccer coach*?" The trooper's eyebrows rose by a few inches. "Had you had any previous altercations with Mr. Cullen?"

Cyrus glanced over his shoulder at Vanessa. She stopped fiddling with her robe. Her face went pale. The trooper followed Cyrus's gaze, now focusing on her.

"He's been stalking my wife," Cyrus finally answered.

"Is that true, Mrs. Grey?" the trooper asked.

She loudly swallowed. "Y-y-yes. Yes, it's true. He's been stalking me. He thinks . . . he thinks h-h-he's in love with me."

"He calls the house," Cyrus elaborated. "He calls asking for her all the time. You can even ask our son, Cy Jr. I told that man to stay away from my wife, but he wouldn't listen, Officer. I guess he thought if he could get rid of me, he could have her all to himself." Cyrus exhaled. "The man is crazy! I don't know what else to tell you."

"Is there a reason you haven't filed a report about this?" the trooper asked. "Why didn't Mrs. Grey file for an order of protection against Mr. Cullen if he's been stalking her?"

She opened her mouth to answer, but nothing came out. Cyrus cleared his throat.

"My family has been through a lot these past few months. We're already in the newspapers constantly. His behavior was scary, but we didn't want to bring attention to ourselves yet again by going to the police about this."

He glanced out the kitchen window at the police cruisers outside his house and the ambulance parked along the curb. "But I guess we can't avoid it now."

The trooper flipped his notepad closed. "I'm sorry this happened to your family, Mr. Grey. But none of them were hurt. At least they're all safe thanks to your quick thinking."

Cyrus nodded. "You're right. You're absolutely right. And thank you for all you help, Officer."

An hour later, the cops left. Cyrus and Vanessa stood in their foyer, watching through the glass window as the cruisers drove off and their nosy neighbors trudged up their yards and driveways to return to their homes.

"I protected you tonight," he whispered from over her shoulder. "I won't do it again."

"I'm . . . I'm sorry, Cy." She kept her eyes focused out the window as she spoke. "I didn't know Bilal would do something like—"

"Don't insult me by lying to me. You set this shit up from the beginning. You've been planning and plotting against me this whole time, Nessa. The only thing that kept me from telling the cops what you did and letting you rot in prison with your side nigga was one thing and one thing only. And it isn't even that you're the mother of my children and my wife. Shit, I could find another one. I'd let her raise our kids. Raise them right." He placed his hands on her shoulder and squeezed. Despite his gentle touch, she winced. "No, the truth is I enjoy seeing you miserable. Your misery brings me joy. But that will only protect you but so long, baby. Think about leaving me . . . turn on me again and I won't turn you over to the cops. I'll kill you, Nessa. I almost did it before. You didn't know that, did you? And I won't hesitate to try it again. I really will kill you the next time around. Understood?"

She didn't immediately respond, so he tightened his grip on her shoulders until it was almost painful. "*Understood?*" he repeated.

"Understood," she whispered with eyes downcast, and he finally released her. She turned away from the window. "I have to check on the kids. Make sure they're okay."

He watched as she fled across the foyer, climbed up the stairs, and disappeared down the hall.

Chapter 24

Noelle

Noelle tiredly rubbed her neck as she drove.

It had been a long, emotionally exhausting day. She'd had to let go of two of her part-time employees at Azure—one a perky, hard-working college student named Janise, who was using the money she earned at Azure to pay for her schoolbooks, and the other Inez, a single mother of three who badly needed the extra income she got as a sales clerk to take care of her family. Noelle said goodbye to them and gave them their last paychecks, trying to hold back tears and remain stoic, but with all the pregnancy hormones and fatigue she hadn't succeeded. She'd blubbered like a baby.

Noelle hadn't wanted to fire them, but the bills were stacking up with no more money from Cyrus. She was only a month or so away from no longer being able to cover overhead. She'd had no choice.

That's not true, she thought as she turned the wheel. She could spot her neighborhood in the distance.

Tariq had offered her the money to cover all her expenses and bills so she wouldn't have to fire anyone, but she hadn't accepted his offer. She couldn't, especially now that she trusted him even less than she trusted her husband, and she didn't think she would ever say that. The truth was Tariq absolutely terrified her.

She hadn't seen him in almost two weeks, not since the day she'd met Diamond for lunch and found the cache of guns in Tariq's closet. He'd called her quite a few times since then, asking to meet up, but she'd always beg off and come up with an excuse.

"Not tonight. I'm just too tired, honey," she'd lied to him only two days ago when he asked if he could come over.

"*Still?*" He'd sounded worried, or maybe suspicious. She couldn't tell. "Is something up? Do you need to see a doctor?"

"No! No! They say a lot of women experience fatigue the first few months. It's perfectly normal. I'm gonna stay in tonight and go to bed early. I'll talk to you when I feel better tomorrow."

But she hadn't called him back and didn't intend to. She didn't know what to say or how to act around Tariq. What could she say? He was a liar and likely, a killer. He'd manipulated her into falling in love with him. She'd even been foolish enough to get pregnant by him. But she wasn't a fool anymore. She couldn't afford to put her life and the life of her baby at risk being around a man like Tariq. But Noelle knew she couldn't avoid him forever; she'd have to face him at some point.

She rounded the corner and saw a black Porsche roadster parked in her driveway. It was Tariq's.

Noelle cursed under her breath. Her grip tightened around her steering wheel. Her throat went dry. What the hell was he doing here?

Should've called the cops on him when I had the chance, she now thought. But every time she'd picked up the phone to do just that, she'd hung up. He terrified her, but she also couldn't work up the nerve to turn him in, to tell the cops what she suspected about him. She just wanted to wash her hands of him. Of Cyrus. She wanted both of them out of her life, but neither would go away.

Noelle slowed to a stop and watched as Tariq climbed out of his Porsche. He leaned down to gaze at her through the driver's side window. "There she is! There goes my baby! Where've you been, girl?" he chided playfully.

Noelle didn't answer him, making him cock an eyebrow at her.

"You gonna get out of the car?" he asked.

She slowly nodded. With shaky hands she turned off the car's engine and opened her door. She stepped out.

"Are you okay? Still aren't feelin' well?" he asked, reaching for her.

She stepped out of his grasp and closed her door behind her. "I'm . . . I'm fine. What . . . umm . . . what are you doing here, though? I didn't know you were coming over."

Her pulse was racing. Her palms were starting to sweat. Was he carrying one of his guns? Could she get away from him if she had to?

"One of my meetings ended early," he replied, still eyeing her. "I hadn't seen you in a while so I thought I'd surprise you and stop by."

More like ambush me, she thought, unable to meet his gaze. She scurried to her front door, ready to flee inside her home and away from him.

"Well, I'm sorry you came all this way, honey," she began, "but I've had a hard day and I really wanna—"

"Relax?" he finished for her. "I figured. That's why I came armed and ready."

He reached inside his lowered car window and her breath caught in her throat. Noelle froze, horrified at what he was about to pull out. She watched as he removed a grocery bag sitting on the passenger seat. When she saw the produce and bottle of wine sticking out of the canvas bag, she started to breathe again.

"I bought enough food on the way over to make you a home-cooked meal because we both know cookin' isn't exactly your forte. After that, I'll massage your feet," he paused to take a step toward her and let his eyes rake over her hungrily, "and just about anything else you'd like me to massage until you fall asleep."

She wanted to tell him no, but she didn't know what excuses she could make to get out of it at this point without being obvious, so she nodded.

"Sure. Why not?" she said weakly before unlocking her front door. They both stepped inside and she tried not to wince when the door closed behind him.

As Tariq cooked pasta and shrimp and they ate dinner, she tried her best to keep up a façade that everything was fine and she wasn't frightened of him. She shared in their usual playful banter. She even kissed his cheek and forced a smile or two, but playing the part was draining. Noelle didn't know how Tariq and Cyrus did this all the time. It was starting to wear her down.

Just one more hour, she told herself. *Let him stay another hour, then tell him that you're tired and ask him to leave.*

But she could feel herself slowly becoming unraveled under the pressure. She needed some relief.

"I'll be right back," she whispered suddenly, rising from the dinner table. She didn't wait for his response.

Noelle walked up the stairs and rushed to her bedroom, closing the door behind her.

Now her hands weren't the only things shaking; her entire body was. She grabbed a bottle of Zoloft sitting on her night table, removed the lid, and shook a pill into her hand. She tossed it into her mouth and swallowed before falling back onto her bed. Noelle closed her eyes. She took several deep breaths.

"What's going on?" she heard Tariq suddenly ask.

Her eyes shot open. She looked up and found him standing in her doorway, leaning against the frame.

She opened her mouth and closed it. She fidgeted on the bed. "Uh . . . uh . . . I'm just ti—"

"And don't say you're tired. That's not it. Something is up with you. You've been acting like this for weeks. What aren't you telling me?"

She shook her head, feeling her panic rise again. "I don't know what you're talking about."

"Yes, you do." He strolled into the bedroom, gazing at her like he was studying her. "I told you. I know you well. Every expression. Every gesture. And I know when something isn't right." He tilted his head. "You act like you don't want to be around me. Like you're scared for some reason." He reached out to touch her face, making her pull away despite herself. He nodded knowingly, now having evidence to support his theory. "I just want to know why you're scared."

"I'm not . . . I'm not scared of you, Tariq," she lied. "That's crazy!"

Her eyes drifted to her night table drawer. One of Cyrus's pistols was inside. She wondered if she could reach it.

"Yes, you are," Tariq insisted, now looming over her. "Did something happen? Is it something Cyrus said? Because you know he lies, don't you, baby?"

"He didn't say anything!" She eased closer to the night table.

"I don't believe you." He took another step toward her. "You know he wants to tear us apart," he urged, reaching for her again. "If you'd just tell me what he told you, I could—"

He didn't get to finish. She tugged open the drawer and whipped out the Smith & Wesson Shield 9mm she'd tucked underneath her bras and thongs. When she did, Tariq looked at her in surprise.

"Step back! Step the hell back!" she yelled.

He did as she ordered and she rose to her feet. The bastard had the nerve to burst into laughter. He was smiling even as he raised his hands into the air.

Tariq was insane. Full-on, batshit crazy. She was sure of it now.

"I knew something was up with you," he said with a chuckle. "I'm rarely wrong."

"Shut up!"

"Noelle, baby, all this," he said, gesturing to the gun, "ain't necessary."

"Don't call me 'baby'!" she shouted back, still pointing the gun at him. "And don't you dare tell me what's necessary. I don't even know who the fuck you are!"

"Yes, you do. I'm the man who loves you . . . who would do anything for you. I—"

"No, I don't know who you are—T. J.!" When she shouted his name his smile evaporated. "I didn't even know you went by that name. You didn't even tell me you had a brother!"

"How . . . how the hell did you find that out?"

"From Diamond. She told me your brother Darius is her lawyer, that you hired him for her."

For the first time that night, Tariq didn't look amused; he looked annoyed. "I should've known he couldn't keep a secret to save his damn life. Couldn't since he was little. He's been a snitch since he was in diapers. When I see him I'mma beat his ass."

"But there was no reason to keep all that a secret if you weren't trying to do something underhanded. You told him to get Diamond off her attempted murder charge because you knew she didn't do it. *You* did, didn't you? *You're* the man who tried to kill my husband. You were the reason why Cyrus was shot!"

He didn't respond.

"Cy getting shot had nothing to do with him stealing from his clients like you said. You set him up, Tariq! You worked with Big El . . . or . . . or paid him to do it. The job you wanted done that he messed up, right? You hired him to kill Cy!"

He narrowed his eyes. "You want to shout that shit a little louder? Maybe the neighbors didn't hear you."

"Just answer the question! Tell me the truth!"

He rolled his eyes. "So what if I did? Some niggas deserve to die. Cyrus Grey is one of them."

Her eyes flooded with tears. So it *was* true.

"Look, I'm sorry you had to find out this way." Tariq took a step toward her. "But baby, if I hadn't done it, things would've been a lot worse. Trust. You don't—"

"I said stop calling me 'baby'! And if you come near me again, I swear to God, I will shoot you!" She took one step back from him, then another. But Tariq kept pressing forward anyway, like he hadn't heard her—or he wasn't scared of a bullet.

"You're upset. I get it. But you've got no reason to be. I may have tried to kill your husband, but I would never hurt you," he assured her, holding up his hands again, as if to show her that he meant no harm. But his body language told a different story. He still kept coming forward. He still kept invading her space, pressing down on her.

He reached for her again and she lurched back, hitting the wall. She'd run out of space. Somehow he'd managed to back her into a corner. In her terror, she hadn't noticed, but he obviously had.

"Noelle, I'm *not* gonna hurt you. Put down the gun."

He sounded so calm, like she was the one who was crazy, but she knew she wasn't. *He* was.

Tariq was a murderous liar and probably a sociopath. Noelle looked frantically around her. There was no way to get out of the bedroom's corner, boxed between a wall and her night table, unless she fought him, shot him, or both—then ran for it. There was no other means of escape. If she didn't do it, he was going to hurt her, maybe kill her. Why wouldn't he? She knew too much about him now. He had to get rid of her.

Her breath came out in sharp bursts. Her heart was beating so fast, she thought it might pound its way out of her rib cage. The gun wasn't steady in her sweaty hands, but she still kept her finger on the trigger.

"I told you not to come near me! For the last time—step back! I *will* shoot you!"

He shook his head again. "No, you won't." He took another step forward. "Because even though you don't trust me anymore, I still trust you . . . and I know you're not gonna do it."

"Tariq, I'm warning you! I mean it! Step the hell *back*! Please!" she begged even as he took another step toward her so that the muzzle of the pistol was almost flat against his chest, perfectly aligned with one of his dress shirt buttons. He didn't shift his gaze from hers. He didn't flinch.

Her vision was blurred with tears now. She urged her finger to pull the trigger, to fire the bullet. It was either him or her. But her finger wouldn't follow her command. She couldn't make it budge.

Tariq was right—she couldn't shoot him. The realization left her both astounded and aghast.

With lightning-quick speed, Tariq grabbed her wrist and wrenched the pistol out of her hands, making her cry out in pain. She didn't have the chance to respond, to even try to wrestle it back. Now in his grasp, she braced herself for him turning the gun on her and firing.

Once again love had made a fool of her, but this time it would get her killed, too. Noelle just hoped it would be quick, that she wouldn't have to suffer too much. Maybe he'd fire a bullet into her temple and it would all be over in a flash.

She closed her eyes when she heard the click.

Chapter 25

Noelle

Noelle waited for the gunfire, for the sensation of the bullet piercing her body, but she heard and felt neither. She opened her eyes again to find Tariq ejecting the pistol's magazine. He dropped it into his pants pocket and tucked the gun into the back of his pants.

The whole maneuver—from disarming her to taking the pistol apart—had taken him less than a minute.

"Are you okay?" he asked, gazing down at her, looking genuinely worried.

"No, I'm not okay!" she cried. "I'm not okay! I thought you were gonna shoot me! Y-you . . . you could've killed me!"

"No, I couldn't. I told you, I would never hurt you."

"And you wouldn't stop walking toward me! Are you crazy? Are you out of your fuckin' mind? I told you to stay back! Why did you keep coming? I could've shot you!"

"Not really. I could see the safety was still on, but I'm happy you didn't pull the trigger. I knew I could trust you, baby."

"The . . . *The safety was on?*"

He nodded.

So he was never in any danger, but she could've been in danger this entire time.

Noelle opened her mouth and closed it. She was shaking all over like the room was chilly. This time when he reached for her, she didn't step back or shove him away. She fell into his arms and cried on his shoulder.

"You don't have to be afraid of me. I love you," he whispered into her ear, rubbing her back.

"No, you don't!" She raised her head to gaze up at him. "You can't. Because if you did, you wouldn't lie to me over and over and over again. You wouldn't treat me like Cy did, like I'm some idiot you can con!"

Tariq winced.

"Just tell me the truth! Tell me the goddamn truth! If you love me like you claim you love me, I deserve that from you. No more lies!"

He squeezed her shoulders. "I don't think you're an idiot and I never wanted to con you. It's just . . . it's just how it worked out."

When she opened her mouth to argue, he spoke over her. "Because sometimes . . . sometimes the truth is too much. Sometimes it makes things worse, not better. I told you the truth about what happened to Cy—and I saw how you looked at me. You think you want to know everything about me, but you don't. Not really. You will never see me the same way again."

"I already don't. The rose-colored glasses are gone! I know that you're a liar and you almost committed a murder. What else could you tell me at this point that would shock me? It can't be any worse than what I've heard."

He staunchly shook his head.

"Trust me like I've trusted you from the very beginning!" she shouted. "Tell me the truth! If you can't do that, then stay the fuck away from me! You hear me? If you can't do that, I want nothing to do with you! I want you out of my life, Tariq."

He stopped shaking his head and loosened his hold on her shoulders. The bedroom fell silent for a long stretch after that. She watched his Adam's apple bob as he swallowed.

"Fuck. I'm gonna regret this shit. I know it," he mumbled before sucking his teeth. He looked down at the floor. "What do you want to know?"

"Is it true that you killed people?" she asked, deciding to ask the worst question first. "Is that what you did before . . . for your crew? Did you do it for Cyrus, too?"

He seemed to hesitate, then gradually nodded, making her light-headed. So that part was true as well. Her heart started racing again. Noelle tamped down her hysteria to ask her next question.

"If you used to kill for Cy, why did you turn on him? Why would you want to kill him? What did he do to you?"

"Nothin' more than the shady, self-involved shit he usually does." He tilted his head. "I had to kill him, though. It was either him—or you."

"What?"

"You heard me. I said it was either him or you . . . well," he shrugged, "you and Vanessa. If I didn't take him out, he was going to take you two out. That's what he asked me to do."

Noelle's stomach dropped. "What are you saying?"

"I'm saying that husband of yours wanted you dead. He wanted me to kill you and Vanessa so he could cash out your insurance money. Running three households and keeping three beautiful women happy ain't cheap. Cy quickly figured that shit out. He was up to his ears in debt.

He asked me for money and I told him I didn't have that kind of cash on hand. He had been skimming money from some of our clients. I knew that. But it still wasn't enough. He needed *more* . . . a lot more. He needed a way out, and from what I understand, he'd taken out insurance policies on both of you. It would have given him about three and half mil . . . maybe four, just enough to pay off all the money he owed."

Noelle stared at Tariq, dumbfounded. Was all this true? She vaguely remembered Cyrus giving her some insurance paperwork a few months before the shooting, but he was always having her sign papers, claiming they would help their investment portfolio or financial outlook. She hadn't given the insurance papers a second thought. Was his plan really to have Tariq kill her and cash in the policy? Or was Tariq weaving an elaborate tale again? He'd done it before, telling her about clients who were angry that Cy had been stealing from them so they'd hired a hit man to kill Cyrus. Meanwhile, the person really doing all the plotting had been Tariq.

"But why me and Vanessa, though? Why not—"

"Because y'all had become a pain in the ass. Thanks to some investigator, Cy knew Vanessa had been cheating on him for a while. He knew that ho wasn't loyal! And he told me things were getting bad between you guys. I didn't know shit about his vasectomy, but I knew he wondered if you were gonna leave him if the baby stuff didn't work out. I guess he knew it wouldn't. He said he felt like either one of you might file for divorce soon, and he couldn't let that happen."

"Why not?"

"Cy thought a divorce would reveal the truth about him. A lawyer might dig up that he had other wives. He could get charged. It would fuck things up for him, and he wasn't willing to take that chance, so he—"

"So rather than go to jail, he told you to kill me? To kill *us*?" she finished for him.

Tariq nodded. "I tried to talk him out of it. I told him he was being paranoid . . . that there had to be some other way, but he wouldn't listen to me. He just wouldn't let that shit go."

"Wouldn't it be conspicuous if both of us were killed? It seems like it would've brought more attention to him to have different women he had policies on die within weeks of each other."

"I told him that, too. He said he had different policies with different companies and he was hoping that two murders in different states wouldn't raise too many red flags. Finally I told him I couldn't do it myself. I said you knew me too well . . . you would see it coming. I said I had to hire someone else. He told me he didn't care. Just to get it done by the end of the month."

Listening to Tariq recount how her husband supposedly discussed and plotted her murder was surreal.

"'Get it done by the end of the month,'" she whispered.

She could be dead right now.

"That was my deadline, too, after he told me that. That was the deadline I gave myself to get rid of his ass. I knew the history he and I had, but I couldn't let him kill you. I had to do it to protect you."

It was a good story, but she still wondered if it was the real one.

He eyed her. "You don't believe me, do you?"

Was she *that* easy to read?

"It's not that I don't believe you," she began. "It's just that—"

"I lied to you in the past, so now everything I say, you're giving me the side-eye," he finished for her. "I get it. But I ain't lying this time and I'll prove it to you!"

She watched as he reached into his back pocket and grabbed his phone. He sat down on her bed and began tapping buttons on the screen. She took the spot beside him, curious as to what he was doing.

"Cy's usually a smart nigga. I'll give him that. But when he gets desperate, he gets sloppy. He started leaving these dumbass messages on my phone. I kept them as insurance if this shit ever went left. I'm glad I did. He left this one back in April," he said before pressing the screen.

"*Tariq!*" she heard her husband's voice erupt from Tariq's cell phone speaker. She watched as Tariq turned up the volume. "*Where the hell you been? You haven't come in the office all damn morning. I told you we needed to talk. Did you find somebody or not? We gotta do this and we gotta do this soon. I don't care how it happens . . . car accident . . . hit and run . . . whatever! Make it look like a break-in and a robbery or rape . . . I don't give a fuck!*"

Noelle's eyes went wide and her mouth fell open in horror.

"*Just get it done,*" her husband continued. "*Call me back and give me an update. All right?*"

Cyrus hung up. She stared down at the phone screen.

"*Rape me?* He wanted you to pay someone to rape and murder me?"

This whole time Cyrus had been painting Tariq as the monster, when it sounded like he was worse.

Tariq groused. "He might have just meant Vanessa. Shit, I don't know!"

"Does it make a difference?" she cried.

"No, it doesn't," he conceded. "I know it sounds bad either way. I told you he was desperate. He didn't give a fuck anymore."

"So why not warn me?" she cried. "Why not tell me he

was talking like this? That he was saying these deranged things?"

"So you could do what? *Tell the cops?* Cops only make shit worse! You saw what they did to Diamond . . . how they fucked up that whole investigation. Besides, we handle our own shit. We have since the beginning. Cy knows I would never go running to the cops unless there's no other alternative. He won't either. We could *both* end up in jail for all the shit we've done. And I should've handled it myself this time around and not handed the job off to Big El. All he did was fuck it up! We wouldn't be in the situation we're in now if I had shot that motherfucka myself! And I would've made sure he was dead."

This was the side of Tariq that he'd kept hidden from her. She didn't know what to make of it. But she'd heard what Cyrus had asked him to do, the savagery her husband had been willing to permit to get what he wanted. Tariq, however his methods, had kept him from doing it to her and Vanessa. He'd saved them.

"You said you wanted to know the truth. So there it is. This is what happened. This is who I am. I'm laying it all out for you. No more lies, like you said."

She nodded. "Thank you for not lying to me for once. Thanks for finally telling me the truth—even if it scares the hell out of me," she said with a shudder.

He gazed at her, now looking apprehensive. "So what now? You're gonna go running out of here screamin'? You're gonna call the cops?"

She slowly shook her head. "You know I wouldn't do that to you," she whispered.

"But it's over between us, right? Cy said you would never stay with a man you couldn't trust . . . that you couldn't respect. I know I've done things that . . . well . . .

that most people wouldn't give a pass." A pained expression crossed his face. "I know you want an upstanding-citizen type of dude, one who pays his taxes, gives to charities, and definitely hasn't killed anybody, but that ain't me, Noelle. It never will be."

She didn't respond. She didn't know what to say.

"And I guess I could tell you that I feel bad for what I've done and I wish I could take it all back, but you told me to stop lying to you. The honest truth is, only about half the shit I've done I regret. But most of the niggas I popped, if I didn't kill them, someone else would've." He smirked. "And I was good at what I did. Like numbers, I've got a talent for taking niggas out."

She cringed.

"Too much?"

"*Yes!*"

"Fine, I won't talk about killing people anymore. And the truth is, I hadn't done it in years. I came out of retirement to handle Cy."

"So . . . so those days are behind you?"

"I want it to be. I'm willing to go cold turkey if you'll still have me. But now that you know everything, where do we go from here?"

She should end it with him. She knew any sane woman would. He had lied to her repeatedly, even though he claimed he'd done it to protect her. He was dangerous, and the way he talked about killing people sounded more than just a little nuts. But he loved her. He'd proven it time and time again. He was proving it now, too, by entrusting her with enough incriminating knowledge about him that she could send him to prison for a very long time.

For that reason alone she raised her hand to his cheek. "I told you that if you trusted me with your secrets, I'd trust you. You love me . . . and I love you, too. That . . . that hasn't changed, Tariq."

He reached up and took her hand in his own, kissing the inside of her palm. He leaned forward to kiss her lips, but she shifted back, just out of his reach.

Noelle wanted nothing more than to let him kiss her and hold her, to take away all her fear and unease, but she knew she couldn't.

"Things can't continue like they were," she continued. "I accept you for the man you really are, but it's gonna take some time getting used to . . . well . . . all of this. It's a lot to take in. I'm gonna . . . I'm gonna need a little time."

His face fell. He looked disappointed. "I get it," he said, sounding resigned. "I figured something like this would happen eventually. This was one of the best-case scenarios."

"But it doesn't mean we're done. This isn't over," she rushed out, gazing into his eyes. "Not for me anyway."

"Not for me, either," he replied.

"It's more like a . . . a pause. I'm just saying I need some time to orient myself. Okay? Can you give me that?"

He loudly exhaled. "I guess I have no choice but to."

She walked him to her front door a few minutes later. They stood in the doorway, listening to the crickets and the passing cars.

"During this pause . . . while you're orienting yourself and whatnot," Tariq said, "if you ever need me . . . I mean if you ever need *anything*, you—"

"I'll call. Don't worry."

He stepped forward and embraced her. Noelle closed her eyes and held on tight. She didn't want to let go. Standing here, it reminded her of the first night they'd held each other like this, when it felt like her world was crumbling around her and Tariq said he could be her rock, that he would take care of her. Shockingly, despite everything, he'd kept that promise.

"I love you," she whispered, fighting back the tears.

"I love you, too," he whispered back. "I always will."

He let her go and stepped onto the walkway. She watched his retreating back and his bowed head as he walked back to his Porsche. She watched as he climbed inside and pulled off. Her eyes stayed on him until his car disappeared down the street.

Chapter 26

Diamond

"Two whiskeys on the rocks and one Bud Light, Jake. Thanks," Diamond said before setting down her serving tray on the counter. Then she turned and looked at the barroom, surveying the customers. The crowd was thin tonight, but she expected it to pick up in the next few hours when the last of the stragglers got off from work.

"Drinks up," Jake said behind her.

Diamond nodded absently. She was about to turn back around, but paused when she spotted a familiar face striding through the Tavern's door, making her heart take flight.

Darius had his suit jacket tossed over his forearm and his tie loosened. She wondered if he had just come from the courthouse. He scanned the room in search of her, adjusting his glasses as he did it. When he finally noticed her standing on the other side of the bar, he waved.

Since that day at his office, they'd spent almost every night together—either at her place or his. She never would have suspected Darius would be such a good lover, so attentive and tender—with stamina to boot. He made her feel sexy, adored, and loved. She was even starting to eat again and put on some weight.

Diamond knew she'd had a bad track record with men, from her former pimp to her current husband, but she hoped her luck was finally changing. She felt like she had something special with Darius.

She held up her finger. *Be right there*, she mouthed to him before getting her tray of drinks. She carried them to the patrons sitting at table number five, then strolled across the room to where Darius stood.

"Hey," she said, rising to the balls of her feet to give him a kiss, not caring if it looked unprofessional or if people stared.

She was in a bar where people were smoking in the open, for Chrissake.

Worry about yourselves, Diamond thought as she looped her arms around his neck.

But Darius didn't accept her kiss; instead, he turned his head away, making her frown.

"What's wrong?" she asked, loosening her arms around his neck.

"Can we talk? Can you take a quick break?"

"Sure. Of course!"

Diamond led him to one of the vacant booths, her frown deepening along the way. She wondered what he had to tell her. It didn't sound like it was going to be good whatever it was. They sat down and she watched as he dropped his gaze to the tabletop.

"Bad day?" she asked.

He nodded before taking off his glasses and roughly running his hands over his face. "This was one of those days when I wished I wasn't sober."

She grabbed his hand and squeezed it. "Why? What happened?"

"Well, my brother is still freezing me out for betraying him, even though I've apologized to him about thirty times, and one of my clients was found guilty today. Two counts of armed robbery. He could face more than forty years in prison, but I know he didn't do it. Even if none of the jurors believe me. The cops got the wrong guy. I know they did! Even one of the victims recanted their initial statement and said they were wrong . . . that it wasn't him. But it doesn't matter because he's still going to jail."

Diamond cringed. She knew how it felt being accused of doing something you didn't do. And it sounded like Darius's other client was experiencing Diamond's worst-case scenario: being found guilty of it.

"I just . . . I just feel like I failed him."

"No, you didn't, honey! I know you. I know how prepared you are when you go in that courtroom. You tried your best. You shouldn't blame yourself!" she said, but he didn't look convinced.

"Well, anyway, after my client was taken away and the mother of his four children walked out of the courtroom sobbing, I gathered my stuff, pulled myself together, and had a moment of reflection." He looked up from the table-top and met her eyes. "We have the trial coming up next month."

"Yeah," she said, nodding but wondering where he was going with this, "I know."

His hold tightened on her hand. "And I'd like to—with your permission, of course—file a continuance so we can postpone the trial."

"What? *Why?*"

"Because it feels like if I put you up in front of that jury, I'm just throwing you to the wolves. What if our testimony isn't convincing? What if they find you guilty?"

Diamond was at a loss for words.

She could deal with her own self-doubt and worry, but she wasn't used to seeing Darius questioning himself like this.

"I'm just gonna tell them the truth . . . like you said," she argued. "We've practiced over and over again. Waiting another month or two isn't going to change any of that, Darius."

He started shaking his head, like he wasn't listening to her, silently arguing with her—or both.

"Why? Why do you want to postpone? Do you think I'm not ready?"

He stopped shaking his head. "No, *I'm* not ready! I'm not ready to lose you. Not this soon. Hell, this thing between us just started."

Her heart took flight again. He really did care about her as much as she cared about him.

"Honey," she said, raising her hand to his face, "you don't—"

"No, listen to me! I can't tell you when was the last time I've been in a relationship . . . hell, I can't even remember when I've been on more than two dates with any woman. And I'm not crazy about the fact that when I finally take a leap like this, I'm doing it with my married client. But it is what it is, right? I wanna try to make this work if . . . if we can."

"We *are* making this work. Nothing is going to stop that—the court system or my husband. You know damn well that Cy and I don't have a real marriage. Not on paper and not much in real life either lately."

Darius tilted his head. "But does *he* know that? Does he know it's over?"

Diamond thought back once again to the last time she'd seen Cyrus, how he'd grabbed her face and threatened her. He'd talked to her not like she was his wife, but like he owned her. And she acted like he would never let her go. But Cy had a wife and family of his own. He had a whole life he'd carried on for decades without her, where she didn't even exist. Why couldn't she finally have a life of her own as well? Why couldn't she finally move on without him?

"He probably doesn't." She leaned across the table and gave Darius a kiss. "But it's about time that he does."

At the end of her shift, Diamond strolled outside, tugged her cell out of her back pocket, and squinted under a street-lamp. She shivered a little, and not just because a breeze had kicked up off the Chesapeake Bay and made its way to her street in Little Italy and she'd left her jacket inside, but because she was going to call her husband to tell him their marriage was over. The very idea made her quake in fear.

She didn't know how Cyrus would react, but she expected that it wouldn't be pretty.

At least he can't grab me over the phone, she thought. *At least he can't dangle me over a bridge.*

She pressed the button on the screen and listened to the ringing on the other end. Finally the ringing stopped and she heard Cyrus coughing and clearing his throat.

"Cy?" she said.

"Diamond . . . baby, what are . . . do you realize what time it is?" he asked, mid yawn.

"Yeah, I do, Cy, but I wanted to talk to you." She started to pace on the sidewalk. "I need to talk to you."

"And this can't wait for another few more hours? I mean, damn . . . at least until the sun comes up?"

"No, this . . . this can't wait. I-I have to do this. I have to say it."

He sighed impatiently and smacked his lips. "Okay, fine, baby. Say whatever you gotta say so I can go back to sleep."

She took a deep breath and closed her eyes. "Did you know I fell for you the same night I met you?"

"Huh?"

"You were smooth and charming," she continued. "I thought, *That is one fine ass man. Just look at him!* And I wasn't the only one thinking it, either. I remember more than one woman at the restaurant staring you down, trying to get your attention. But you ignored every single one of them. Your focus was all on me, and I felt so, *so* special. And every day after that, the feeling didn't fade because I was yours and you were mine. It didn't even disappear when I found out you were hiding the fact that you were married to two other women."

"Now wait a minute! You were hiding some shit from—"

"Because I was just happy to be with you at all, Cy," she pressed on, speaking over him. "As long as you treated me like I was your princess, I didn't care that I had to share my prince with two other women. I didn't care what the world said. I didn't care what the law said. I would've stayed with you until the end. Until death do us part—like I promised. But you don't treat me like a princess anymore. You don't treat me like you love me. It's more like you *own* me, Cy. Just like Julian did. Just like all those other assholes in the past who used and abused me." She stopped pacing. She blinked back tears, bracing herself for what she was about to say. "So I can't do this anymore. I'm . . . I'm ready to end this. Please let me go."

The other end of the line went silent for so long that Diamond wondered if her husband had hung up on her.

"Cy?" she asked hesitantly. "Cy, are you still there?"

Finally she heard a soft rumbling that sounded like laughter. It got louder and louder, to the point that she had to pull the phone from her ear. Why was he laughing?

"You dumb bitch," he said as his laughter died down to a chuckle. "You dumb, ungrateful bitch."

She sniffed and wiped at the errant tear that had spilled onto her cheek. "What did you call me?"

"You heard me! I damn near emptied out my bank account to bail your ass outta jail when everybody else left you to rot. Guess I should've saved the money and left your ass in there, too."

She shook her head. "This is what I mean! You never used to talk to me like this! You never—"

"Yeah, well, I should've! I should've treated you like the cheap whore you are. The low-class hooker you've always been. You wonder why I don't treat you like you're a princess anymore? It's because you're not. You're no Snow White or Sleeping Beauty, sweetheart. You're my fucking pet. You're the stray cat I picked up off the street, fed, and cleaned up. Do you know how much money I've given you? Invested in you? I do fuckin' own you! Paid in full. Talking about how I don't treat you like a princess. What kinda bullshit is that? And now you wanna leave me? Did you find some other nigga? Is that it?"

"That has nothing to do with this!"

"Guess that answers my question," he said with a snort. "You've probably already started fuckin' him, haven't you? I can't believe you woke me up for this shit! I swear, none of you understand loyalty! Not a single fuckin' one!"

"I was always loyal to you, Cy," she choked. "I-I defended you when—"

"Oh, save your breath, honey. Let me just cut this short so you don't waste any more of my time and I don't waste any more of my sleep. If you wanna leave me, baby . . . fine! I ain't gonna stop you. I'm so done with all of you. You all caused me more pain than you're worth. No good deed goes unpunished, huh? But just know that I dole out my own punishments."

Diamond wanted to hang up. Nothing good could come from continuing to listen to his threats, but she couldn't hang up for some reason. Maybe it was old conditioning to abusers, but she continued to listen. He had to hang up first.

"All of you are gonna learn that lesson," Cyrus said with an eerie calmness. "Maybe you'll walk out the door one day and get taken out by a stray bullet. Maybe you'll climb into your car and it will blow up on you. You never know. But you'll see what happens when you cross Cyrus Grey, honey. I always come out on top and I always have the last word. So watch your back!"

He finally hung up on her, leaving her staring at the phone in shock and horror.

Chapter 27

Vanessa

"Stop hogging the cereal!" Bryson shouted.

"I'm not hogging the cereal," Cy Jr. argued, shaking some into his bowl and slamming the box back onto the kitchen table. "You don't even like Froot Loops!"

Bryson grabbed the box and shook some over his bowl. Only a few colorful loops tumbled out. "See! Now it's all gone!" Bryson yelled, climbing to his knees in his chair and holding the box aloft. "Junior ate all the cereal, Mommy!"

"Kids, please stop arguing. There is more than enough cereal in this house," she lamented.

But they ignored her. The arguing continued, rising in volume. Vanessa reached for the glass of OJ sitting on the counter that she had been nursing all morning. She took a gulp. It was spiked with vodka. She didn't usually drink this early in the day. She definitely didn't usually drink in front of the children, but she'd been doing it off and on for the past two weeks, since the night of the shooting and Bilal was arrested. She needed alcohol to get through her days now because she remained stuck here in her own private hell. And her husband was her own private Satan, lording over his domain, taking joy from her pain and suffering.

She couldn't leave him. She couldn't kill him. She'd just have to wait around for him to die, and who knew how long that would take?

Vanessa took another drink from her glass, finishing off the rest of it. She licked her lips, deciding she might make another.

"What's that buzzing sound?" Zoe asked with a mouth full of Cheerios.

Cy Jr. glanced over his shoulder. "I think your phone is ringing, Mom."

Vanessa nodded as she walked to the other end of the kitchen counter, where her cell phone sat. Cy Jr. was right; her phone was buzzing. As she drew closer, she saw the letters, "ANNE ARUNDEL CTY DETE CTR" appear on screen. Anne Arundel County Detention Center. She knew instantly who was calling her from there. She wavered for only a few seconds before picking up the phone from the counter.

"I'll be right back, guys," she called to her children before rushing out of the kitchen into their adjacent mudroom. She pressed the green button to answer.

"You have a call from the Anne Arundel County Detention Center. Would you like to accept the call and all associated charges?" the automated voice asked.

Did she want to accept the call? Cyrus said he would kill her if he thought she'd betrayed him again. But she never got a chance to explain to Bilal what had happened when the cops arrived. She never got a chance to apologize for dragging him into this mess. He wouldn't have tried to kill Cyrus if it wasn't for her. He wouldn't be in jail, either. She'd been wracked with guilt over it.

"Y-y-yes," she whispered into her phone.

"We are connecting you to the inmate," the automated message said. "This call will be recorded."

"*Nessa*? Vanessa, you there?" she suddenly heard Bilal's voice erupt over the line.

"I'm here," she whispered back.

"Bae! Damn, it's good to hear your voice! I miss you, luv! Are you okay? He hasn't touched you, has he? Has he hurt you?"

Even though he was the one in prison, he was worried about her safety. *That poor boy*, she thought.

"I-I'm fine. He hasn't . . . he hasn't hurt me."

"How's the baby?"

She glanced down at her flat stomach. "Uh, o-okay."

"I'm glad y'all are okay. I'm not, though. I hate it here, bae. Some of the niggas they got in here are crazy as fuck! I've gotta get out. My mama begged my uncle to post bail, but he don't want anything to do with me. He's pissed that I used his gun. Mama managed to get enough money together to hire a lawyer for me. He said they got me on breaking and entering . . . attempted murder. I figured that. But they got me on a stalking charge, too. I told them it was a mistake though. That shit had to be because I didn't stalk you."

"Cy . . . Cy told them that you did."

"Then why the hell didn't you tell them he was lyin'? I never stalked you! We were always together! We planned this shit together!"

She looked over her shoulder, paranoid that she'd heard footsteps behind her. "I had to. I had no choice!"

"Like you left me lying on the floor of your bedroom with your husband standing over me? Like he was going to kill me? You had no choice with that either, huh?"

"I didn't want to do it! I had to think about my children. I had to—"

"Yeah, but what about *our* child? Did you forget about that? What about our baby, Nessa?" he shouted back. "You said he wouldn't let you keep it if he found out. And here you are—"

"There is no baby, damn it!" she said impatiently, cutting him off.

"What? You got rid of it already?"

"No! I'm not pregnant. I-I never was. There never was a baby."

He went quiet. "So you lied about that, too?"

"I had to! I had no choice! If I didn't tell you I was pregnant, you never would've—"

"You always had a choice, Nessa! And you chose to lie to me over and over again. Your man's an asshole, but he was right about one thing: I was stupid to listen to you. I was stupid to ever trust you! Now look where it's got me. Now I'm stuck in here!"

"You think you're the only one who's stuck? You think I want to stay here *with him*? This is agony! He hates me and I hate him, but he won't let me go. He won't let me go!" she cried hysterically. Her eyes flooded with tears. "Instead he keeps . . . he keeps torturing me and—"

"Oh, shut up! Poor you, stuck in that big ol' house with your big ol' pool and your fancy cars! Poor you with all your clothes and your jewelry and your facials. You know what, Nessa? I'd be happy to switch places with you, bae. Why don't I stay stuck in that house while you come here? Let you sleep in a bed that's only a foot away from a toilet in the cell you gotta share with three other dudes, so every time somebody pees in the middle of the night you gotta worry about getting piss dribbles on your face. Let you have niggas keep threatenin' to whup your ass or spread your cheeks, you selfish bitch! You wanna trade places with me, huh? You wanna trade?" he yelled.

"I'm sorry! I am so, so sorry, Bilal," she wept.

"No, I'm sorry. I'm sorry I ever met you." He sounded like he was crying, too. "My mama said I wasted my life . . . and she's right. I'm sorry I believed all the shit you were feeding me. And when I finally get outta this place, I'll show you how fuckin' sorry I am!"

He hung up after that and she stood barefoot on the cool tile in their mudroom, staring down blankly at her cell phone.

"What are you doing in here, Mommy?" her daughter asked, scaring her and making her drop her phone to the floor and clutch her chest in alarm.

Vanessa turned to find Zoe gazing up at her searchingly.

"Oh, hi, honey!" Vanessa said, wiping her wet cheeks. "What do you need?"

"I wanted to tell you that we finished breakfast."

"Oh, well, then I'll clean up." She picked up her phone and rushed across the room to her daughter. "You guys should grab your stuff so we can head out."

The little girl glanced at the phone. "Who were you talking to? Why were you crying?"

"An . . . an old friend." She sniffed. "But don't worry about that. Go get your lunch box, and don't forget the toy you were going to take to show-and-tell today. Okay?"

Zoe still eyed her suspiciously, but she nodded and turned to head back to the kitchen.

Vanessa waited for another minute or two, getting herself back together. She decided after she dropped the kids off at school she would make herself another drink.

Chapter 28

Cyrus

Cyrus strode down the stairs to find his wife Vanessa lounging on their leather sectional in their living room with a glass in one hand and the remote in the other, staring up at their flat-screen TV. Some morning talk show was blaring on the hidden speakers, filling up the room with uproarious audience applause. When Vanessa heard Cyrus descend the last riser and loudly clear his throat, she turned to stare up at him.

"Well, look at you, strolling around in broad daylight like someone who ain't pretending to be sick!" she slurred.

"Well, look at you—drunk as a skunk before noon," he replied with a curl in his lip.

She snorted and held up her glass. "I need all the alcohol I can get if I'm forced to stay married to and live in a house with you, oh, husband of mine. So . . . cheers!" She took another sip.

"You're lucky the kids are at school and can't see you like this."

"And *you're* lucky that out of all our kids, only Junior is old enough to realize what a piece of garbage you are."

"Watch it, Nessa. Don't get cute. I've never backhanded you across the face, but I could start makin' it a habit."

She didn't respond. Instead, she shoved her mussed hair out of her face and turned back around to look at the television. She took another drink.

"I'm heading out. I'll be back in a couple of hours," he called to her before striding across their foyer and heading to their mudroom, then the garage.

"Hope you don't come back at all," he heard her mutter under her breath as he walked away.

That's what he had to deal with lately: constant disrespect from the women in his life. If it wasn't Vanessa, then it was Noelle. If it wasn't Noelle, then it was Diamond. He knew he'd been right months ago; he should have killed those bitches. But instead of stopping at just two wives, he should've gotten rid of all three.

Would've been better off, he now thought as he strolled down the garage stairs, then to his car.

But hindsight is 20/20, Cyrus decided before opening his car door and climbing behind the steering wheel. There was no point in belaboring the past and fretting over his previous mistakes. If he was finally going to get out of this mess his life had become and settle old scores, he had to focus on the present and look toward the future.

Thirty minutes later, Cyrus pulled to a stop in his reserved parking space in the lot next to his office building and turned off the engine to his BMW. When he hopped out, he stared up at the glass exterior. The building went on for fifteen stories and had a stone courtyard with a water fountain. Cy remembered when he and Tariq took a tour of the building five years ago. The real estate agent had planned to show them one of the vacant offices on the fourth floor, but Cyrus had refused to sign on the dotted line until they looked at one of the offices several floors above.

"Are you crazy?" Tariq had whispered as they rode back down after seeing another vacant office on the seventh floor—the one they would ultimately rent. "This shit is about fifty more dollars a square foot than the other one. Let's just get the cheaper one on the fourth floor and call it a day, man. Hell, they look the same."

"Nah," Cyrus had said, shaking his head, "the one on the seventh floor has better views . . . more of a presence. The kind of clients we're lookin' for are expecting that, Tariq. They want it when they walk through the door. Besides, you know the old saying, 'Go big or go home.' That's what we gotta do. Always."

And that's exactly what Cy was doing right now. He was about to go big—because he had nothing left to lose.

Cyrus slammed shut his car door and strode across the parking lot, then the courtyard, bracing himself for the task at hand.

He and Tariq were still locked in their chess match; it was a game they'd been playing for quite a while. Tariq had been at least two steps ahead for most of it, leaving Cy scrambling to catch up. Cy had already lost several of his pieces—his wealth, two of his wives, a few of his homes, and almost his life. To any onlooker he would seem to be down and out and on the verge of losing the game entirely, but they didn't know he had one last maneuver up his sleeve. Tariq didn't realize it either and Cyrus was counting on that. If all worked out as planned, Tariq wouldn't know what had hit him before Cyrus declared "checkmate."

A couple of minutes later, Cyrus stepped off the elevator and walked down the carpeted corridor to his old office. When he pushed open the door and stepped inside, he found their receptionist and office assistant, Kelsey, sitting at her desk. The waiting room looked the same as he remembered it, from the paintings on the wall to the sofa and three armchairs, and the magazines splayed at the center of the coffee table. Nothing had changed in the months of his absence. He didn't know why he'd expected it would.

"Mr. Grey?" Kelsey squeaked, gawking and rising to her feet. "What are you doing here, sir? I had no idea you were coming! I thought you were still recovering at home."

Kelsey was always a cute little thing. Today the petite young woman with the ready smile and curly hair was wearing a blue, short-sleeved blouse, a black pencil skirt, and high heels. She looked a lot like Vanessa in her younger days.

Too bad I never got to fuck her, he now thought. He'd wanted to make a move on Kelsey within weeks of her starting the job, but Tariq had barred him from doing it. He'd said it wouldn't be a good thing to sexually harass their employees.

"She's here to work—not to suck dick. Just let her do her job," Tariq had argued.

Now Cyrus wished he hadn't listened to him. For all he knew, Tariq could've been fucking her behind his back the whole time—like he'd been fucking Noelle.

Yet more "advice" from his backstabbing business partner that he should've ignored.

"I was feeling better and decided to make the drive over here," he explained as he gave Kelsey a quick hug. He stepped back and stared down the hallway leading to their offices. "Is Tariq in?"

"Yes, he is! He's on a call right now, but I bet he'd be happy to see you." She gestured down the hall. "Just knock on his door."

Cyrus nodded, turned, and walked toward Tariq's office. But when he approached the polished wood and heard Tariq talking on the other side, he didn't knock like Kelsey had suggested. Instead, he turned the knob and shoved the door open, catching Tariq by surprise—as he'd intended.

The younger man had been leaning back in his chair at his desk as he spoke on the phone, but he suddenly sat upright. He turned to face his doorway where Cyrus now stood.

"Ain't expect to see my ass here anytime soon, did you?" Cyrus asked.

"Uh, Justin, something just came up. Let me call you back." Tariq lowered his headset from his ear and dropped the phone back into its cradle. His eyes zeroed in on Cy as Cyrus shut the office door behind him. "I figured you'd have to stop pretending you were broke down and sick and quit hiding in your house eventually, but I heard you got shot at again just a few weeks ago. Maybe it was a better idea for you to stay your ass at home."

"You know me. I take a lickin' and keep on tickin'. Not one of you niggas have managed to take me out yet. I'm indestructible."

"Yeah, whatever. What do you want, Cy? Why the fuck are you here?"

Cyrus strolled across the office before sitting down in one of the armchairs. "You know why I'm here. I came to finally end this shit . . . to settle it once and for all."

As he spoke, he noticed Tariq's hand disappear beneath his desk, like he was reaching for something. Probably a gun.

Cyrus held up his hands. "Hold up! That isn't necessary. I'm not tryin' to settle it *that* way." He shook his head and adjusted in the armchair. "Nope, I'm over all this shooting. I have a proposition for you instead. You might like it when you hear it."

Tariq brought his hands back to the tabletop. His raised eyebrow went even higher. He was incredulous—something else Cyrus had expected.

"Okay." Tariq nodded but still looked doubtful. "I'm listenin'."

"I came to you months ago, asking to borrow some money to take care of my debts," Cyrus began.

"If by 'some' you mean *three and half million* dollars . . . yeah, I remember. And?"

"Well, I still need the money, but this time I'm not asking to borrow it. I want it outright."

Tariq squinted. "Are you fuckin' with me?"

"Nah, I want three and half mil—and I want *you* to give it to me."

Tariq burst into laughter. He slowly shook his head. "You're funny, Cy. You know that? Why the fuck would I give you that much money when I wouldn't even let you borrow it damn near five months ago, especially after all the shit that's happened since? Besides, I told you before that I don't have that kinda cash on hand. I can't pull it outta thin air!"

"I know you've got it, Tariq. You can get it. You're good for it."

"Even if I could, I wouldn't do it for *you*, nigga."

"You would . . . to make me go away. You'd do it to get me out of your and Noelle's life, once and for all."

Tariq stilled.

Cyrus knew he had his attention now so he pressed on.

"Give me the money. Wire it to my account by the end of the week and, as far as I'm concerned, all this shit between us is over. I'm done with Greydon Consultants. I'm done with Noelle. She doesn't want me anymore." He shrugged. "Fuck it! You can have her! I'm ready to move on, but I can't do that if I'm still drowning in debt, Tariq. Take those shackles off of me and I'll call us even."

"You really expect me to believe your psychotic ass is ready to just give up? Bow out?" Tariq slowly shook his head again. "Get the fuck out of here! I wasn't born yes-terday."

Cyrus opened his suit jacket and reached inside, mak-ing Tariq reach under his desk again.

"Hold up! Slow your roll!" Cy shouted, gesturing with his free hand. "I just wanted to show you these so you know I'm serious."

He removed two thick documents he had folded and tucked into his inner pocket of his jacket. He set them on Tariq's desk. "There! That's a draft of a contract dissolv-ing our partnership and company. That's my annulment that stipulates Noelle becomes sole owner of Azure, both the store and the trademark. Agree to give me the three and half million dollars and I'll sign both of them."

Tariq hesitated before finally picking up the stack of stapled papers. He flipped through them both, reading them silently. After a few minutes Tariq set the papers back on his desk. He leaned back in his chair and folded his hands over his chest, still shaking his head.

"What?" Cy asked. "Don't like the terms? Want your lawyers to review it?"

"No, the terms are fine. *Too* good, to be honest. But I still can't figure out why you're doing this. Why walk away? Throw in the towel? Why now? This ain't like you."

"I told you why. I'm tired of this shit! It was hard be-fore juggling three wives. Keeping all those balls in the air. Now it's only gotten worse. Noelle left me. Now Diamond claims she's fallen in love with some nigga and is leaving me, too. Nessa hates me. I've been shot and shot at! I am *tired*, Tariq," he said, sounding tired as well. "You won. It's over. It's over!"

Tariq still didn't look moved. He still looked uncertain.

"Look, you might enjoy seeing me suffer like this, but what about Noelle?" Cyrus leaned forward in his chair, knowing that if his sales pitch was going to work, he had to seem earnest. "Shit, I'm offering you two a chance out of this! You gonna keep letting her suffer, too, just to leave me hangin'?"

Tariq's face changed with those words. His stern expression softened.

Look at this stupid motherfucka, Cyrus thought, chuckling to himself.

The whole time he'd thought Tariq had cast a spell over Noelle. Now he realized it was the other way around; she was the one who had Tariq pussy-whipped. The old Tariq would have laughed in Cyrus's face.

Oh, now I know you're full of it. You don't give a shit about her! The same woman who you wanted me to kill, now you care about her suffering? Take your contract and get the fuck outta my office, man, the old Tariq would have said.

But the new Tariq, who had fallen head over heels in love with Noelle, was seriously considering this.

"If you do this, y'all can finally have your happily ever after," Cy persisted. "You can finally get her all to yourself."

"It's not about that. It's about her having peace of mind . . . not having to look over her shoulder checkin' for you all the damn time."

"You have my word as a gentleman. I'll stay away from her."

"Your word don't mean shit, but . . . *but* I'm willing to take the chance that you actually mean what you say—for her sake. If I give you the money, you promise all this is over? You accept the annulment and leave her alone?"

"I've said it about five hundred times, but I'll say it again: It's over. The shit between you and me is done and I'm out of her life once and for all. But I have to have all my money by the end of the week."

Tariq tilted his head as he eyed Cyrus. "I swear to

God," he whispered through clenched teeth, "if you are bullshitting me . . . if I find out that you double-crossed me . . . double-crossed *us*, I will make you sorry, Cyrus. You won't know what—"

"I won't double-cross you! I told you . . . I don't have the energy! So do we have a deal or not?"

Tariq seemed to waver a bit longer before grudgingly giving a curt nod. "Yeah, we got a deal. You'll get the money, but you better sign all this shit now. You get a copy. So do I. We'll get them notarized once the money is wired to you."

Cyrus left his old offices a few minutes later. He strode back to the elevators holding back a smile. That had gone better than expected. Tariq had bought the lie.

Cyrus was back in the game—finally—and he was lining up his pieces for the win.

Chapter 29

Noelle

"These boxes are ready to load, guys," Noelle said to the movers after she smoothed down the tape on one of the lids of the cardboard boxes.

The young men stepped forward and carried two of them out of her bedroom, grunting as they did. Noelle bent down to take one of the smaller boxes they had left behind, intending to carry it herself to the moving truck downstairs waiting in her driveway.

"Ah, ah!" Tariq shouted as he stepped into her bedroom, like he was chastising a disobedient toddler. "What do you think you're doin'?"

He was actually wearing a T-shirt, basketball shorts, and sneakers today. She didn't even know Tariq *owned* basketball shorts, let alone seen him wear a pair in the five years she'd known him. But he was always full of surprises, wasn't he?

He was dressed casually to help her move out of the house she'd shared with Cyrus. Now that her husband had agreed to her terms for the annulment—even allowing her to keep ownership of Azure—and his lawyer had submitted it to the court two weeks ago, they were going their separate ways and selling their home.

She didn't know why Cyrus had suddenly changed course. She didn't ask him. She was just relieved that it all was finally over. Now she was moving into a one-bedroom-with-loft apartment in DC that was a lot cheaper than her mortgage and was a fifteen-minute drive from Tariq's place. She figured it was a way to be closer to him, but also still maintain some distance and independence—something she'd told him was necessary for their relationship to work.

Noelle had accepted that she was a woman hopelessly in love and didn't want to be away from Tariq anymore, regardless of what she now knew about him, but she still was a woman who wanted to stand on her own two feet for once. No more Noelle dancing around on some man's puppet strings. No more control and manipulation. She was responsible for herself, which was why she was annoyed that Tariq wouldn't let her carry one little box.

"I can do it!" she lamented as he snatched the box out of her grasp. She stood upright and dropped her hands to her hips. "It's not even that heavy."

"I'm not letting you carry a damn thing except the package you're already totin'," he said, reaching down to give her belly a soft pat. He then gave her a quick kiss. "That's more than enough."

Tariq patted her stomach all the time now, especially because she was now approaching her fifth month and showing it.

"I can't get over how big you've gotten," he'd told her two nights before while they lay in bed together.

"Oh, thanks!" she'd cried sarcastically.

"Just look at you!" He'd caressed her bulging belly as she'd reclined back against a stack of pillows. "It's like it happened overnight. Nothing there. Perfectly flat stomach, then . . . bloop!"

"*Bloop?*"

"You know what I mean," he'd said before kissing her navel and making her laugh again.

Noelle couldn't begrudge him for his observation; she couldn't help marveling at her own belly either. She did it in the shower and when she stood in front of her mirror. She was pregnant; there was no denying it now. She was finally going to have the baby she'd longed for.

She and Tariq had even found out they were having a girl, and Noelle couldn't wait to meet her. A new apartment. A new man. A new baby. Noelle couldn't believe her luck.

She followed Tariq out of her bedroom and down the stairs to the first floor, which was already emptied out, save for three or four boxes.

Cy had already come through the night before to remove all that he wanted. Now the house was bare and hollow—a perfect metaphor for their marriage.

"What are you thinking about?" Tariq asked from the doorway.

She'd turned to find that he'd already loaded the box on the truck. Over his shoulder she could see the moving crew was winding down and would take everything to her new apartment soon. Noelle gazed around her living room, slowly turning in a circle while clutching her stomach.

"I never would've believed this would be my life a year ago. Hell, six months ago! Leaving Cyrus. Moving out. I still might have to close Azure, too, even though I plan to use the proceeds from the house sale to help keep it open. The money still may not be enough. So much change in so little time—but I'm still happy. I'm happier than I've been in years! Does . . . does that sound crazy?"

Tariq walked toward her and wrapped his arms around her. "No, it doesn't. It makes perfect sense." He kissed her bare shoulder, then the nape of her neck. He squeezed her tight, careful of her belly.

"It's okay." She patted his arm reassuringly. "You don't have to comfort me. I'm not about to cry again. Not even happy tears. The first trimester is well behind me, so I'm not as much of an emotional mess anymore."

"I didn't think you were gonna cry," he said, turning her around to face him. "I just wanted to know where your head was at. I wanted to make sure you were okay."

"And you claim you can read me!"

"Every expression. Every gesture. I know when you're happy, when you're sad. Shit, I even know when you're suspicious. But I still can't read your mind. Give me ten or fifteen years and I might be able to do that, though."

"I'm honored you want me around that long," she said, chuckling.

"We'd spend our entire lives together if it were up to me, but I'd be happy with just ten. That's probably the most we'll get anyway."

Her grin faded. "Why just ten? You know something I don't?"

For the first time, Tariq went somber. "Men . . . hood niggas like me who've done their dirt don't get happy endings, Noelle. A lifetime together . . . well . . . that's just not in the cards for us. I've got too much bad karma to deserve something like that."

"That's not true!" She raised his hands to his face, clasping his cheeks. She stared up into his eyes. "Look, you're far from perfect. I realize that. But you deserve a happy ending just as much as the next person. We *both* do, honey."

He shook his head. "No, I don't, but I'm willing to take the closest I can get with you. If it all ended today, I'd be grateful for it either way."

She wrapped her arms around his neck and kissed him, long and hard, pouring all her love into it, hoping it would reassure him. She only pulled back when she heard someone loudly clear their throat.

"Uh, we're almost done, ma'am," one of the movers said. He gestured over his shoulder to his truck. "We're loading the last of the boxes and leaving soon."

She stepped out of Tariq's embrace, but still clutched his hand. "Thanks," she said to the mover.

When the last box was loaded and the door to the panel truck was slammed shut, Noelle gave one last glance at her home and closed the door behind her. It was symbolic. She was closing the door on her marriage, on her life with Cyrus, which had been built on a foundation of lies, and, hopefully, she was closing the door on the pain of her past.

"I'll meet you at the apartment," she said to Tariq as she followed him to the parking lot where his car was parked. She watched out of the corner of her eye as the moving truck pulled off. "You have the address, right?"

"Yeah, I got it," he said as he pressed the button to unlock his car door and then to turn on the engine. It rumbled to life. "I still wish you would let me drive you."

"Tariq, I may be pregnant, but I haven't lost the ability to drive a vehicle. Besides," she glanced at his black Porsche, "I trust me behind the wheel more than you! You drive crazy as hell in that thing!"

He laughed. "Fine. Have it your way!"

"See you soon," she said as she walked back to her garage, where her car was parked. She only had a couple of bags full of last-minute items and cleaning supplies to load in the trunk before she was ready to go. She waved goodbye to Tariq over her shoulder.

When she neared her garage she saw him still sitting behind the wheel of the Porsche, watching her. She shook her head in bemusement. He was so damn protective. She hoped he wouldn't be like this her entire pregnancy. She made a shooing motion.

"Go!" she shouted to him, fighting back a smile.

Okay, okay! he mouthed. He held up his hands in surrender and began to back out of the parking space.

Noelle turned and pressed the remote to turn on her car's engine. She felt the explosion before she heard it. The searing-hot heat that licked at her skin and her tank top and shorts. The force of it sent her and the garage door flying into the air. It knocked her out of one of her sandals and the wind out of her. She crashed against the hood of a neighbor's car, then rolled to the asphalt. She finally heard the roar of the explosion just as she heard Tariq shouting her name over and over again, but she couldn't see him through the blood gushing into her eyes, through the fire and the smoke.

"Tariq? Where . . . where are you?" she called out hoarsely, but she could feel herself fading.

Noelle heard the thunder of footsteps, the crackle of fire and breaking glass, and screaming. So much screaming. Was her house on fire? Someone picked her up. They lifted her off the ground, but she couldn't see who because, by then, she could sense the heavy sleep that was tugging at her was going to have its way. The grayness of the smoke gave way to black, then everything went silent.

Chapter 30

Diamond

Diamond lay on the couch, snuggled in one of Darius's robes while he stood in his kitchen in sweatpants, making them both dinner. The robe was soft and comfy but so large on her that she had to keep rolling up and shoving up the sleeves. Diamond didn't mind, though. She was happy to wear it. She was happy to spend one of the few evenings she had off from the Tavern with Darius, listening to old jazz albums on his stereo, basking in the high of love and freshness of a new relationship. Nestled on his couch, it felt like nothing could harm her here, though part of her still wondered whether Cyrus would follow through on the threats he'd made the last time they'd spoken a couple of weeks ago.

Diamond now shivered at the memory of his words. She tightened the collar of the robe around her to ward off the chill.

Would Cy come for her? Would he hurt her? She'd woken up in the dead of night at her apartment more than once, questioning whether she'd heard the creak of her front door or a breaking of one of her windows only to climb out of bed and find her home silent and still. But she didn't want to think about any of that or Cyrus right now. Not when everything felt so peaceful and seemed so right.

"So how do you like your burger? Medium well or well done?" Darius tossed over his shoulder.

"Medium well is fine with me," she said, resting her chin on the back of the sofa cushion to gaze at him as he cooked.

"Medium well it is," he said with a lopsided grin. He took one of the burgers and placed it on a toasted bun that was already covered with lettuce and a sliced tomato. He carried the plate to her.

Diamond closed her eyes and took a whiff. "Mmm, thank you," she whispered before taking a bite.

"Does it taste as good as my kisses?" he asked, leaning toward her ear.

She chewed her hamburger and laughed simultaneously. "Almost! Maybe a close second."

"Good answer." He leaned down again and kissed her cheek.

Just then his phone buzzed. Darius strolled across the living room to his cell phone that sat on an end table. He picked it up and stared down at the screen.

"Hey, what's up?" Darius answered after pressing the button on screen. His face broke into a grin. "I haven't heard from you in a hot minute. You've finally forgiven me?"

Diamond stopped chewing. She lowered her burger back to her plate, not wanting to listen to their conversation but doing it anyway.

It's T. J.? she mouthed.

Darius nodded.

She guessed his brother was no longer angry at him for sharing his secrets if he was calling him again. Darius said they hadn't spoken in weeks.

His grin suddenly evaporated. "*What?* . . . Wh-why are

you at the hospital? What happened? . . . Wait! Wait, slow down!" Darius shouted. "Just tell me what happened!"

She rose to her feet, tightening the robe belt around her waist.

"Oh, God," Darius whispered as his face went ashen. "God, I am *so* sorry, T. J. Is she gonna be okay?"

What happened? Diamond mouthed, but Darius only responded by shaking his head and holding up his hand, motioning her to be silent.

"What do you need me to do?" he asked his brother. He nodded as he listened. "Okay . . . Okay . . . Yes, I can get that stuff for you. . . . Yeah, you can have that, too, but why? What happened to your car? What the hell are you . . ." He closed his eyes and pushed up his glasses on the bridge of his nose. "Yes, I heard you. . . . Yeah. . . . Yeah, I can be there in a little more than an hour. . . . I got it. . . . Yeah, I got it. . . . Bye." He hung up.

"What happened?" she asked again as he set down his phone.

"T. J. is at a hospital in Virginia. He said he was helping Noelle Grey move out of her home when her car exploded."

"*What?*" Diamond cried, rushing toward him. "How . . . how did it happen? Is Noelle okay?"

"He doesn't know how it happened, though he has his suspicions. He said the police are investigating it now. Meanwhile he's been at the hospital for hours. Noelle's alive and stable, but they're worried about the baby. T. J. . . . he's not . . . well, he's not takin' any of this well for . . . for obvious reasons."

"Did he ask you to come to the hospital? Do you have to leave?"

Darius nodded as he walked to his bedroom with her trailing behind him. "But he wants me to pick up some stuff at his place first. Clothes . . . toothbrush and . . . uh . . ." He paused, opening one of his bedroom drawers. An expression she couldn't decipher crossed his handsome face. "A few other things."

"Can I come with you?"

When he started shaking his head, she grabbed his arm. "*Please*, Darius? I like Noelle! She and I were both married to Cy. And . . . and we both know who he is. What he's capable of."

It wasn't lost on Diamond that what had happened to Noelle was one of the things Cyrus had threatened to do to her. When Darius had said that Noelle's car had exploded, a shiver had gone up Diamond's spine. She still felt that chill now.

It could've been me.

"Does T. J. think Cy did it?" she asked.

Darius took out a T-shirt and closed his drawer. He looked away.

"That's one of his suspicions, isn't it? That Cy made her car explode? That he's behind it?"

"Yeah," Darius finally answered. "He was ranting about it on the phone. He didn't just sound upset that Noelle is hurt . . . that they could lose the baby. He sounded furious. He sounded crazy, Diamond. I think he's gonna go after your husband and I'm hoping I can talk him out of it. My brother has his faults . . . he's done some bad things, but I don't want him to rot in prison for the rest of his life for this. He saved me, but I don't know if . . . if I can save him this time. I don't know if he'll listen."

She stepped forward and wrapped her arms around him. She held him close. He was worried about his big brother. She was worried about Noelle. She couldn't believe Cyrus would do this. Did his violence and cruelty have no limits?

"I have to go," Darius said a few seconds later, making

her unwind her arms from around him. "T. J. is waiting for me."

He turned to open another drawer and she gazed at him, crestfallen.

He glanced down at her. "You better hurry and get dressed, too. They're not gonna let you in that hospital just wearing a robe."

So he wasn't going to leave her behind.

Diamond quickly nodded. He didn't have to tell her twice. She tore off his robe and scrambled around his bedroom, gathering her clothes.

Darius pulled into the hospital parking lot an hour and a half later.

"Are we ready?" he asked her, removing his key from the ignition.

Diamond nodded before unlocking her seat belt.

At least she would be able to get out of the car this time. When they'd stopped at his brother's house in DC before driving to the hospital, she'd waited in the car until Darius returned with a bulging duffel bag and a black briefcase. She'd stared curiously at the case when he placed it in the back seat.

"What's in there?" she'd asked Darius as he'd climbed back into the driver's seat.

"I don't know," he'd mumbled, slamming the car door closed behind him. "And I don't wanna know. He just told me to bring it."

Both the briefcase and the duffel bag were still in the car as they strode to the hospital entrance and then through the sliding glass doors. When they rode up in the elevator, Diamond reached out to hold his hand. He interlocked his fingers through hers and held on tight.

They spotted Darius's brother as soon as the elevator

doors opened. He was pacing up and down the hall. His face and shirt were covered in soot and smudged blood. He looked like he had been through hell and back.

When they stepped out of the elevator and T. J. aka Tariq finally noticed them, he stopped pacing and stared.

"What the fuck is she doing here?" he asked, pointing at her.

Darius winced. "Calm down. She just wanted to—"

"What the fuck is she doing here, Darius?" he asked in a harsh whisper. It sounded more like a growl.

She suspected it probably would have been a shout if they weren't standing in the middle of a hospital hallway.

"This isn't a road trip where you can let your little girl-friend tag along! You know damn well what I gotta do and I don't need—"

"He didn't want me to come, but I insisted. I came for Noelle," Diamond said, stepping forward, standing in between the brothers. "I wanted to see her. How . . . how is she?"

Tariq's tense stance relaxed a little. His expression soft-ened.

"She's stable. She's asleep now. The doctors and nurses took good care of her, stitching up the few cuts from the broken glass and bandaging the second-degree burns from the explosion, but they said those will heal with time. She had some . . . some bleeding, too. The baby's heart rate . . . dropped."

His voice shook. He blinked over and over again like he was holding back tears. He was getting choked up. She could tell. Tariq loudly cleared his throat, getting himself back under control.

"But . . . uh . . . they said our little girl might pull through this, too." He sniffed. "They've got Noelle on oxygen. They're pumping her full of drugs and keeping her on bed rest for a while. They said it should help."

"I am so, *so* sorry, Tariq," Diamond said. "I'm sorry for what Cy did to her."

"What Cy did to . . ." Tariq's words drifted off as he shifted his gaze back to his little brother, now looking irritated all over again. "Jesus Christ, are you gonna tell her every goddamn thing I tell you?"

"I didn't have to tell her. She figured it out herself. Cyrus was her husband, too. Remember? She knows how he is."

"He threatened to do the same to me," Diamond confessed. "I thought . . . I *hoped* he was just talking crazy. I didn't know if he would follow through with it. I didn't . . . I didn't know."

"Well, Cyrus Grey *is* crazy," Tariq said. "He's out of his fuckin' mind! And I was out of my damn mind to fall into his trap and believe he really was done with his bullshit! But I'll make sure he's done this time. Did you bring the stuff like I asked you to?"

Darius reluctantly nodded. "It's in my car downstairs, but I don't think confronting him right now is a good idea or very smart."

"Yeah, well, I didn't ask you what you thought."

Diamond stood silently to the side, observing the two brothers' angry exchange.

They looked similar in the chin, eyes, nose, and even had the same tall, lanky build. She wondered why she hadn't spotted the resemblance before. Maybe it was because their temperaments were so different. Whereas Darius came off cool and calm as a soothing creek in the forest, Tariq was a sleeping volcano, with bubbling magma just beneath the surface, ready to explode when you least expected it. Unfortunately for Darius, a creek couldn't quell a volcano, no matter how hard he tried.

Darius slowly shook his head. "Why do you do this? Why do you always . . . *always* do this? Do you have some kinda death wish? You finally have a woman you love. You've got a baby on the way. You need to stay here *with her*, at her side in that hospital room—"

"Don't tell me what I fuckin' need to do," Tariq said, balling his fists at his sides.

"—and not go running after some asshole who may or may not have done this!"

"He did it! He did, goddamnit!" Tariq yelled, drawing stares from the other people in the hallway. He got into his brother's face. "There's no may or may not! I *know* he did it!"

"Fine," Darius said, shoving Tariq back. "He did it! Does knowing that make you feel any damn better? Will going after him solve anything?"

"It'll end it. It'll end it once and for all!"

"So tell the cops. Let them do it!"

"Oh, come on! They ain't gonna do shit! They never do!"

"We won't know until we try," Darius argued, making Tariq suck his teeth in disgust and start pacing again. "Go to them with evidence. I'll . . . I'll go with you. Tell them everything you know about Cyrus so his ass will finally go to jail."

"And I can go to jail, too?"

"If you do what you plan to do, you'll still go to prison, T. J.," he said, dropping his voice to a whisper. "And if they find out I'm connected to this, they could charge me with aiding and abetting. I could get disbarred."

"Don't worry, lawyer boy. I've got it covered. It won't get back to you. And even if it does, just tell them I threatened you and forced you to do it. I don't care!"

Diamond watched the two men with growing frustration. Tariq was bullying his little brother and dismissing every valid argument. Couldn't Tariq see that Darius was only trying to help? Couldn't he see what going down this path was going to cost him in the end? His life with

Noelle. But in the back of her mind she knew Tariq was right about one thing: Cyrus would never stop unless someone or something stopped him. She'd heard it in Cy's voice that day they last spoke. She'd seen it in his eyes on that bridge. Cyrus would always be the bogeyman lurking in the shadows of their lives.

"You have an answer for everything, don't you?" Darius asked. "But this could go left ... *way* left. Don't handle this on your own. Don't throw your life away! You don't have to do this!"

"Yes, I do, because I was supposed to protect her. I promised her that I would and ... and I didn't." He cringed as if he was physically in pain. "Noelle could've died. We could still lose our baby. I-I can't live with myself for letting that happen. I'm not gonna just roll over and accept it. He has to pay for what he did, Darius. And I'm not waiting for the cops to conduct an investigation and maybe ... *maybe* file charges. I'm asking you as my brother to help me. But if you aren't gonna do that, then stay the fuck outta my way. Okay?" He reached into his pocket and held up a set of keys. "Take these. Now give me your car keys and tell me where you parked."

Darius stood silently for several seconds. He seemed to waver. Finally he closed his eyes before reaching into his back jeans pocket and tugging out his own car keys. "Third row, next to the entrance."

"Thanks." Tariq snatched Darius's keys out of his hand. He did it so fast that Darius couldn't change his mind and withhold them even if he wanted to.

"Don't you thank me for this shit." He looked pissed and sad at the same time. "Even if you don't regret this, I know I probably will for the rest of my life."

Tariq gave a wry smile. "Lil' brotha, if there's anything I wish for you, it would be the ability to not feel guilty about every damn thing. Especially shit you can't control—like your strong-willed older brother. It'll make your life so much easier." He glanced Diamond. "If you and him do stay together, please help him to lighten the fuck up." He then pressed his keys into Darius's limp, out-stretched hand, walked to the waiting elevators where doors had just opened, and stepped inside.

When the doors closed behind him, Darius's dropped his head. His shoulders slumped.

"I'm so sorry, sweetheart," Diamond said, placing her hands on his back. "I'm sorry he wouldn't listen. You tried. You know you did!"

He turned to face her. She saw so much bleakness in his eyes that it scared her. "I'm sorry, too, because I don't think I'm ever gonna see my brother again."

Chapter 31

Vanessa

"I'm going to bed now, Mom," Cy Jr. called out.

Vanessa raised her head from the leather sofa cushion, wiping the drool from the side of her face. She squinted with bleary eyes at her eldest son, who was standing on the stairs, staring down at her.

How long had she been passed out on the sofa cushions?

Vanessa remembered making dinner, sipping a vodka orange as she cooked, setting the table, and calling the kids to come downstairs and eat. She hadn't wanted to eat with Cyrus at the dinner table so she'd gone into the family room to watch TV and wait him out, but everything after that was a blank.

"Uh . . . o-okay," she now slurred. "Good night! Sweet dreams!"

Cy Jr. frowned. "You aren't gonna say anything about me going to bed so late?"

"Huh?" She reached again for her glass that sat on the coffee table. She cursed under her breath when she realized it was empty. "It's not that late."

"It's eleven thirty, Mom!"

Vanessa turned to look at the clock on their bookshelf. "Well, I'll be damned," she muttered.

It was eleven thirty. She'd been out for almost five hours.

Maybe it was time to slow down on the alcohol consumption. She thought she was being more responsible by keeping her heavy drinking to the evenings after that unfortunate incident when she was picking up the kids from school and she'd run a red light. She'd almost gotten sideswiped by an oncoming tractor trailer. It had sobered her up within seconds.

Cars had blared their horns. The children had started yelling in the back seat. Zoe had screamed like she was in some slasher horror movie. It'd taken a good half hour to calm her down.

After that waking nightmare, Vanessa swore she would never do that again, but she didn't want to go cold turkey. She still needed alcohol to get her through this daily hell.

"You're right, baby." She now pushed herself to her wobbly feet. "You should've been in bed about an hour ago." She made a shooing motion. "Go on! Get some sleep so you'll be bright-eyed and bushy-tailed tomorrow."

Cy Jr.'s frown deepened. "Are you okay, Mom?"

She nodded, then stopped because the nodding was making her dizzy. "I'm fine, baby. Why?"

"It's just . . . you don't seem . . ." He halted and slowly shook his head. "Never mind. Good night." He turned and climbed up the stairs to his room.

Vanessa dazedly watched her son walk away. She wanted to follow him, to reassure him, but she didn't know what to say to him. What could she say?

Your father is an even bigger bastard than you think he is, Junior. He's gonna kill me if I turn on him again—or try to leave him, she thought sadly. *I thought I was a lioness who could protect you, but I can't do a damn thing. I can't even protect myself.*

She strolled back to the kitchen with her empty glass, grabbing the wall to steady herself when she stumbled. She rolled her eyes in annoyance when she saw dirty dishes were piled in the sink.

"The son of a bitch doesn't know how to use the dishwasher?" she mumbled before opening one of the bottom cabinets and taking out a bottle of Smirnoff. "Well, I'm not cleaning up after him anymore!"

She unscrewed the bottle's lid and poured some into her glass. Just then she heard footsteps behind her. She looked through her kitchen entryway and saw her husband striding down the stairs.

"Well, if it ain't the devil himself," she murmured as he walked into their kitchen. "Heading out this late?" she asked him.

"I'm surprised you even know what time it is, considering how drunk you are all the time now."

She held up her finger. "Correction. Not all the time. Just between the hours of five P.M. and midnight." She looked him up and down. "So where are you headed anyway? You were gone most of the day."

He turned to her and smiled. "I had a few errands. Just one more and then I'm done."

At eleven thirty at night?

"Don't rush back home on our account," she said before taking a sip from her glass. "In fact, if you want to make a whole night of it, be my guest. Maybe two nights . . . or three or—"

"I've told you about that mouth of yours," he said firmly, narrowing his eyes at her. "I've already taken care of one wife. Keep testing me and I'll take care of you, too."

At that, she stilled.

Happy with her cowed response, Cyrus's easy smile

broadened. He walked the remaining distance across their kitchen into their mudroom, opened the door leading to their garage, and shut it behind him.

Vanessa walked to one of the kitchen windows and yanked back the curtains to watch her husband slowly back his car out of their garage and driveway.

She said a silent wish, hoping that his BMW would veer off the road and go careening into a tree at seventy miles an hour, sending him flying through the windshield, or maybe a car would sideswipe him and send him sailing over the side of a bridge to a watery grave.

"I could never get that lucky," she muttered just as she watched him turn on his headlights. Soon after, his BMW backed into the street and pulled off.

She was about to close the curtains and turn away from the window when she noticed an SUV pull out of a parking spot across the street without its headlights on. Vanessa didn't recognize the car or the driver from this distance. The car drove in the same direction in which Cyrus had just disappeared but did it at a crawl, accelerating when it reached the end of the block.

"Humph," she murmured before closing the curtains and taking another sip from her glass.

Then she walked out of the kitchen and returned to the sofa, not giving it another thought.

Chapter 32

Cyrus

Cyrus tapped his fingers on the steering wheel and hummed along to the music playing on his car stereo. It was a bouncy, '90s New Jack Swing groove that he'd listened to on an endless loop back in the day, when he was a young man with a high-top fade and his name etched in his hair. The music seemed fitting for tonight. Cy felt revitalized, refreshed, and about twenty years younger. He was downright triumphant.

He was finally on the comeback. He had finally beaten Tariq at his own game, and with luck, both Tariq and Noelle were dead.

"Checkmate, motherfucka," he whispered.

Everything had gone as planned with minimal hiccups. He'd gotten the three and a half mil he'd wanted out of Tariq, as promised. It was now in an off-shore bank account that even the Feds didn't know about. And Noelle and her bastard baby were no more.

She had forgotten that Cyrus still had the spare key to her car from when he'd purchased it for her as a gift years ago. Thank God he'd kept it. It allowed him to plant the bomb inside her vehicle that was triggered to go off when she turned on the engine—a little trick he'd picked up from Tariq long ago, but one he'd never tried out himself.

Cyrus had stuck around the neighborhood in a rental car to wait for the fireworks. He'd been close enough to know that she and Tariq had been at her house that day, carrying out boxes. He'd guessed the happy couple were moving in together. Cyrus had also been close enough to see the explosion when Noelle had turned on her car. He'd watched as Tariq rushed into the smoke and flames, but he'd been far enough away that when he drove off no one would suspect that the guy in the Honda Civic wearing the hat and sunglasses had anything to do with it.

Now Cyrus was off to finish the next and final item on his checklist. He was headed to Diamond's place to plant evidence of the explosion on her and make the cops believe she was behind it. Why wouldn't they? According to them, she had tried to have Cyrus killed. It would make sense that she would go after one of his wives, too, especially one she claimed to have befriended. Jealousy and spite were great motivators, especially in women.

Any detective worth his salt knows that, Cyrus thought.

Diamond had decided to pretend she was friends with Noelle to pick off the competition, the cops would conclude. Finding Noelle's spare car keys hidden at Diamond's place—which Cyrus would tell them she took from him without his knowledge—would only solidify the cops' theory. And Cyrus would have to reluctantly . . . grudgingly admit that maybe he had been wrong about his wife Diamond and the authorities had been right all along; Diamond Grey was a merciless killer, a deceitful whore who should spend her remaining years in prison.

Serves her right, he now thought. *Turn on me and see what happens.*

He still had to figure out how to get into her place to

plant the evidence, but he assumed he'd come up with a solid idea before he arrived there. Until then, Cyrus would continue to enjoy the music on his satellite radio. He leaned over to turn up the volume, but paused when a Jeep Cherokee that was driving in the lane beside him suddenly accelerated and got in front of him, almost cutting him off.

"The fuck," he muttered aloud.

All this maneuvering wasn't necessary; the two cars were alone on this stretch of road this late at night. The only other things that seemed to be out here with them were the trees, the moon, and maybe a few skittish forest animals.

Cyrus changed lanes to try to go around him, but the car abruptly jumped over, blocking his path.

"What is this crazy son of a bitch doin'?" he asked his empty car while changing lanes yet again, only for the other driver to pull the same maneuver.

Cyrus was no longer annoyed. He was starting to get pissed off.

Just as he shifted the wheel and gunned the engine to make his third attempt to go around, the driver in front of him slammed on his brakes, catching him off guard. Cyrus stomped on his brake, too, but he wasn't fast enough. He crashed into the SUV, making his airbag inflate in less than a second with all the force of a heavyweight's punch, knocking the wind out of him. When the airbag deflated he swore he could see stars. He could also see that the car's hood was completely caved in. His engine and internal wiring were exposed. Smoke was filling the car.

"What the hell?" he murmured as the driver in the SUV threw open his car door and started to climb out. Cyrus unlocked his seat belt and door, attempting to do the same, but winced at the pain in his chest, a residual injury from the shooting that was flaring up again thanks to the airbag. "Are you fuckin' outta your—"

Cyrus's words died on his lips and his eyes widened when he saw who the driver was, who was striding to his car—a very much alive Tariq.

Panicked, Cyrus reached for the center console, where he stored his Glock, but Tariq was faster. He yanked open Cyrus's car door and hit him in the face once . . . twice . . . three times with the butt of his gun, pistol-whipping him and blinding him in the process. Cyrus tried to fight back, to take a swing, but he couldn't see.

"Do you remember what you said to me the first time you asked me to kill somebody for you?" Tariq said as he yanked Cy's collar, dragging him out of the car and making him fall face-first onto the pavement. "Huh? Do you remember what you said, Cy? 'Don't make it quick. I want him to feel it.' Well, I'm gonna make sure you feel this shit tonight." He then hit him with the butt of the gun again, making Cyrus cry out in pain.

"Let me fix the settings on this so I can see. There we go," he heard Tariq say over his shoulder as a spotlight shone down on him.

Cyrus turned to look up, stunned to find Tariq holding a pistol in one hand and his cell phone in the other. Tariq gazed into the phone as he spoke.

"My name is Tariq Jalen Donovan. It is 11:47 P.M. on Wednesday, September the fifteenth, and I am about to kill this man over here. His name is Cyrus William Grey."

He then turned the phone's camera so it faced Cyrus.

"But before I do, I want him to make a few confessions. First, I want you to say what you did today, you sack of shit! I want you to confess who you tried to kill."

Cyrus was still sprawled on the pavement. He blinked blood out of his eyes as he pushed himself up to his elbows.

"Yeah, that's right." Tariq goaded him. "I said *tried*!

You thought Noelle was dead, but joke's on you. You tried to kill my woman, but you didn't."

"She's not your woman!" Cyrus yelled as he reached out and grabbed Tariq's ankle, making him yank himself out of Cy's grasp and almost stumble back in the process. Cyrus crawled and tried to push himself to his feet, ready to charge. "She was my wife! My wife, motherfucka! And you stole her from—"

His tirade was cut short when Tariq fired, sending a bullet through Cyrus's outstretched hand, making him screech and roll around on the gasoline-soaked asphalt.

"Do that shit again and see what happens," Tariq growled, lowering the pistol. "See what I fuckin' do to you."

"What difference does it make?" Cy whimpered, slumping back against his car, clutching his bleeding hand. "You're gonna kill me anyway!"

Tariq nodded. "You're right. I am. But the difference could be a quick shot to the head when all this is over, or a bullet to the ankle . . . then the kneecap . . . then the gut." He pointed to Cyrus with his pistol. "You'll still die, nigga, but I'll make sure that shit is as slow and painful as possible. It's up to you. You might be crazy, but you forget—I'm *a lot* crazier."

Cyrus took a shaky breath, then swallowed the lump in his throat. His mouth was going dry from breathing so hard. He tried desperately to think of a way out of this, but the searing-hot pain in his hand and chest were screaming louder than the scrambled thoughts in his head.

"Now do what I asked," Tariq said in a measured voice, "so we can get this over with." He turned his camera phone to face Cyrus again. "Did you try to kill your ex, Noelle Grey, today?"

"She ain't my ex!" he said through gritted teeth. "She's still my goddamn wife!"

"Stop dancin' around my question and just fuckin' answer it!"

"Fine! You wanna hear it?" he shouted. "Yes, I tried to kill that bitch! And she deserved to die! Fuckin' around behind my back. Getting knocked up by the same man who tried to kill me. Any man with any pride would do what I did!" He glared up at Tariq. "And I wanted you there to see it. I wanted you to watch that bitch die! If it was up to me, you would've died with her."

"And it wasn't the first time you wanted her dead," Tariq continued. "Keep goin', Cy. Get it all out. You asked me to kill her back in April. You asked me to kill your other wife, Vanessa, too, didn't you?"

"Yeah, I asked you to do it; instead you tried to have me killed!"

"That's right. I tried to kill you. Not your third wife, Diamond Grey. We should enter that into the record, too."

"The record, huh? Should we talk about those other times, too, when you didn't bat an eye before you pulled the trigger? How many people have you killed in your lifetime, Tariq? How much blood is on your goddamn hands?" His voice was starting to slur. He was feeling light-headed thanks to the loss of his own blood. "Why don't you confess that shit to the camera?"

"Because this is your story, Cy, not mine."

"We were partners! Damn near brothers—until you betrayed me! Now you wanna act like you suddenly grew a fuckin' conscience?"

"I don't know." Tariq shrugged. "Maybe I did."

"Bullshit! You wanted what I had. You always did. You wanted my life. My marriage. You wanted *her*!"

"Maybe." Tariq shrugged again, ending the video and dropping the phone into the pocket of his shorts. "Maybe in the back of my mind I wanted Noelle since the day I first saw her on your arm in that restaurant in New York, and I didn't even realize it. Maybe in the back of my mind I was just waiting . . . waiting for you to fuck it up like you always do, but this time I wasn't gonna clean up after you."

"Clean up after me? Don't act like it was all one-sided! Like you were doing me all the favors! You were happy to tag along behind me like a goddamn puppy for more than fifteen years. I helped you! I gave you a brand-new life. The suits you wear . . . the house you live in . . . the car you drive . . . I made you a goddamn millionaire! I made *you*!"

"No, Cy, we made each other, but those days are over." He leveled the gun at Cyrus again.

"Wait! Wait!" Cyrus yelled, holding up his hands. He thought furiously for an excuse. Anything to stall. His gun was still inside the car. He might be able to get it if he had enough time.

"Just let me say goodbye to . . . to my kids." He blinked his eyes, trying to bring on tears. "Don't let them wonder what happened to me . . . how I died. Let me get my phone, Tariq. Let me call them. Please!"

"Nigga, your kids are fast asleep. Besides, they'll know what happened to you. I'm sending this video to the cops, the local news . . . hell, I'll even upload it to YouTube."

"So you're just gonna rip me from my family?" he asked as he scooted to his right. "You're gonna let my kids grow up without a father?"

"We both know they're probably better off without you."

"If you kill me, that's it!" Cyrus rushed out, shifting again. "There goes your chance of ever being with Noelle. You'll either go to jail for life or have to go on the run. You can never come back! You know that, don't you?"

At that, Tariq paused. His brows drew together.

"She'll be all alone," Cyrus persisted, easing to his right by another few inches.

He was sitting next to the open door now. He could see his handgun lying on the driver's side floor, underneath the pedals.

"No man. No money. Nothing and no one to protect her," Cyrus said. "And she's so fragile. Always has been. You know that. Is that what you want for her? For her and your kid?"

Tariq's gun seemed to lower by a few inches. He slowly shook his head.

"No, I don't. I don't want to leave her. But she's stronger than you think, than even *she* realizes. I need her a lot more than she needs me. She'll be okay without me . . . and the world will be much better off without you," he said, raising his pistol again.

As he did it, Cyrus scrambled for his Glock. He grabbed it, turned, and was about to fire just as he took a bullet to the temple—dead center.

Chapter 33

Diamond

The wipers whipped back and forth rhythmically as the rain pinged on the sedan's roof and windshield. Diamond gazed out the window at the people streaming from the gravesite, all cloaked in black and holding umbrellas, trudging back to their cars parked along the gravel roads of Cedar Hill Cemetery. Some were crying silently. Others just looked shell shocked.

For her part, Diamond couldn't work up any tears, even though it was her late husband being buried.

Once Diamond had loved Cyrus. She'd even dreamed of spending her life with him. And yet, as she walked with the rest of the parishioners toward the front of the church earlier that day to say her last goodbye to him while he lay in his satin-lined casket, all she could think was, *They did a good job with his makeup. You can't even see any of the bullet holes*, and *If it hadn't been him, it would've been one of us.*

He had nearly succeeded in killing Noelle. Who's to say he wouldn't have tried to kill her or Vanessa in the end?

Cyrus was gone and they were now safe, but it had required a huge sacrifice on Tariq's part.

The video of Tariq's confession and Cyrus's reluctant
admission of his crimes as well had been splashed all over
the news, even making some of the national broadcasts.
After the prosecutors saw the video, they decided to drop
the charges against Diamond, no longer feeling they had
that strong a case for attempted murder. They now had
murder charges against Tariq instead, but the cops still
didn't know where Tariq had gone and couldn't arrest
him. They'd questioned Darius several times—holding
him overnight once—but he told them the truth: He had
no idea where his brother had disappeared to.

"I don't know if he's still in the country," Darius had
lamented to her in the wee hours of the morning when he
couldn't sleep. "I don't even know if he's still alive."

Noelle, who was still on bed rest, also didn't know
where Tariq had gone, though Diamond doubted she
would tell the police the truth even if she did. She owed
him her life. They all did.

The rain ended. Diamond watched as the last trickle of
people left the cemetery. Only a few cars remained. When
it looked like the gravesite was empty, when it looked like
not a single soul lingered under the black tent on the hill-
top, then and only then did she open her car door and
begin the treacherous climb to Cyrus's grave. The ground
was wet and muddy. Her heels sank slightly in the terrain.
In retrospect, she should've worn flats or maybe tennis
shoes for a hike like this. Or maybe she could have saved
herself the labor and just not come here at all, like Darius
had suggested.

"You know you don't have to do it," Darius had told
her that morning as they sat in his kitchen, eating break-

fast. "You don't owe him a damn thing. Definitely not mourning or grief. That bastard can rot in hell for all I care."

"I know. But I feel like I have to do this. I need the closure, Darius," she'd confessed.

He'd lowered the coffee and sighed. "You want me to come with you?"

"No," she'd said, shaking her head, though she'd reached across the table and squeezed his hand, warmed that he was willing to take the journey with her. "I have to do this alone. I feel like I should."

Now at the graveyard, she finally neared the top of the hill. She saw the tent, where a dozen empty fold-up chairs were arranged in front of the casket. At least twenty freestanding floral bouquets were on display. A smiling, framed photo of Cyrus in all his handsome glory was set on a golden easel. Beneath it was the engraving, "Loving husband, father, and friend, Cyrus Grey."

Diamond rolled her eyes at how disingenuous it sounded. She stepped under the tent and drew closer to the picture frame, placing her hand on the cool glass as she gazed at her late husband's image.

"Oh, Cy," she whispered. "I thought you were my knight in shining armor. Goddamn, was I wrong."

"I thought it was you," a familiar voice said behind her, making Diamond almost jump out of her shoes. She whipped around to find Vanessa standing a few feet away, wearing a black tailored suit, Louboutin heels, and a feathered, wide-brimmed hat that could be seen from an airplane.

"H-h-hey," Diamond stuttered.

Vanessa didn't return her greeting. Instead, she crossed her arms over her ample chest, on full display even in her suit. She cocked an eyebrow.

"I thought I saw you back at the church, but then I thought, *there is no way in hell she would show up today. Not today of all days,*" Vanessa snapped. "But then, I thought, *of course she showed up! She has to remind everyone that she's Cy's widow, too.* Definitely with all the damn news cameras around. She has to rub it in that—"

"I didn't come for any of that." Diamond held up her hands in surrender. "I came in peace, Vanessa. I just wanted to pay my respects. I purposely stayed in the background."

She'd sat in one of the back pews, attempting to be inconspicuous with her head lowered and a veil drawn over her face. Luckily, the church had been packed with so many people—a mix of family, friends, business acquaintances and curious onlookers who were there to see the man who had monopolized local headlines for months— that Diamond had faded into the background. Even though the press and cameras had lingered around the church doors as they entered, she hadn't been spotted by anyone. Or at least she thought she hadn't. She now realized she'd been wrong.

"I didn't want to start any drama today," she now explained to Vanessa. "I'm past all that. Especially after all that's happened."

"Don't tell me you're actually sad to see him gone," Vanessa said, strolling toward her.

Diamond shook her head. "No, not really. I guess in some way I just . . . I just wanted to make sure he was dead. It doesn't seem real. You know?"

"Yeah, I guess I get that. When the police told me Tariq had killed him, the first thing out my mouth was, 'Are you sure? Don't play with me!' When they said they were sure, I started sobbing—with relief," Vanessa said as she opened her purse. "That bastard was finally dead and gone. Hallelujah," she muttered dryly.

To Diamond's surprise, Vanessa pulled out a silver flask, unscrewed the lid, and took a sip. To Diamond's even greater surprise, she offered her a drink.

Diamond shook her head. "No, I'm good. But . . . uh . . . thanks."

"Humph, oh well. More for me," Vanessa said with a shrug before raising the flask to her lips and taking a longer pull of whatever was inside.

"How . . . how are the kids taking it?" Diamond ventured.

Out of all the people affected by the past events, she felt the worst for Cy's three children. They were innocent of their father's shortcomings and crimes.

"Not too good. He was their father, of course, but we'll work through it. My mama and I are taking them to Disney World to cheer them up. And I'll have another man in a year or two to take his place. Having a new daddy will help them get over it."

Diamond grimaced. She wasn't as convinced as Vanessa that a getaway vacation and a new stepfather could erase the memory of Cyrus for the children, but she kept that thought to herself.

"Well, they have my condolences. You . . . you do, too, Vanessa."

Vanessa chuckled as she screwed back on the lid of her flask. "Girl, don't waste your condolences on me. Like I said, I'm glad he's dead. Good riddance to trash." She looked like she was about to turn away but paused, abruptly hocked back and spat on the picture of Cyrus before wiping her mouth with the back of her hand. She then casually dropped her flask back into her purse and adjusted her suit jacket. "I should get going. I made up an excuse to come back here. Mama and the kids are waiting for me."

"I . . . I understand."

Diamond watched as Vanessa walked off. She looked again at Cy's photo, at Vanessa's spit as it slowly dripped down the glass. Diamond then loudly exhaled. "Goodbye, Cy," she whispered before walking away, too.

Chapter 34

Noelle

Nearly two years later . . .

"Happy birthday to you! Happy birthday to you!" the partygoers sang in unison in Noelle's living room. "Happy birthday, dear Kayla! Happy birthday to you!"

Noelle surveyed the room. She had spent all night getting the party ready. She'd pushed her furniture to the walls and corners to accommodate all her friends, neighbors, and her daughter Kayla's little playmates from Baby Gym. Now they were all huddled shoulder to shoulder in a room awash in pink balloons, streamers, and silver sparkles.

"Blow out the candle, honey," Noelle whispered into her daughter's ear, beaming with pride that her little girl was now one year old.

The squirming, squealing infant she had nursed for six months, changed countless times, and spent endless nights rocking to sleep was officially a toddler. Though Noelle had been terrified those first few months as a single mom, overwhelmed and sleep-deprived, Noelle now marveled that she'd managed to do it all on her own. She'd made it out alive and with her sanity intact. She felt like the party was just as much for her as it was for her daughter.

"Go ahead and blow, Kay!" someone called out before blaring a party horn, making everyone laugh.

"*Bow*?" Kayla asked.

She sat on her mother's lap and twisted slightly as she shifted her gaze from the candle at the center of the birthday cake and back up to Noelle, as if seeking approval from her mother. When their eyes locked, Noelle's big smile waned.

More than once someone had pointed out that Kayla had the most unique eyes, not in color or shape. They were the eyes of an "old soul"—way too wise and world-weary for her age.

"She's probably been here before," one older woman had once said as she gazed down at Kayla in the grocery store. But Noelle knew the truth.

Kayla wasn't an "old soul." Her dark eyes were identical to her father's. Any world-weariness she had, she'd inherited from him. Tariq had always had a cynical view of life and people. He'd never had patience for rose-colored glasses or fairy tales. She used to find his outlook refreshing, even funny sometimes, but she wondered now if that cynical view of people and the world had made it easier for Tariq to leave in the end. Did it help him to not have any misgivings about disappearing on her because he never believed they had a real chance to begin with?

Noelle painted a smile back on her face. She would not let thoughts or memories of Tariq mar today. It was a celebration. She refused to be sad.

"Want Mama to help you?" she asked Kayla and kissed her daughter's brow. "Okay."

She leaned forward and blew out the candle for Kayla, making the room erupt into applause.

Three hours later Kayla was sitting, babbling on her play mat in the living room, interested more in a glittery gift bag than her new toys, while Noelle stood nearby in the kitchen, soaking dishes in soapy water.

"All right, I think we got everything," Diamond announced as she walked into the kitchen with Darius trailing behind her, towing two bulging trash bags. "Every stray party hat, streamer, fork . . . you name it!"

"Thank you, guys," Noelle said while shaking soap bubbles from her hands. "You two were sweet to do that. I really appreciate it. Seriously, if there's any trash lingering around, Kay seems to have the magic ability to find it. And she still puts everything in her mouth. I'll be happy when she grows out of that!"

"Well, all trash is secured. I'll take these to the garbage shoot down the hall. Is there anything else you need us to do for you before we go?" Darius asked.

Noelle shook her head and wiped her wet hands on a dish towel. "No, you've done more than enough! Thank you again."

And she wasn't just referring to helping her clean up after the party. After Tariq killed Cyrus and disappeared, Diamond and Darius had been helping her and checking in with her regularly. The engaged couple even babysat Kayla on occasion.

"She's my niece. It's my job to look out for her," Darius had confided in Noelle once. "My brother would want me to."

Noelle hadn't told Darius that if Tariq was so concerned with the welfare of his daughter, he would have done a lot more than leave a voice mail to her mother while she was stuck in a hospital bed, professing his love and saying goodbye to them both forever. Over the past two years, Noelle had listened to that saved message about three hundred times. She tried to decipher some code word he might have said, some hint to let her know when he would come back to her, but after one week stretched into the next and several months passed she realized the voice mail was exactly what it seemed to be—just a long good-bye. She didn't have the heart to erase it, though; it was all she had left of him. One day, she might let their daughter hear it, too.

"The party turned out nice," Diamond said, throwing on her jacket. "That cake was adorable. Where did you get it? From that bakery up the street?"

"No, I tracked down the baker on Instagram. I shouldn't have splurged on it, though," Noelle said with a laugh, glancing over her shoulder at Kayla, who was still babbling quietly as she played. "Especially because she won't remember any of this. But I couldn't help myself."

"Do you need any money . . . for the party, I mean?" Darius asked. "I can chip in, you know."

"I'm fine," she said, waving him off.

He stepped forward. "Are you sure? Because—"

"Yes, Darius. I'm sure. You don't have to worry about me. I'm all set. Trust me."

She wasn't hurting for money, though she couldn't tell him or anyone else that. Soon after she finally left the hospital and within days of arriving at her new apartment, she'd found a padded envelope on her doormat filled with thousands of dollars. None of her neighbors had seen who left the envelope, but Noelle had her suspicions. She'd dipped into the cash every now and then, only when she needed it the most. It pissed her off that she had to. She didn't want Tariq's damn money. She wanted him here with her, helping to raise their daughter, spending their lives together, but him murdering Cyrus had made that almost impossible. She'd played with the idea of giving all the money away, but Azure was just starting to make a profit. Taking care of herself and her baby took precedence over her pride and heartache.

Noelle now watched as Darius and Diamond exchanged a look.

"What?" Noelle asked, staring at the couple. "What did I say? I really am okay, guys. I've got it all covered."

"I'll go take out the trash," Darius muttered, looking evasive. "Diamond, I'll wait for you downstairs, okay?" He set down the bags, walked to Kayla's play mat, knelt down, and kissed his niece on one of her plump, brown cheeks. The little girl raised her chubby fingers to his face and gave his beard a tug, making him laugh. He pretended to nibble at her fingers and she squealed.

Watching them, Noelle ached a little. They seemed so much like father and daughter, but Kayla's real daddy wasn't here and probably never would be.

"Bye-bye, honey. Uncle Darius will see you soon, okay?"

Kayla babbled her reply before returning her attention to her building blocks. Darius kissed her cheek again, rose to his feet, then turned. He gathered the trash bags without another word, walked across Noelle's living room, opened her front door, and walked out, shutting the door behind him.

Both women gazed at the closed door.

"He's a good guy," Noelle said.

Diamond nodded thoughtfully, turning around to look at Noelle again. "I know."

"You're lucky to have each other."

"I know that, too."

"He loves you—a lot. I can tell."

"I love him, too. I guess I should be thankful to Tariq for bringing us together."

"Maybe," Noelle murmured bitterly to herself, walking back to her sink.

"Noelle, are you . . . are you really doing okay?"

"Why does everyone keep asking that?" She grabbed a sponge, feeling the first prickles of irritation. "Don't I seem okay?"

"Actually you seem great. You always do!" Diamond pulled out one of the stools at the kitchen island and sat down. "Which is making Darius kinda paranoid. And honestly, it has me wondering, too. He wanted me to talk to you one-on-one about it. You know . . . girl talk? He thinks you would feel comfortable . . . being candid . . . if he wasn't in the room."

"There's nothing wrong. There's nothing to be candid about," Noelle insisted, shaking her head as she scrubbed a pan in the sink. "Darius is worried for no reason."

"Noelle, it's me you're talking to. I went through that stuff with Cyrus just like you did. And we went through *a lot*, girl. He threatened to kill me. He damn near almost killed you and—"

"But he didn't. We're alive!" Noelle gestured to herself and Diamond, then returned to her washing. "You're not on trial anymore and you're in a healthy relationship now. I'm the mother to a beautiful little girl, which is what I always wanted. We got through it. We got through it stronger . . . better!"

"But those scars from the past just don't disappear."

"Mine did. You can barely tell I had burns or stitches."

"Don't play dumb. You know what I mean! The invisible scars. They don't just disappear. The sadness doesn't, either." Diamond inclined her head and rested her elbows on the counter. "Don't . . . don't you miss Tariq?"

Noelle paused from scrubbing her pan, then resumed.

"You haven't mentioned him in months. You don't seem to even want to talk about him anymore."

"Why talk about him when he isn't here?" Noelle asked. "What's the point?"

"You know he did it all for you, right? That's why he killed Cy. He thought he failed you by letting you get hurt and almost killed so he—"

"So he went on a revenge spree, tortured and killed my crazy-ass husband, made a video of it, and disappeared into the wind," Noelle said, tossing her sponge aside and whipping around to face Diamond.

"The video was to protect you and to get the cops off my back," Diamond argued. "He wanted everybody to know the truth about what really happened. And you know why he hasn't come back. He—"

"Look, Diamond." She held up her hand and took a step toward the counter. "I know you mean well, but don't defend Tariq to me, okay? Honestly, you can't. I knew Tariq. I understood him better than most. He was one of the smartest, most conniving, and charming men I have ever met. Even more than Cy—and that says a lot. If anyone could find a way to get out of a mess, it was him. If anyone could find a way to come back to me, it would be him. And he hasn't because he doesn't *want to* for whatever reason. At first I didn't understand why. He said he loved me. That he always would love me! But then again, he said we wouldn't get our happy ending, either. He predicted it." She bit down on her bottom lip, fighting back tears. She pointed to her kitchen window. "And if he's out there somewhere, creating a new identity and making a new life, why shouldn't I do the same?"

Diamond slowly shook her head. "No one's saying you shouldn't, girl. But you have to allow yourself time to mourn, to—"

"I mourn every damn day," Noelle said. "I miss him *every* damn day. Sometimes I even wonder if he's dead and his ghost is hanging around, because I swear I think I can feel him around me. A few steps behind me. It makes me feel like I'm insane!" She winced. "I can't hang on to this anymore. It's gonna eat me up inside and I have to be strong for myself . . . for my little girl." A tear trickled onto her cheek. "I . . . I have to let him go. I have to let him go."

"Damnit, now you're gonna make me cry," Diamond said with a sniff and reddened eyes. She stood up from her stool and walked to Noelle, enveloping her in a hug.

They held each other tight as they wept, pulling apart minutes later.

"I know a few single guys that I could set you up with if it'll make it any better," Diamond offered, making Noelle laugh.

"Oh, God! I got asked on a date last week by a guy at the post office," Noelle said, wiping her face.

"*Really?* Was he cute? What did you say?"

"I gave him my number but we haven't set up anything," Noelle began. "I'm still very gun-shy for obvious reasons. You know?"

"I mean, it's understandable," Diamond said, taking a seat at the kitchen counter. "Especially with some of the men out there, girl!"

As the two women talked, Kayla continued to stack blocks ten feet away, oblivious to her mama and her auntie.

Chapter 35

Darius

"Leaving already?" Diamond asked tiredly, turning onto her back and smacking her lips while she stretched.

"I'm afraid so." He tossed the strap of his satchel onto his shoulder and adjusted his coat. "If I'm gonna make the conference, I should head out now."

She adjusted the pillow behind her and pushed herself up to her elbows. "Well, drive carefully. Don't forget to call me when you get there, okay? I'll be pissed if you don't."

Darius gazed down at her.

Diamond lay in their bed with puffy eyes, wearing a pink silk bonnet. He remembered how many nights she'd spent at his place before she finally let him see her this way. He'd thought it was odd when he woke up in the morning to find her hair softly tousled, her face fresh and glossy, and not even sleep in her eyes. It wasn't until she caught the flu and he saw her at her worst that she finally did away with the subterfuge.

"It's what Cy expected of me," she'd confessed bashfully. "To look beautiful and perfect all the time. I know you aren't Cy, but old habits are hard to break. You know?"

"I don't want perfection," Darius had confessed, gathering her snotty tissues and her bowl of half-eaten soup. "I just want you."

And he'd meant it. As far as he was concerned, they were two broken people who had found each other and made something whole. And after the prosecutor dropped the attempted murder charge against her, they were free to start a new life. They were getting married in two months. Darius wouldn't have it any other way.

He now leaned down and kissed her goodbye, then nuzzled her neck, taking in her smell, absorbing her warmth. She giggled, clasped his face in both hands, and gave him a lip-smacking kiss.

"Go! And call me when you get to Charleston," she ordered.

He nodded. "Of course, love," he whispered before waving goodbye.

"I still don't understand why you aren't flying down there," she called to him. "It's such a long drive, baby!"

"It's cheaper to drive and I don't mind the time on the road," he lied. He blew her a kiss and backed out of their bedroom. "Bye, baby."

"Bye!" she called.

Darius sighed wearily as he crossed the South Carolina border. He'd been driving for more than six and half hours—stopping for a BLT with a side of fries at a diner in Norfolk, Virginia, along the way—and he still had another hour or more to go before he reached the law conference's hotel in the scenic part of Old Charleston. More than the views, he was looking forward to room service and a warm bath after all this time on the road, but before Darius enjoyed any of that, he had to make a detour. It was something he'd done twice before, and every time it made his stomach twist into knots. It made his palms sweat. He'd wanted to tell Diamond where he was going, what he was doing. They made it a policy not to keep secrets from each other, but sometimes he had to make an exception. He hoped in his heart of hearts that she would understand.

"Take the next exit on your left," his phone's automated voice said.

He turned the wheel, following its command.

The exit led to a long, lonely road bordered on both sides by corn and alfalfa fields, cows and dilapidated barns. He saw American flags and even Stars and Bars flying on the exterior of the few ramblers and doublewides he passed.

"Where the hell am I?" he whispered to himself with a slow shake of the head, even though his phone told him exactly where he was—on an old stretch of Route 221.

Seeing his current surroundings, under normal circumstances, Darius would make a hard U-turn and head back to the exit and the highway. There was no God-given, logical reason why his black ass should be out here on the back roads of South Carolina. But then again, he wasn't operating on logic. He was here out of obligation. He was here because of a promise he'd made long ago, and he planned to keep it.

Darius finally saw the red motel sign in the distance. Only three cars sat in the motel's lot: two pickup trucks and an understated tan sedan. Darius pulled into one of the empty spaces in front of an aging Coca-Cola machine. He removed his cell from his holder and pulled up one of his old text messages.

" 'Room 8,' " he read aloud. Considering how small the hotel was, the room shouldn't be hard for him to find.

Darius climbed out of his car and strolled to the door with the rusted "8" dangling on the exterior. He knocked.

"Door's unlocked," a voice called out.

Darius opened it and found his brother, Tariq, reclining on one of the double beds with a remote control in his hand. He wasn't wearing one of his signature suits. Instead, his clothes reminded Darius of how he used to dress back in the day, before he made his money—stained T-shirt, grubby jeans, and scuffed kicks. Tariq looked like he had just finished toiling away in one of the nearby tobacco fields. He turned from the television screen to gaze up at Darius. His face widened into a smile.

"Well, damn! You grew a beard, too, huh? Just got tired of shaving or your ass hiding from the law like your big brotha?"

"Funny," Darius muttered before closing the hotel door behind him. "And why the hell would you leave the door unlocked? Anyone could burst in here."

"Who? *The cows?*"

"No," Darius said, securing the lock, then the dead bolt, "the FBI or the South Carolina State Police or the dozen other law enforcement agencies who've been told to be on the lookout for you. It's a risk you don't need to take, T. J.!"

Tariq tossed aside the remote and threw his legs over the side of the bed. "Man, save the damn lecture. I wanna see pictures of my kid, but before that, take this and make sure Noelle gets it." He reached for a padded envelope that sat on the night table in between the double beds and tossed it to his brother. "It's about sixty grand in there. That should hold her over for a while."

Darius stared at the envelope now in his hands. He'd held a similar envelope after another clandestine meeting with Tariq almost fourteen months before. He'd left the envelope on Noelle's doormat in the wee hours of morning, like Tariq had asked.

"Don't let her know that you got it from me," he'd told Darius. "Don't let her know that you know where I am. She'll wanna come with me. She'll ask me to come and get her, and I won't be able to resist coming back—and I might as well sign my own arrest warrant. I'd end up taking her down with me in the process, too. I don't wanna do that to her."

"I'll give it to her," Darius now said, tucking the envelope into his satchel, "but I don't think she needs it."

"How the hell not? I gave her the other money more than a year ago! She has to have run out by now."

Darius shrugged. "She's pared down a lot. Noelle lives pretty conservatively. I ask her all the time if she needs anything . . . any money. She always says no."

Tariq seemed to contemplate his answer. "Well, give it to her anyway. Think of it as a birthday present for Kayla." He tilted his head. "How is my baby girl, by the way? Is she as big as the last time you sent me a picture?"

"No. Noelle said she's grown about two inches in the last couple of months and put on about three pounds." He smiled despite himself as he took out his cell phone. "She's becoming quite the cute little butterball."

Tariq sat forward as Darius sat down, taking the spot on the bed beside him. The two men scrolled through his camera reel, and Tariq stared at the images of the birthday party two weeks before.

Darius knew these meetings were dicey. He was risking his law career and jail time and his brother was risking a life in prison every time they met. Though Tariq had been on the run for a year and a half, he still found his way to secretly reach out to his little brother to find out what was happening back home. Their conversations were always done via burner phone and painfully short, but he would ask the same question no matter what: "How is she? How's Noelle?"

He asked it even now as he stared down at the images on the screen.

Darius shrugged. "Okay. She's starting to see some success with her dress shop."

"That's good," Tariq said absently with a nod, smiling down at the photo of Kayla sitting in front of the glowing solitary candle on her birthday cake.

"She's hoping to maybe expand to two shops in a couple of years."

"She should. She has a knack for business," Tariq murmured, flipping to another image. "I really wish she would just post this shit on Instagram or Facebook. It would make it a lot easier to catch up with her."

"She won't do it. She said after all the media attention she got because of her marriage to Cyrus, she doesn't want to put her life out for public consumption anymore."

"Makes sense," Tariq said, zooming in on one of the photos. Both men fell silent.

"She misses you."

Tariq smirked. "Well, I ain't a nigga who's easy to forget."

"Stop it with the goddamn jokes, will you?" Darius snapped, not remotely amused. "I mean it! She misses you."

Tariq's smirk faded. He nodded again, looking grim. "Yeah, well, I miss her, too. What do you want me to do about it?"

"I want you to know how this is affecting her, affecting your kid. I thought you loved her."

"I do, but again, what the hell do you want me to do about it?" Tariq asked tightly.

"She tries to put up a brave front, but she's still taking this hard. Diamond said she even broke down into tears when they were alone. She's sufferin', T. J. Don't you feel like shit about any of this? Don't you even care? You left the woman you love and your baby to fend for themselves and—"

"Now hold the fuck up!" Tariq shouted, dropping the phone to the mattress and shooting to his feet. "Don't you dare even form your goddamn mouth to say I left them to fend for themselves, let alone ask me if I even fuckin' care about her! Like I'm some asshole . . . some deadbeat! I just gave you sixty grand to give to her and I sent eighty grand before that. I chased down the nigga who tried to kill her and I killed him! I gave him pass after pass after pass. But I couldn't do it anymore. If she was gonna survive . . . if *any* of them were gonna make it . . . *your* girl included," he said, pointing down at Darius, "Cyrus had to die! You and I both know that! I didn't have—"

"I understand all that you're sayin'," Darius began calmly. "I understand the hard decision you had to make. But the end result is that you left. You left her! Nothing will change that fact. Kayla will never get to know her father and Noelle is struggling alone. She's finding it hard to let you go!"

Tariq crossed his arms over his chest. "So you feel the need to be my conscience . . . that little voice in my head that says I fucked up and ruined whatever chance she and I could've had of being together? Well, let me tell you that you don't have to be. I know what I did and I deal with the consequences of that shit every fuckin' day." He loosened his arms and dropped them to his sides. "If she's finding it hard to let me go, that shit is mutual. It's been a battle to stay away."

Darius squinted up at him, remembering something Diamond had mentioned about her conversation with Noelle after the birthday party. It took on new meaning now, listening to his brother's words.

"Noelle told Diamond that you were like a ghost still

haunting her. She said sometimes . . . sometimes she even still feels like you're there." He paused. "When you said it's a battle to stay away . . . you aren't . . . you haven't come back to DC, have you? You haven't been to her place? You aren't crazy enough to follow her around, are you?"

Tariq didn't answer him and it was all the answer Darius needed.

"Jesus Christ," Darius said, dropping his head into his hands, openly groaning.

"Calm down. No one saw me! And I did it at a distance! She was at the playground with Kayla. She wasn't even worried about me. She—"

"T. J., she could've spotted you!" he said, dropping his hands. "Anyone could've recognized you!"

"First you accuse me of deserting her, now you're on my ass for checkin' in on her! Decide what the fuck you're gonna lecture me about. Make a damn choice."

"You want me to make a choice?" Darius asked, glaring up at him. "Okay, how about this? I wish you would've fuckin' listened to me that night at the hospital when I warned you that you were throwing your life and your happiness away because of the rage you couldn't let go. Admit that protecting Noelle was only half of the reason why you killed him! The other reason is that you and Cyrus Grey were locked in a battle and you refused . . . you *refused* to let him win. He took your money, he *tried* to kill your woman, and he wounded your fuckin' pride, and you could not . . . you would not let that shit slide! You could've run away together. You could've disappeared and I would've been happy for you, but you wouldn't listen. And you still aren't listening. You've always had a hard head and a death wish and its fuckin' irritating!"

"Fuck you! You're irritatin', too!"

"Really? That's your comeback?"

"Yeah, really!"

The two brothers glowered at each other. Only the sound of the TV filled the motel room during their stare down. Tariq finally relented, loudly exhaled, and slumped on the bed beside Darius. He stared down at the tan shag carpet beneath their feet.

"I know it's stupid to go back there. I don't do it all the time. Just . . . just when the need gets bad. When being away from them gets to be too much. Seeing her and the baby helps." He sucked his teeth. "Shit, sometimes I think about how I was probably better off before I met her. At least then I didn't give a fuck about what I did, who I hurt. Now I think about it constantly. How this is hurting her. How badly I want to hold my baby girl. Noelle made me a better man, but she made me *feel* worse. I hate it! I hate this shit so much!"

Darius looked up at Tariq, wounded by the pain he saw on his brother's face, in his eyes.

He'd wanted to avoid this, but he guessed Tariq had always been on this path. He'd been driving down this lane his entire life. Tariq was a hustler. A survivor. A chameleon. Darius swore Tariq had nine lives—unfortunately, he suspected all those lives would be lonely ones.

"I want her to move on without me, even if I find it hard to move on without her. I want her to be happy." Tariq looked up from the carpet and met Darius's gaze. "I mean that, bruh. She deserves it. If you can figure out a way to communicate that to her for me without telling her I said it, I'd appreciate it."

"I will. I will. Don't worry." He glanced at his cellphone screen, checking the time. "I better get back on the road. I told Diamond I would arrive at the hotel a little after four o'clock at the latest. If I'm too far after that—"

"I get it. You gotta go." Tariq nodded. "I understand."

They both rose and stood awkwardly in front of each other. Even when they were younger, they were never affectionate. Tariq had been more likely to punch his little brother or smack him in the back of the head than to drag him into a hug. But to Darius's shock, Tariq did it now, even slapping him on the back.

"You take care of yourself and that fiancée of yours," Darius said. "And watch out for my girl and my kid."

"Of course I will. And I'll make sure Noelle gets the money you sent her. I'm . . . I'm gonna hear from you again, right?"

"Yeah, we'll meet up again. Trust. I'll reach out."

"See you, okay?"

"Yeah."

As Darius turned to unlock the door and walk out of the motel room, he took one last glance at his brother. Tariq was already reclining on the bed again, staring at the television as if he didn't have a care in the world, but Darius knew different. In fact, Tariq carried the weight of the world on his shoulders.

He's a hustler, a survivor, and a chameleon, Darius reminded himself. *He'll be all right no matter what.*

Darius closed the door behind him and headed back to his car, bracing himself for the next leg of his journey.

Chapter 36

Vanessa

"Whoa, there!" Vanessa's date said with a chuckle, grabbing her around the waist just as she stumbled on her stairs. "I got you!" he assured her as his hand veered dangerously close to the underside of her breast.

"Whoopsie!" she cried, before breaking into giggles.

Vanessa didn't know why she found almost falling so amusing. Maybe it was because she had worn these ridiculously high, crocodile-skin pumps because she'd thought they made her look extra sexy, but she hadn't achieved her goal thanks to her stumbling around in her high heels all night. Or maybe it was because of the four . . . make that five glasses of pinot gris she'd had during their dinner date, but either way, she was finding all this funny as hell.

"Just lost my balance for a sec, Harry. I'm good now, though," she gushed while gazing up into his eyes.

Harry Tavett was a little shorter than she usually preferred, wasn't that handsome, and had an unfortunate case of halitosis, but he was also the fifty-two-year-old owner of five chicken joints, twice divorced, and currently had a net worth of more than eight million dollars.

Meanwhile she was a single mother of three children with a murdered husband and bills to pay.

Instead of removing Harry's invading hand from around her waist, she leaned into him, rubbing her breast into his palm. She placed a hand on his chest and batted her eyelashes seductively. Vanessa had to turn on the charm and turn up the heat. She had to win him over.

Harry gazed down at her, eagerly licking his lips, blowing hot, rancid breath into her face.

If it wasn't for you, I wouldn't have to do this shit, Cy, she now thought.

She had the same thought every morning when she woke up and every night when she went to sleep. Vanessa had thought with Cyrus being gone she'd be a free woman, able to do whatever she wanted now that she was no longer stuck in her gilded cage. But he'd had one last surprise waiting for her. She bet the son of a bitch was laughing in his grave.

Yes, Cyrus's death had freed her from her marriage and left her with a house and money, but her dearly departed husband had neglected to mention before he was killed that he was up to his eyeballs in debt to creditors and lawyers. By the time everyone else got their cut of his estate, Vanessa was left with hardly any money and a four-thousand-square-foot home with a double mortgage and utilities she couldn't afford to pay.

She'd been forced to downsize and now rented a simple town house in a neighborhood where her neighbors had plastic birdbaths on their front lawns and minivans and Volvos in their driveways. Her mother helped financially, but gone were Vanessa's weekly facials and shopping trips to Neiman Marcus. Gone were the private schools for her kids and summer vacations in the Caribbean. Vanessa was officially on her own and on a budget and, frankly, she was over it. She wanted her old life back and she figured ensnaring Harry was the means to do it.

His gaze drifted from her mouth to her low-cut top. "Maybe I should walk you inside," he said, licking his lips hungrily again. "You know, just to make sure everything's okay in there."

"That won't be necessary," a voice answered.

Vanessa and Harry broke their mutual gaze to turn and look at her doorway, where Vanessa's mother, Carol, now stood. Her arms were crossed over her chest. She was scowling.

"Hey, Mama!" Vanessa cried. "Come and meet Harry! Harry, say hi to my mama!"

Harry nodded awkwardly. "Good . . . good evening, ma'am."

"Thank you for bringing my daughter home safely, Harry. Much appreciated. I can take it from here."

"No, Harry, stay!" Vanessa cried, wobbling up the rest of her walkway to her front door. She grabbed the handrail when she almost tripped again. "Come in and meet my babies! Mama, why don't you—"

"I don't think that's a good idea, Nessa. It is after midnight. Your children are in bed. He should go home."

"Mama, this is *my* house! I say who comes and goes—not you." She grabbed his hand, roughly tugging him forward toward the door. "Come on, Harry! Come inside."

Harry took one step forward, but seeing the severe expression on Carol's face, he immediately took a step back.

"Maybe some other time," he mumbled. "I'll give you a call later this week, Vanessa." He then slinked away.

"Harry! Harry!" Vanessa shouted after him as he fled to his car. "Don't listen to her! You don't have to go, honey. Come back!" she yelled when he pulled off.

"Vanessa Nicole Grey, stop making a goddamn fool of

yourself," her mother hissed. "Bring your ass inside! The neighbors can hear you."

"Oh, who gives a damn!" Vanessa waved her hand dismissively as she stomped up the stairs. She shoved past her mother into her entryway, yanking off her earrings and kicking off her high heels before slamming the front door behind her. "If I had my way, I would've been out of this goddamn neighborhood months ago. Harry was my chance to get out—and you *ruined* it! He's never gonna call me back now that you—"

"You really thought strutting around like some drunken hussy and inviting a man home was gonna whisk you away from this place?" Her mother slowly shook her head. "If it didn't work the other half dozen times with the rich men you've dated since Cyrus's death, why the hell would it work this time, Nessa?"

"Oh, don't preach to me! You're the one who taught me to spread my legs for any man with a seven-figure bank account. That's how I met Cy in the first place. *Remember?* I'm just doing what you taught me, Mama. I'm doing what needs to be done!"

"Keep your voice down," her mother whispered. "The children will hear you."

"So what if they do!" She tripped as she stalked toward the stairs but caught herself by grabbing the railing. "Junior is away overnight with friends and Bryson and Zoe don't know what the hell we're even talkin' about anyway!"

"Do you really think your children are that stupid, Nessa? You don't think they know what it means when you wake up too late to take them to school, or when you do finally wake up, you stumble around slurring your words? You don't think they hear what you do with these men on the other side of their bedroom walls? You are an embarrassment! Don't you see that? I spent all those years teaching you and nurturing you, and this is what you turn into? For the sake of your children, stop drinking and get your damn life together!"

"I hate you! I hate you! I hate yoooooou!" Vanessa screeched, stomping her feet like when she was a little girl and her mother made her wear a dress she didn't want to wear.

"Mommy?" Zoe called.

Vanessa turned to find Zoe and Bryson standing in their doorway in their pjs, staring at her worriedly.

"Why are you up?" Vanessa yelled. "Go back to bed, goddamnit!"

"Vanessa!" her mother admonished.

Bryson sniffed as his lower lip trembled. Zoe burst into tears.

"Oh, for love of . . ." Vanessa rolled her eyes. "Why are you crying?"

"They're crying because they are frightened. They are frightened at how you're behaving." Carol motioned frantically to them. "Come, babies! Come with Grandma. You're gonna spend the night at my house."

"No, they are not! They are gonna stay right here and go back to their damn beds!"

"Vanessa," her mother said before charging up the stairs and grabbing her arm, almost yanking her off the staircase, "I am taking these children home with me tonight. I will not leave them here with you in the state you're in."

Vanessa opened her mouth to argue, but her mother cut her off before she could.

"And while they are gone," the older woman continued, "you are gonna sleep this off and sober the hell up, or so help me God, I will call Child Services and file a complaint. I will ask for you to be declared negligent and take custody of my grandchildren. Do you understand me?"

Vanessa glared down at her mother. If anyone else had made that threat, she would call their bluff. But she knew even in her drunken haze that her mother could be ruthless and determined when she wanted, especially when she felt like she was protecting her own.

"Fine," Vanessa snapped, yanking her arm out of her mother's grasp. "Take 'em."

"Come on, babies," Carol said, gesturing to them again, "don't worry about gathering some clothes. Grandma has some at her house."

"Go on! Go with your grandmother," Vanessa echoed.

But she didn't have to say anything. Her children were already rushing down the stairs, Zoe with her stuffed animals in tow. They took an uneasy glance at Vanessa as they went by, giving her a wide berth, like she was a bomb that could go off at any moment.

"Grab your coats," Carol ordered, and they promptly removed their down jackets from the wall hooks by the door. "Head to the car. I'm parked in the driveway."

They nodded and opened the front door. Bryson grabbed Zoe's hand, tugging his still sobbing little sister out into the cold night.

When they were gone, Carol turned back to face her daughter. "I hope you can pull yourself together. I hope you can go back to being the woman I remember you to be. I hope Cyrus Grey didn't take the best of you with him when he died on that road in Baltimore County two years ago. You are better than this! No daughter of mine is this weak."

"Just go," Vanessa muttered, turning away from her mother and continuing up the stairs. "Make sure you have the kids back in enough time for them to get to school tomorrow or you can take 'em yourself if you insist on being in charge of every damn thing."

She walked to her bedroom, only pausing when she heard her front door slam. She tossed her crocodile pumps to the floor and strolled to her dresser, where a half-filled wineglass she hadn't finished earlier awaited her.

"Don't mind if I do," she said before grabbing the glass and taking a gulp.

As far as she was concerned, she didn't have a drinking problem. She could stop whenever she wanted. Her mother was just being controlling and melodramatic. And Vanessa would call Harry back tomorrow, if he didn't call her. In a date or two she'd give him a little somethin', somethin', and he'd forget this whole episode. Over time she'd wrap him around her finger and be on the rebound. Tonight would be nothing but a bad memory.

"Mama will see and that'll shut her up," Vanessa said before finishing the rest of her wine. She then set down her glass and flopped onto her bed. Within minutes she was fast asleep.

Chapter 37

Bilal

No one noticed he was there. To a casual onlooker, he probably was just a dark figure lingering underneath an overgrown maple at the end of the block. But he doubted there were any onlookers. It was almost one o'clock in the morning and most of Vanessa's neighbors were fast asleep.

Bilal stood across the street from Vanessa's new home with his hands shoved into his pockets to ward off the chill, but his teeth were chattering anyway and he was shivering thanks to the thirty-degree temperature. He probably should be wearing a coat, but these were the only clothes he'd been able to swipe from the giveaway dumpster. They served their purpose; they helped him to blend in, unlike the bright orange prison jumpsuit he'd ditched that morning.

Bilal removed his hands from his pockets to raise his hoodie when Vanessa's mother's sedan drove by. He turned his head slightly so neither the old woman nor Vanessa's kids, who were in the back seat, would see him. He didn't want to run the risk that the old woman would recognize him. She'd seen him a couple of times years ago, back when he and Vanessa were carrying on their affair. If she saw him now, lurking in Vanessa's neighborhood in the dark, she might wonder why he was here. She might even call the cops.

But then again, maybe not. When he looked in the mirror, he didn't even recognize himself anymore. He was no longer the Bilal from back then—the handsome, confident young man he used to be. Two years in prison may not seem like a long time to most, but it had been long enough to make him slump-shouldered and twitchy. It had taken away the luster in his skin and beard and had robbed him of more than twenty pounds. It had also made him angry, *very* angry.

The things he had to do in there to survive still made him shudder in disgust, even now standing outside in the fresh air, rather than trapped like a rat in a cage with Omar, his three-hundred-pound cellmate. Omar didn't seem to know the difference—or care, for that matter—between Bilal and the Playboy Playmates he fantasized about on the regular. Omar couldn't get his hands on Miss July or Miss November, but he definitely could get his hands on Bilal and did so—frequently.

But if it wasn't for Omar, Bilal supposed he never would have worked up the courage to finally stand up for himself after the rape and the beatings he'd taken on the cell block and try to kill one of those bastards. And he would have succeeded if the correctional officers hadn't heard Omar's bloodcurdling screams during the night. Funny, they'd always seemed to go deaf when Bilal had cried for help.

Their rescue had kept Omar from bleeding to death, but Bilal still managed to exact his pound of flesh. The inmate was now undergoing corrective surgery to reattach it, but, according to his doctors, the outlook wasn't good.

The infraction had landed Bilal a transfer to a maximum security prison in Western Maryland. That morning, a female driver had arrived in a paneled van to transport him. Lucky for him, she happened to find him cute. Unlucky for her, she was the one obstacle between him and escape. Bilal had talked her into pulling over on a deserted roadside for a romantic interlude and strangled her with his handcuffs. After dumping her body and driving her transport van until the gas ran out, he'd eventually managed to find his way here.

Discovering where Vanessa had moved hadn't been as challenging as he thought it would be. Her old nosy neighbors had been more than happy to detail Vanessa's fall from grace when he'd lied and said he used to work for her as part of the grounds crew and was looking for her.

"Oh, honey, does she owe you money?" one of her elderly neighbors had asked. "I'm not surprised! She and that dead husband of hers owe just about *everybody* money. Having that big house and driving around in those fancy cars and couldn't even pay their bills!" She'd shook her head. "Well, anyway, there have been plenty of people coming around here, knocking on our doors, asking after her. I just give them the same forwarding address the post office gave me when I got tired of all the callers."

The elderly woman had handed him a sheet of paper with the address for Vanessa's new home written on it. He'd thanked her and walked and hitchhiked the seventeen miles.

"Oh, Nessa," he murmured sadly, now gazing up at the exterior of her row house, at the shabby shutters with their peeling paint and the chain-link fence.

He bet Vanessa felt like a deposed queen, having to live in a place like this. She'd lost her home, her money, her cars, and her status as a trophy wife.

Bae, I bet you're so miserable, he thought.

Well, he was here to put her out of her misery. He was

here to kill the bitch like he'd promised, but time was running out. He bet the detention center was already looking for the van and him. Eventually they'd find the driver's body, and her face, along with Bilal's, were bound to appear on the morning news under a "LATE BREAKING" banner.

"Escaped convict Bilal Cullen murders corrections officer and is now at large," the broadcast would say, and it would only be a matter of time before they found him.

He had to get this done before he got caught.

Bilal stepped out of the shadows with his head bowed and walked across the street. He had a slight limp now thanks to Vanessa's husband shooting him in the shin. He was the lone moving figure on the block besides a stray cat a few houses down and a rustling leaf tapping its way toward a storm drain.

He kept walking up the sidewalk and then Vanessa's driveway, quietly opening the back gate leading to her backyard. He then climbed the short wooden staircase leading to the back door. He pulled the sleeve of his oversized sweatshirt over his fist and bashed open one of the back windows. Bilal then reached inside, undid the lock, and opened the door by a few inches. He waited for the beep of a house alarm or the bark and growl of a dog but heard neither. He slowly smiled.

"I'm comin', bae," he whispered before opening the door farther, stepping inside, and closing the door softly behind him.

He made his way by moonlight through the kitchen— grabbing a knife from the butcher block as he passed it, then down the hall and up the stairs to Vanessa, eager for their long-overdue reunion.

TRUTH, LIES, AND MR. GREY

Shelly Ellis

ABOUT THIS GUIDE

The suggested questions are included
to enhance your group's reading of
Shelly Ellis's *Truth, Lies, and Mr. Grey.*

DISCUSSION QUESTIONS

1. Though Cyrus has been caught in his lies and now faces bigamy charges, he refuses to give up and insists he can still come out on top, keeping all his wives and taking revenge on Tariq. What do you think motivates him to continue with his manipulations and lies even though the stakes are even higher?

2. Diamond has lost faith in everything and everyone, except Cyrus. Why does she continue to trust him despite what she now knows about him? What do you think he represents for her?

3. Now that Noelle knows that she's pregnant and has lost all financial support from Cyrus and will lose her home, she refuses to take money or move in with Tariq even though he's offering her the stability and nuclear family she once craved. Do you think it is as simple as her not wanting to be dependent on a man again as she claims, or does she sense inherently that something is "off" with Tariq?

4. Vanessa finally decides to move forward with her plan to murder Cyrus after she finds out he's been pretending to be ill the entire time she was nursing him. Why do you think that was her catalyst to proceed forward?

5. Do you think Cyrus has a right to feel betrayed by Tariq, his former friend and business partner, even though they're both criminals and conmen? Why or why not?

6. Diamond realizes that her lawyer Darius is a lot more complex than he initially seemed. Why does

that make her draw closer to him instead of running away when she finds she's falling for yet another man with secrets?

7. Even though Noelle has finally figured out the truth about Tariq, she still can't pull the trigger and shoot him when the moment comes. Would you have made a similar choice?

8. Tariq finally explains the full story of why he tried to have Cyrus murdered. Do you think he would have carried out his plan if *only* Noelle's life was on the line? Why or why not?

9. Tariq chooses to kill Cyrus himself, going on the run and ruining his chances of ever having a life with Noelle. Do you think his brother was right in saying it was motivated by a selfish desire for revenge/tit for tat, or was Tariq right in arguing that it was the only way any of them could finally be free?

10. Do you think all the characters ultimately got what they deserved in the end, or were there some surprises?

Want to see how it all began?

Be sure to read

THE THREE MRS. GREYS

Available now

Wherever books are sold

Connect with Us

Visit us online at
KensingtonBooks.com
to read more from your favorite authors, see books
by series, view reading group guides, and more.

Join us on social media

for sneak peeks, chances to win books and prize packs,
and to share your thoughts with other readers.

facebook.com/kensingtonpublishing
twitter.com/kensingtonbooks

Tell us what you think!

To share your thoughts, submit a review,
or sign up for our eNewsletters, please visit:
KensingtonBooks.com/TellUs.